PRAISE FOR

Amy Lillard

"Amy Lillard never disappoints! Her writing is always fun, fresh, and fabulous!"
—*USA Today* bestselling author Arial Burnz

"Amy Lillard's novels are funny, sweet, charming, and utterly delicious. Reading her stories is like indulging in gourmet chocolates: You'll savor every delightful page, and when you reach the end, you'll always wish there was more!"
—*New York Times* bestselling author Michele Bardsley

"Amy Lillard's characters will tug at your heartstrings and leave you wanting to meet more!"   —Laura Marie Altom

"At the top of my autobuy list, Amy Lillard's romances always leave a smile on my face and a sigh in my heart."
—RONE finalist A. J. Nuest

"Amy Lillard is one of my go-to authors for a sexy, witty romance."   —Readers' Choice finalist Kelly Moran

"Amy Lillard weaves well-developed characters that create for lovers of romance a rich fabric of love."
—Vonnie Davis, author of the Wild Heat series

"Funny, warm, and thoroughly charming. Make room on your keeper shelf for Amy Lillard!"
—Karen Toller Whittenburg

Loving a Lawman

A CATTLE CREEK NOVEL

Amy Lillard

A SIGNET ECLIPSE BOOK

SIGNET ECLIPSE
Published by New American Library,
an imprint of Penguin Random House LLC
375 Hudson Street, New York, New York 10014

This book is an original publication of New American Library.

First Printing, July 2016

For more information about Penguin Random House, visit penguin.com.

ISBN 9781101990933

Printed in the United States of America
10 9 8 7 6 5 4 3 2 1

Designed by Laura K. Corless

Penguin
Random
House

To Rob, my very own lawman.

Acknowledgments

When I first started this book, I had no idea that it would come to mean so much to me. And even more, that it would come to mean so much to the people around me.

Thank you, Stacey Barbalace, for always believing in Seth and Jessie and for all your hand-holding support. This book would not have been the same without you! Love ya, babe!

To Sarah Grimm, author extraordinaire, who always finds the time to read "one little bit" to make sure it "works" even though it's midnight her time. Your friendship means more to me than you will ever know.

And a big, big thanks goes out to Deona Thompson. Through the course of my researching and writing this book, she has not only become a good friend of mine, but also had the forethought not to call the police when I sent e-mail after e-mail asking about the specifics of the town of Big Lake, Texas. Even when I asked how many deputies worked for the county and how many were on duty at any given time. Deona, you're the bestest!

Thank you, Laura Marie Altom and Karen Crane. Who knew that day in the coffee shop that it would come to this? That day I turned to the both of you and said, "I have a cowboy story I want to write." I love you both!

Thanks to Julie Gwinn, my superagent. You helped me get the book of my heart into print. I'm forever grateful!

And super thanks to editors Laura Fazio, for taking a chance on me, and Katherine Pelz, for picking up the torch. I'm so grateful to be a part of the New American Library family!

And to my family, the Teen and the Major, who smile politely when I talk about Seth and Page County as if they're real. You mean the world to me!

Chapter One

࿇ ✴ ࿇

By the time Sheriff Seth Langston pulled his patrol vehicle to a stop in front of Manny's Place, there had already been one casualty.

It had taken him exactly seven and a half minutes to reach the scene of the crime, but a crowd had already gathered in the graveled parking lot in front of the bar. The area was dim, lit only by the neon beer signs in the windows and twin security lights that buzzed and hummed and attracted moths.

The onlookers were talking amongst themselves, pointing to the body, and shaking their heads. No big wonder why. In a town the size of Cattle Creek, Texas, not much happened.

Ever.

And given the rare occasion when something noteworthy actually *did* happen, everyone lined up to be the first to see it.

Seth switched off the strobe lights and slid from the seat of his Explorer as his chief deputy parked his own car in the closest available spot and got out.

"Clear the scene," Seth said strictly out of habit. "And find out if there're any witnesses."

Dusty nodded, then limped toward the crowd of about twenty people, all of whom had been enjoying an evening at the honky-tonk before the goings-on outside Manny's got more interesting than the goings-on inside the bar. "You folks get on back to what you were doing. There's nothing more to see here. Go on with you."

Seth took a deep breath. It was damn near one o'clock in the morning. He was tired, hungry, and tired. This was the last thing he needed.

This was their third call of the night—not counting ol' Johnson Jones. Jones had been booked so many times Seth was about ready to give him his own key to the jail. Seth *expected* Jones to show up somewhere drunk as a skunk, so he figured he couldn't exactly count that arrest in the evening's tally.

Three calls in one night, plus Jonesy. Yeah, it was a busy night in Cattle-town. And this call was the worst by far. This one he hadn't expected.

At Dusty's direction, the crowd reluctantly shuffled back into the bar. Every so often, one of them glanced over their shoulder and grumbled about history repeating itself.

"It's just like Homecoming '08," Seth heard someone say, before he turned his attention back to the matter at hand.

The victim.

His brother's truck.

Or at least what was left of it.

Seth slowly walked around the crumpled body of the once shiny, candy apple red four-wheel-drive. It was a cryin' shame. The windshield was busted, taillights busted, headlights busted. Tires slashed, driver's-side door dented, windows . . . well, Seth couldn't tell if the windows of the Ford were rolled down or gone. But judging by the amount of glass that sparkled like misplaced diamonds across the ground surrounding the truck—and the fact that Jessie McAllen was a loose cannon—he'd put his money on gone.

The waitress in the parking lot with the baseball bat.

Given time—and a good paint and body man—the victim might possibly make it. His brother . . . well, Seth wasn't so sure about Chase.

"Get her outta here," Chase yelled. "Before I kill her. I swear to God, Seth. I'll do it."

And then there was the perp—*alleged* perp. Jessie McAllen stood next to one of the weathered railroad ties that created a barrier in front of the tiny bar. Her arms were folded across her waist, chest heaving. Her straw cowboy hat shielded her face from view, but Seth had been a witness to this too many times not to know that her eyes were blazing, her freckled cheeks flushed.

Seth thumbed back his buff-colored Resistol and ignored the dueling pair. "Anybody see who did this?"

"What are you talkin' about? She did it," Chase yelled.

Seth looked to the three men who stood between Chase and Jessie. The two biggest, Joe Dan Stacey and Buster Williams, both worked at the Diamond, the Langston family ranch. The other, smaller man was Skeeter McCutcheon, a rodeo friend of Chase's. All three of them shook their heads and held their ground. Their attempt to protect Jessie from the full brunt of Chase's wrath was noble but questionable all the same.

Regardless of Chase's threats, Seth—and everyone in Page County for that matter—knew he expended effort for only two things. Rodeo and sex. Even the destruction of his truck wouldn't change that. Not that the youngest Langston had to expend any significant effort toward his favorite pastimes. Rodeo was in his blood. And women seemed to serve themselves up on platters whenever he was within a hundred feet of them. Or yards. Sometimes even miles. His charmed record of riding the rankest bulls around wasn't the only reason they called him Lucky.

Tonight was no exception. Despite the fact that he had to be in New Mexico early tomorrow afternoon, Chase stood with his feet apart, the fingers of his right hand curled around the neck of a bottle of Bud, his left braced on one Wrangler-clad hip. Not far behind him stood a tiny bleached blonde with jiggly breasts and glossy lips.

Seth cut his eyes from the buckle bunny back to Jessie. It wasn't fair to make comparisons. The little blond thing in her shiny satin halter top and skintight jeans oozed sex, whereas Jessie in her pink gingham and secondhand denim was as wholesome as white bread. But the rodeo groupie was a one-night stand—two if she was lucky—and Jessie had been Chase's girl since she was seven years old.

"Anybody see anything at all?"

"Arrest her," Chase continued. "Jail's the only safe place for her now."

Seth's gaze centered on each of the men standing before him. "Nobody saw anything."

"No, but—" Joe Dan started.

"But what?" Seth asked.

The big man shrugged and looked to Buster as if he had all the answers.

"Somebody tell me."

It was Buster's turn to shrug. "It's just that . . . well . . . you know."

"Yeah." Seth glanced back toward Jessie. At least she didn't have the baseball bat any longer. "I know."

When he'd gotten the call he expected to have to talk her down, have Dusty distract her while he snuck up from behind, snaked one arm around her waist, and used his other to snatch the bat from her grasp. Then despite her kicking and screaming, he would have used his hold on her to haul her pretty little ass to jail.

Uh-hum . . . did he say pretty? He meant . . . feisty. Yeah, that was it.

Inside the bar, someone's quarter dropped in the jukebox,

and George Strait gave way to Toby Keith. *How do you like me now?*

"If you're not a witness, then get on back inside," Seth said.

The three men hesitated a fraction of a second before they ambled toward the blue-painted door of Manny's, feet dragging as if they'd rather do anything but leave their friend and the firebrand waitress behind. Joe Dan stopped only to give the bat to Seth, then followed behind the others.

"I mean it. I want to press charges. I don't care how long we've known each other. It ain't right to do that to a man's truck."

"I'll handle it, Chase." Seth tried to keep his words calm and controlled, even though he wanted to smack his brother upside the head for being so damned stupid and even though he wanted to shake Jessie till her teeth rattled for . . . well, for being so damned stupid.

"Just how am I supposed to get to Santa Fe, huh?"

The blonde nodded in solemn agreement and slipped her arms around Chase's waist in a gesture of support. He took an angry swig of beer and made no attempt to stop her as she possessively ran her hands over his torso.

Jessie didn't move despite the interloper's familiar manner.

Seth raised a brow at the girl hanging all over his brother like a bad case of Spanish moss, but Chase just shrugged as if to say, *Can I help it if I'm irresistible?*

Nights like this made Seth feel old and worn down and more than just a little tired of cleaning up after his baby brother.

He mentally counted to ten before asking, "Is she of age?"

The blonde tittered—Lord help him, she actually tittered. "He's funny."

"Yeah," Chase agreed. "A real riot." But he wasn't even smiling. "What do you think?"

I think you've hurt Jessie—again—and deserve more than just having your truck smashed in.

"I think you have some explaining to do," he said.

Chase actually had the cheek to look affronted. "Hey, I'm the victim here."

Blondie bobbed her head again.

"You want to give me your side of the story? Alone," Seth added when Chase opened his mouth to speak.

His brother looked none too happy but didn't protest. He simply nodded, then disentangled himself from the buckle bunny's clutches. She shoved her hands into the back pockets of her designer jeans as if she didn't know what else to do with them if she didn't have Chase to maul. Then she pouted in a put-on sort of way as Seth led Chase a few feet away where they couldn't be overheard, but he could still keep an eye on his perp.

"You stay right there," Seth said to Jessie.

She looked as if she might protest; then she flopped down on the railroad tie to wait it out as Seth turned his attention back to his brother.

"Why're you here, Chase?"

The youngest Langston shrugged. "I just needed to blow off some steam. You know how it is."

He didn't, but there was no gold in telling Chase that. "In Texas," Seth clarified.

"I found a litter of kittens out on 81 in Kansas."

"You brought them here." It wasn't a question.

The trip was at least twelve hours out of his way, but Seth knew better than to point this out to Chase. Lucky Langston was always picking up strays of one kind or another. Seth resisted the urge to let his gaze wander back over to where the buckle bunny waited.

"Their mama had been hit by a truck. I couldn't just leave them there."

"Where are they now?" Seth knew even before the words left his mouth that he wasn't going to like the answer.

Chase grinned in his good-old-boy, "aw, shucks, ma'am" kind of way that pretty much got him through life.

"You'd think the sheriff would know better than to leave a spare key under the welcome mat."

Seth counted to ten again. There was no key. Hell, there was no welcome mat. Which meant Chase had used his legendary charm to convince Nita to let him into the garage apartment Seth rented from her. "You left a litter of kittens at my place."

"It's a small litter," Chase said, as if that made everything better. "Only four of them."

Seventeen, eighteen, nineteen, twenty. And Seth had thought the night couldn't get any worse. "Shouldn't you be on your way to New Mexico?"

"Well, since we were already here—"

"You decided to come on out and party down."

"We thought we might grab a beer or two."

"Who's we?"

"Me and Skeeter and Angela."

Business first. He'd worry about the kittens later. "What's Angela's last name?"

Chase shrugged. "Does that matter?"

Yeah, it did. It mattered because a question answered with another question meant Chase didn't know Angela's last name. Details, details.

"You've never brought a . . . woman here."

"I didn't bring her, she followed me."

"From?"

"Nebraska."

"Damn it, Chase, that doesn't mean you have to—" Seth stopped.

Chase took a lazy draw off his beer. "Hell, Seth. If I'd wanted a sermon, I'd've stopped off at the First Baptist."

"Jessie deserves better." It took everything in Seth's power not to grind the words out from between clenched teeth. He'd brought this up once before, but Chase was Chase and Seth had given up. It wasn't his place to interfere.

"Yeah, well, Jessie knows how it is."

"I suppose she does." Even to his own ears, the words sounded strained, though he doubted his brother would notice.

"After a couple of dances, we—me and Angela—" he added before Seth could question him, "decided to get some fresh air and found Jessie out here with a baseball bat."

"You see any of it happen?"

"No, but—"

"But what?"

Chase shrugged again. "Well . . . you know."

"Yeah," Seth said. "I know."

Chase looked back over to his truck, the night breeze ruffling the ends of his blond hair where it stuck out from underneath his signature black hat. "How am I supposed to get to New Mexico?"

"You could ride with Skeeter."

"He was riding with me."

"You could fly."

Chase shot him a "no way in hell" look.

Despite the price of gas and the current pack of professional bull riders who hopped planes to get from one rodeo to the next, Chase found a thrill in driving. In drinking, dancing, and loving until the last possible minute before gunning his truck toward the desired state line.

"Tell Jake what happened. You know he'll let you take one of the trucks from the Diamond."

"You expect me to drive a Chevy?"

Seth shot him a pointed look.

"Fine," Chase said, his disgust apparent. "I'll use a ranch truck. Now what are you going to do with Jessie?"

"I guess that depends on you."

"Throw her in jail," he said flatly.

"Chase—" Seth stopped, giving himself time to temper his words. "If there are no witnesses, it's your word against hers."

"She admitted to it."

"A confession given while someone is yelling that they're going to kill you can hardly be considered admissible."

"If you don't believe me, go ask her yourself."

Seth clenched his jaw to keep from saying more. He was, after all, the sheriff, and he had a job to do. Remain impartial, uphold the law. If Chase wanted to press charges . . . and Jessie had no alibi . . . it didn't matter how much Seth wanted her to be innocent. And it surely didn't matter how much he wished things were different. "All right, then. I'll take care of Miss McAllen. You just give Dusty your statement; then get out of here and go get some sleep before that bull kills you tomorrow."

His little brother flashed a "like that's gonna happen" grin that didn't make it past the corners of his mouth. Seth wasn't sure if Chase was thinking about the possibility of death-by-bull or his non-sleep-related intentions with the flavor of the night. Maybe it was both.

Chase paused as if he wanted to say something more, but changed his mind. He readjusted his hat, then spun away.

"See, darlin'?" he said as he swung the blonde to his side and steered her toward the door of Manny's Place. "I told you everything was gonna be all right. Now let's get ourselves a couple more beers and see what we can do about wearin' a hole in that dance floor."

With a sigh, Seth watched Chase head back into the bar. He loved his brother. But there were times . . .

With a small shake of his head, he crunched his way across the broken safety glass toward the girl he'd known since she was in the second grade.

Jessie sat at the end of the building farthest from the door. Her breathing had returned to normal and her head was down as she contemplated only heaven knew what. Her hands were braced on her knees, and her hat was pulled low over her eyes.

Seth didn't need to see them. He knew what color they

were, had memorized it long ago—storm-cloud gray and just as dangerous, with dark rings around their irises that made them look twice as big as they really were and sooty lashes that should have belonged to a brunette.

"Jessie?" he said softly. It was the voice he used when talking to frightened mares and skittish colts and red-haired angels who had fallen from grace.

She didn't look up, just raised her arms out in front of her, wrists lax, hands dangling, anger spent. "I'll go peacefully. Just get it over with, Seth. Handcuff me and take me to jail."

Handcuff her.

Now, there was an image Seth could've lived without.

He swallowed hard.

Despite his brother's tomcat morals, and the fact that he didn't deserve . . .

Well, despite everything that Chase didn't deserve, including the sassy redhead, Jessie was Chase's girl. Always had been. Always would be.

"I just want to talk to you about what happened tonight."

She dropped her hands back to her lap and shrugged. But he still couldn't see her face, couldn't read what was going on inside that pretty little head of hers.

Uh-hum . . . did he say pretty? He'd meant . . . well, he'd meant something else, that was all.

"What's there to talk about? I confess. The end."

"Jessie." The word was heavy with warning.

Her head jerked up at a prideful tilt. The brim of her hat still shaded her eyes, but the slant of her jaw was unmistakable. "Why are you torturing me, Seth? Everyone knows I did it. Just arrest me and get it over with."

"I'd like to ask you a few questions first."

"Seth," Dusty called.

He turned as his deputy came ambling across the gravel, his uneven gait kicking up a few little pebbles and a whole lot of dust.

Damn, they needed some rain. That was half the problem. It hadn't rained in weeks. Daytime temps soared to over a hundred, and the nights weren't much cooler. Heat like that made tempers flare, made normal people do crazy things.

Like take a baseball bat to their boyfriend's truck.

Dusty stopped in front of him and flipped through the pages of his notebook. "Here's what we know so far. Jessie was working at the bar tonight. Chase came in with another girl—the, uh . . . little blond thing."

"I saw her."

"Apparently Jessie took it for as long as she could, then told Manny she wanted a smoke break—just for the record, she doesn't smoke. From there, it appears she took the base-ball bat he keeps behind the counter to make sure everyone stays in line, and the rest is the stuff legends are made of."

"Anybody see her take the bat?"

"No."

"Anybody actually see her vandalize the truck?"

Dusty shook his head. "But you know . . ."

"Yeah," Seth said with a nod. "I know."

It was Homecoming '08 all over again.

Seth had been in California at the time, but he'd heard plenty of news from home. How Jessie, in a fit of rage over Chase—what else?—had wrecked the car Sissy Callahan was going to ride in during the parade. Wrecked meaning she had taken an ax handle and beat the ever-lovin' shit out of it until the thing was damn-near totaled.

Allegedly.

Not the totaling part, but the part about Jessie actually committing the deed. No one had seen her do it, so no charges had been filed. And Jessie's mama had just passed a couple of weeks before, so no one had the heart to go dig-ging around for evidence. The insurance had paid for the car, and Sissy had ridden on the FFA float with the blue-ribbon goat instead of on the back of a convertible 'Vette.

"The insurance adjuster should be here in a little while."

Seth handed his deputy the bat. "Dust this for prints, and we'll file the report in the morning."

Dusty started to walk away, then looked at the bat, stopped, and turned back to Seth. "But this isn't—"

"Dust it for prints, and we'll file the report in the morning," Seth repeated.

Dusty glanced back at Jessie, then leaned close to Seth so only he could hear. "But this ain't Manny's bat, Seth. Manny's bat's got blue tape around the neck and—"

"I know. Now dust it for prints."

"All right," Dusty said with a small shake of his head.

"And get Chase's statement, will ya? He has to come up for air sometime."

Dusty nodded again as Seth turned back to Jessie. "Get in the truck," he said without preamble.

"Aren't you going to arrest me?" It was the first protest she'd made all night.

"Consider yourself arrested. Now get in the truck, and we'll talk about this down at the station."

All right, so the "station" was little more than a three-story building in the heart of downtown Cattle Creek that also served as the courthouse and the jail for all of Page County. But after eight years with the San Diego PD, Seth hadn't broken the habit of calling it by its proper name.

"Fine," she said with a heavy sigh.

Seth reached out a hand to help her up.

Without hesitation, she slid her palm into his, then closed her fingers around the back of his hand. Seth braced himself against what was to come.

One innocent touch of skin against skin had him thinking about . . . things he shouldn't think about. Had him feeling . . . things he shouldn't feel. He felt like using his hold on her to pull her flush against him, shoulder to shin. He felt like kissing her lips, tipping off her cowboy hat, and burying his hands in the curly strands of her strawberry blond hair. He felt like . . . like . . .

He felt like a bastard.

Damn it. She was his brother's girl.

He would go on telling himself that a few more times, and one day he would actually start to listen. Even believe it. Then he could stop wondering how different it would have been if he'd just seen Jessie first.

But no one was allowed those second chances. And he'd been sixteen the first time he ever saw her. She had been seven with dirty knees and scraggly hair that looked as if it had never seen the business side of a brush. No, it wasn't the first time that was the problem. Or the countless times after. No, the problem came when he'd come home from California for Donna McAllen's funeral and found that the scraggly-haired, dirty-kneed seven-year-old had grown up to be a very desirable young woman.

And she was off-limits. As off-limits as they came.

Chase's girl. They had been on-again, off-again—mostly on-again—for as long as most people in Cattle Creek cared to remember. Seth loved his brother, but he didn't know what Jessie saw in Chase. It wasn't as if he brought a woman back home often, but he seemed to lack compassion and empathy, and that set Seth's teeth on edge. It was his brother's lack of maturity, he was sure. He cared for himself first and everyone else after. Everyone including Jessie.

If she was Seth's girl . . . well, she wasn't. And that was all that mattered.

Ah, the irony. He could have any woman in Cattle Creek . . . hell, the whole county. Except Jessie. She was his brother's girl. Always had been, always would be. And that left him with a pretty bad case of "what you can't have is the one thing you want the most."

But he'd get over it. Just like the time Jake started going out with Miranda Coleman, and she was forever marked his brother's territory. Seth had gotten over that one then; he'd get over this one too. Eventually.

Seth let go of Jessie's hand slowly as not to let her know

her touch burned into his soul and reluctantly because—
bastard that he was—he wanted to go on touching her as
long as he could.

True to her word, she went peacefully, plodding along
in front of him as he followed behind.

Without a word she opened the back door on the passenger's side of his service vehicle and scrambled in.

"Jessie, get out of there."

"Isn't this where all the common criminals ride?"

She might have been a bit dejected, a little down in the
mouth, but he had to hand it to the girl, she was as plucky as
ever.

"Cute," he muttered, but knew from the smoldering gray
coals of her eyes she wouldn't be moving any time soon,
not unless it was what *she* wanted. Damn her stubborn hide.

He knew which battles to fight and which ones to leave
alone.

"Suit yourself." He slid inside the Explorer and started
the engine. Seat belt buckled, he waited for her to fasten
her own before backing the SUV out of the parking lot and
onto the old highway. He pointed the headlights toward
town, glancing in the rearview mirror at his prisoner.
"Why'd you do it, Jessie James?"

"Don't call me that." Her words were quiet and solemn,
just a knee-jerk reaction to the nickname he'd pegged her
with so many years ago.

Despite the dim light and the cage that separated them,
he could see the defiant edge of her jaw. Her arms were
crossed over her slim, compact body, her cowboy hat casting
shadows across the upper part of her face. If he looked really
close, he could just make out the curly stubs of her pigtails
sticking out from underneath her knockoff Stetson.

"You gonna answer?"

Jessie blew out a derisive breath. "Did you see that
girl? Ugh."

"Yeah, she was something, all right," he said, very aware she hadn't answered his question, not by a long shot.

"Why does he do it, Seth?"

Her voice was subdued and tinged with sadness, and he didn't have to ask what she was talking about.

"He's just sowing his wild oats, Jess."

But the real truth . . . Chase was a wild oat farmer, not into merely sowing, but planting and harvesting and rotating crops regularly.

"You like girls like that?"

He didn't, but there was no use in telling her that. Bleached blond and man-made curves couldn't compare to a fiery redhead with a dusting of freckles across her nose and a sweet little body that was just the way the good Lord had intended it to be.

She was quiet, maybe even thoughtful for a long moment, then said, "Tell me about your ideal girl, Seth."

"Brunette, built, and breathing." He'd been hiding his feelings for so long the words slipped out before he even had a chance to think about answering her question any differently. "Not necessarily in that order."

She didn't even laugh.

"That was a stupid stunt you pulled back there."

She made a noise, could have been in agreement. Maybe not. He couldn't tell. Maybe it was just a noise.

"You know you'll have to pay for the repairs."

Another noise. This one just as unintelligible.

"Gonna be three . . . maybe even four thousand dollars." He shrugged, then chanced a look in the mirror to gauge her reaction. She was staring out the window, watching the town slide by. She looked thoughtful, almost peaceful, but he could tell by the taut line of her shoulders under the faded cotton of her shirt she was anything but. Jessie McAllen, the poorest kid in town, didn't have that kind of money.

But she had more than her fair share of pride. How could

she not? It had to take a lot to keep her chin up after everything the McAllen women had endured. None of them had had an easy life, but it seemed Jessie had suffered the brunt of the town's gossip mill. She was a little too spirited, a little too easy to pin things on. He supposed that was what had gotten her into this mess. That and her love for Chase.

Seth couldn't say it was unrequited. As much as his brother liked to play around, Seth supposed that in his own way, Chase loved Jessie. Just not enough to give up the other women. Not yet anyway. But one day, Chase was going to smarten up and realize what he had at home. And that would be the end of that.

In the meantime, Seth had three reports to write and a pretty little perp in the back of his patrol car.

Had he said pretty? He meant . . . Ah, hell, he'd meant pretty.

"Where are we going?" Jessie asked a few minutes later as Seth turned the Explorer onto Larkspur Lane. He didn't know why she asked; she knew where they were headed. Maybe she just wanted to hear him say it.

"Your house."

"You're not taking me to jail?" Her question was hopeful and incredulous all at the same time.

"Oh, I'm taking you to jail, all right. But I think you need to let your grandmother know what happened so she won't worry about you."

Jessie didn't answer as he pulled into the buckled concrete driveway.

In the dark, he supposed, the house didn't look so bad. The shadows of the night hid the faded, peeling paint that had once been the color of freshly churned butter. And it wasn't so obvious that the bottom half of the screen door didn't have screen in it anymore. In the dark, you couldn't see the whitewashed tractor tire planter that hadn't had flowers in it since Jessie's mama died or the missing windowpane that had been replaced with a piece of cardboard that used to be a 409 box from the Safeway.

All right, he could see all that. But in the dark, it wasn't quite as noticeable as it was in the golden glare of the Texas sun.

"You know," Jessie started in a falsely bright tone. "She's probably already in bed asleep. And the doctors don't want her disturbed if at all possible. So we can just postpone this until tomorrow."

Nice try, sister. "There's a light on."

"Oh, she always leaves that one burning."

"Everyone in town knows she's an insomniac." Seth turned in his seat to stare through the cage at her.

Her jaw was set at that stubborn angle she seemed to prefer, but her posture was slumped, as if she'd had more than she could handle for one night.

Welcome to the club.

Except all of this would be over in a heartbeat when he pulled her in front of her grandmother and made her admit what really happened. It wasn't an honorable plan, but it was the best one he had. Jessie might have been raised poor, but she'd been raised right. She wouldn't lie to her only kin.

He got out of the truck and opened the back so Jessie could do the same. She hesitated ever so slightly; then without a word she slid from the backseat. She took a deep breath, pulled at her jeans, then started toward the house.

She didn't say a word to him as she made her way up the creaky porch steps. Nor when he held the screen door open as she fumbled for her key. A sliver of light greeted them as she finally got the door unlocked and pushed it open so they could enter.

The combined smells of liniment and nicotine assaulted Seth as he stepped over the threshold behind Jessie. Old people and stale tobacco smoke. It was the kind of odor that seeped into every crevice and refused to leave. Of course, it didn't help that Naomi, Jessie's grandmamma, had arthritis and smoked like a freight engine. Honestly he didn't know how Jessie escaped the house every day without smelling the exact same way. But she didn't. She smelled like sunshine and strawberries and a field full of daisies after a rain shower.

Seth took off his hat and ran the fingers of one hand through his dark hair in a small attempt at ridding himself of the perpetual indention the Resistol gave him. Like that did any good. He'd been raised on a ranch in West Texas. As far as anyone knew, he'd been born with hat head.

"Jessica, is that you?" Naomi's gravelly smoker's voice floated to them from the room off to the left. He had been here enough times to know that the elder and *Mrs*. McAllen referred to the room as the parlor, though he never had been able to figure out why. No one else in Cattle Creek, Texas, claimed to have a parlor. Hell, no one west of the Mississippi had a parlor—except for Naomi McAllen.

"Yes, ma'am," she said, shooting him a sidelong glance. "And Seth Langston."

"The sheriff?" Naomi coughed, rough and long. Seth was no doctor, but even to his untrained ears, it didn't sound good.

Jessie waited for the fit to pass before she answered, "Yes, ma'am." She picked up the stack of mail lying on the small occasional table just inside the door and flipped through the letters as if she didn't have a care in the world. As if she wasn't a hair's breadth from being arrested.

He bent down low so only she could hear. "Uh-huh," he said, and wrapped his fingers around her arm and marched her into the parlor.

Naomi sat in a delicate-looking wingback chair he supposed really did belong in a formal sitting room. The upholstery was of good quality. Or at least it had been in its day. It was proof there had been a time when Naomi was a prosperous and upstanding member of the community. But that was before . . . well, everything. Now it was faded and threadbare, much like the woman who sat in it.

A sour-faced prune of a lady, Naomi McAllen was convinced that everyone—and, brother, he did mean everyone—was up to no good. Must have been all those years teaching English at the high school. But that was before the rise of football, and once the pigskin became king, Naomi had found herself replaced by a coach who would rather have been on the practice field than in the classroom. Disheartened by what she felt was the fall of civilization as they knew it, and too old and worn-out to do anything else, she had simply retired.

If that wasn't enough to make her lose her religion, there was that incident concerning missing money at the bank where her husband had worked. And then the missing husband, the missing sister, and the missing balance in their personal accounts.

It was about that time that Donna, Jessie's mother, had found out she was pregnant—and had no idea who the father was. She was keeping the baby thankyouverymuch—and she'd moved in, bringing sweet baby Jess along for the bumpy ride. Or at least that was how the ladies at the To Dye For Salon recounted the tale.

"Heaven preserve us, what have you done now?" Where age and illness had softened the angles of her posture and grace, there was absolutely nothing flexible about her attitude.

For the life of him, he didn't know why everyone—even Jessie's own family—always expected the worst from her. Sure, there was the whole Homecoming '08 issue, but other than that—and the high school darkroom explosion of 2006—she hadn't been in much trouble. Much. So maybe she was a little temperamental, a little overly passionate, but what redhead wasn't?

"Nothing, Meemaw." Jessie shot Seth another of her sidelong glances, then turned back to her grandmother. "There

was a . . . an incident at Manny's, and I was a . . . uh, witness.
I need to help the sheriff sort through some details tonight.
We didn't want you to worry."

It wasn't really a lie. There was an incident, and Jessie
could be called a witness, and she really couldn't go home
until they sorted out the details. Like *the truth*.

He'd taken a step forward, bent on telling Naomi just
that, when she started coughing once again. If Seth thought
the first time was bad, then this one was horrendous.

Jessie poured Naomi a drink from the pitcher on a side
table, then shook out a couple of pills in her hand. She
managed to get her grandmother to swallow them between
her spasms; a feat Seth considered a miracle in itself.

The old woman shuddered and wiped her face. She
studied her granddaughter with suspicious eyes, then
turned back to Seth.

"That girl's too impetuous by far," she said as if "that
girl" weren't her only grandchild.

"I'm right here, Meemaw."

"Yes, ma'am," Seth replied, for lack of a better answer.

"Probably end up pregnant," Naomi said.

He saw Jessie stiffen, but otherwise she said nothing.

"No, ma'am."

"Don't you sass me, young man. I may not have money
like your family, but that's no reason to disrespect me. You
understand?" Naomi cleared her throat and for a moment
Seth thought she might succumb to coughing once again.

"Yes, ma'am." He placed his hat back on his head,
adjusted it once, then nodded to the woman. So much for
his not so noble plan. "We'll just be going now." He took
hold of Jessie's arm and half dragged her from the house
as behind them in the parlor, Naomi cleared her throat and
started coughing all over again.

Naomi's health had been slowly deteriorating over the
years, but she was worse than he had ever seen her. He felt

guilty as hell for even thinking of laying Jessie's indiscretion at her feet.

Naomi would find out what had really happened eventually. She didn't go to church or the beauty shop regular, so it'd probably be the next bingo night at the VFW before she learned the facts. That was six days from now, and with any luck he'd have this whole mess straightened out by then.

Chapter Two

꧁ ✶ ꧂

Jessie stifled a yawn as Seth pulled his SUV into its parking spot in front of the Page County Courthouse. She normally worked till after two in the morning. It wasn't even one thirty, but she was wasted-tired. Maybe it was the stress and excitement the night had provided. All she wanted to do now was go home, crawl into her bed, and forget tonight ever happened.

Fat chance.

She wasn't going home tonight, so that knocked her bed out of the running, and she sure as heck wasn't going to get to forget about tonight and Chase's truck. Not for a long time.

Times like these she wished she wasn't so foolhardy. She was forever letting her emotions get the better of her. Everyone in town was still talking about the time she'd let the hog loose on Main Street. But it had looked so lonely in that truck just waiting to be slaughtered and roasted for the Cattle Days Picnic. He had looked as trapped as she felt. What was she supposed to do? She had let her heart lead and left her good sense behind. And then . . . well, as usual, all hell broke loose, and she was the talk of the town once again. Tonight had been no exception.

At first she had been so happy, so surprised to look up and see Chase standing at the bar at Manny's. Then she'd realized he wasn't alone, and that excitement turned into jealousy . . . which turned into its first cousin, rage, and before she knew it, she was the talk of Cattle Creek.

Seth hadn't said a word to her since they had hit the city limits. He drove along in a calm silence that she should have been used to by now. After all, she had known Seth practically her whole life, and he was definitely what *Cosmo* would call "the strong, silent type." He never wasted words. Always seemed thoughtful and never missed a thing.

Just as she expected, he didn't say anything to her as he opened the back door of his patrol car. But Jessie knew: he might be quiet now, but the time of reckoning was near. Real near.

"Yoo-hoo, Seth. Sheriff Langston."

Jessie turned in time to see Darly Jo Summers-Eden Burnett slam the door of her tiny silver convertible and mince her way across the street in her shocking-white high-heeled sandals. The top she wore was Barbie pink and formfitting, her shorts very white and very . . . well, short. She had pulled her barely shoulder length, streaky blond hair into the perfectly curled little ponytail she preferred, the bangs sprayed in defiance of the West Texas wind. Her makeup was artwork unto itself, her eyeliner perfectly drawn, eyebrows perfectly arched, and lips perfectly painted. No wonder she was Miss Page County three years in a row.

Next to her, Jessie felt like a female version of Oliver Twist.

Whose lipstick actually looked like that at this hour of the night, for heaven's sake!

Seth stopped and waited for Darly Jo to make her way toward them. He was too well mannered to do anything else, but Jessie rolled her eyes. Everyone in town knew Darly Jo was looking to get married again, and she had set her sights on Seth.

And she wasn't the only one. Half the women in the county would like nothing more than to walk down the aisle with the sheriff. The other half was still mourning that they'd already made that trip with someone else.

"I was listening to the police scanner, and I heard what all happened tonight. I was afraid you wouldn't have time to eat. So I said to myself, self, you ought to take the new sheriff some of your enchilada casserole."

"Why, thank you, Darly Jo." Polite to a fault, he took the pan from her.

Could she be any more obvious? It was the middle of the night, she was done up like it was happy hour, *and* she had food?

"I didn't have any of those disposable pans, so I just cooked it up in my good Pyrex and brought it straight on over here."

"That was real nice of you."

Sure it was, Jessie thought, surprised at her own rudeness, however internal. That gave Darly Jo the perfect excuse to come back tomorrow—or the next day—and pick up her pan. Couldn't Seth see through this obvious attempt of "the way to a man's heart is through his stomach"?

Darly Jo paused as if there was something else she needed from him. Or maybe it was just the expectant look on her face, as though she was waiting for him to pull back the aluminum covering and take a bite right then and there.

"Did you like that Mountain Dew cake I brought you last week?" She laid a hand on his arm in such a way Jessie was sure it had nothing to do with baked goods.

"Best one yet," he said with a smile.

If she didn't know any better, she would have sworn he was enjoying himself. The fact of the matter was, she didn't know better. As one of the most eligible bachelors in the county, Seth probably thrived off all the attention—and food—constantly provided by the husband-trawling women of the county. He was a good-looking man. Single. Virile. Handsome. What more could a girl want?

It was just that Jessie had never seen him like this. With a woman on the prowl.

"Well, I've gotta—" He nodded toward Jessie.

Darly Jo looked startled to see her there, as if she hadn't known anyone else was in the world except her and the "new" sheriff. "Oh. Right," she said, unable to hide her disappointment. She trailed her fingers across his arm as she started to leave. Jessie resisted the urge to roll her eyes one more time.

"Thanks again," he said as she backed toward her car.

"I'll just pick up my pan later."

Surprise, surprise, that innocent little phrase sounded covertly like an invitation to jump headlong into bed.

Or maybe Jessie was just overtired and imagining things.

Darly Jo licked her lips.

Nope.

"That'll be fine," Seth said.

"Okay, then." She waved her beauty-queen wave and turned back to cross the street.

Seth waited to make sure she got into her car okay, then opened the door to the courthouse and escorted Jessie inside.

She collapsed into the hard-backed chair positioned in front of his desk. Another pan of something sat on top of all the unfiled papers and reports along with a round aluminum pie plate that contained—if she wasn't mistaken—Lindy Shoemake's Banana Cream Delight.

She watched as he prowled around the room, turning on lights, flipping through his messages, and checking on Mr. Jones, who had managed to land himself in jail yet again.

Seth's actions were like Western poetry in motion, and despite her near physical and mental exhaustion, Jessie couldn't help but watch him. She supposed she couldn't blame Darly Jo for wanting to snare him as a husband. After all, Darly Jo was the daughter of the "old" sheriff and knew all about life with a small-town lawman.

Then there were the obvious reasons. Seth Langston was about the best-looking man in the county—aside from Chase, of course. But despite the fact that they both had those Langston green eyes, they were as different as two brothers could be. Chase was blond, whipcord lean, and took life as it came. Seth was dark and serious, six foot two of pure cowboy power and grace.

Seth was walking proof that what they said was true: you can take the man out of Texas, but you can't take Texas out of the man. All those years in California hadn't changed him all that much. Maybe added a few lines at the corners of those green, green eyes, deeper slashes at the sides of his sculpted mouth. But that was all. He was still a Texan through and though. Still all cowboy.

Cowboy. That was the sum of all five Langston brothers. Mav, Jake, Seth, Tyler, and Chase. They were all cowboy through and through. As the middle child, Seth was the peacemaker, the lawman.

Jessie could close her eyes and imagine him as the sheriff of Page County a hundred and fifty years ago, with a thick mustache that was the style of the times, black John B pulled low over his brow, and a badge carved out of a silver dollar pinned to his leather vest. But the badge Seth actually wore was clipped to the front of his gun belt. He carried a Glock instead of a six-shooter. Drove an SUV instead of a roan.

Yet some similarities still remained. Without a doubt, Seth had a wild, fiery light in his eyes. The light that had belonged to peacekeepers since the dawn of time. Wyatt Earp, Elliot Ness. Even that sheriff in Arizona who made his inmates sleep in tents and wear pink underwear.

I'm a good man, his eyes said, *but don't cross me.*

And Seth was—a good man and all that. Had been honorable and caring since that fateful day seventeen years ago when she had been terrified out of her mind. That very first time she had met the Langstons—the day Chase had rescued her from the wild coyote and thereby won her heart for all eternity.

Okay, so the animal hadn't been a coyote. And he hadn't really been wild. He'd actually been Heather Clemens's dog, who was about as fierce as a bag of dirty laundry—the dog, not Heather Clemens. But Jessie had been only seven, and the mutt had seemed dangerous enough at the time, so her love for Chase was in no way diminished by those pesky little details.

Her eyes were closed, so she heard rather than saw Seth prop his booted feet upon his desk, the creak of the chair as he leaned back, the rustle of the aluminum foil as he uncovered the casserole dish. Then he asked around a bite of Darly Jo's special recipe, "You ready to talk now?"

"You'll have to use torture, copper, if you want any info from me, see?" She tried to change her voice to the perfect Cagney inflection, but mixed with her slow Texas drawl, she was sure she sounded just plain silly.

But not silly enough that Seth laughed. Not even a small chuckle.

Jessie opened her eyes to find him staring at her, those green orbs so intense she was certain he could see straight through to her bones, all her secrets laid bare for him to examine.

"You can do it tonight or in the morning. Whatever you want."

She didn't *want* to do it at all. Not now, not tomorrow. Not with Seth, not with anybody. Especially not with Seth.

Seth was calm and understanding. He was collected and levelheaded and . . . and everything she wasn't.

"That's going to give you indigestion."

Seth shrugged. "I'm starving. Missed dinner," he said around another big mouthful. "You want some?"

Jessie shook her head. Darly Jo made her enchilada

casserole for every covered-dish potluck the county had, and it always gave everybody a stomachache. "Why'd you miss dinner?"

Seth shoveled in another mountain of the melted cheese and beans into his mouth. He chewed, swallowed, and got another bite ready before he answered.

"The Carvers and the Gibsons were at it again."

The two families were Page County's very own version of the Hatfields and McCoys, and like the famous dueling families neither remembered what the original argument had been about. But that didn't stop them from carrying on with it.

"Amos said Chester let his horses out. Personally I think it was a high school prank. Somebody's been knocking down mailboxes out on Creek Mine Road, and Bert Cottrell's house was TP'd last week."

Jessie nodded. Growing up in a small town had both its advantages and disadvantages. The novelty of summer break had worn off, the nights were hot, and there wasn't a whole lot to do. Except knock down mailboxes, TP the principal's house, and play tricks on Chester Gibson and Amos Carver.

"You gonna give me your statement, Jessie James?" Seth took one last bite, recovered the casserole with the foil, then set the pan on top of his desk. He wiped his mouth with a paper towel and eyed her expectantly.

"Do I have to?" she grumbled, worn to a frazzle and so tired that just this once she would allow him to call her by that awful nickname.

Seth took off his hat and set it down next to Darly Jo's good Pyrex pan. "Yes."

If she knew Seth, he'd had that hat on all day. Instead of looking goofy with a bad case of hat head, he managed to look like the top candidate for Most Handsome Sheriff in Texas . . . with hat head.

"Fine," Jessie grumbled, crossing her arms in front of her and wishing all this was behind her.

But it wasn't . . .

What did it matter anyway? Taking a baseball bat to Lucky Langston's shiny red Ford could only be accomplished by a holy terror like Jessie McAllen. The entire town—Chase included—thought she was guilty. Therefore she was guilty by means of the majority, and no amount of the truth could change that.

Jessie tried to ignore the choked feeling in her chest. It was bad enough eight years ago when she *had* destroyed a fine vehicle out of jealousy. But this time she was innocent. Maybe this was just destiny coming back on her. The thought held no comfort. She had spent her entire life trying to live down her family name. The scandal with her grandfather, her mother's lack of a wedding ring, her own impulsive nature.

"I'll do it now," she finally said.

He nodded—well, really it was more of a jerk of his head. Then he rummaged around in the desk drawer and pulled out an official-looking paper.

Beautiful.

"You know the drill."

Great.

He pushed the form and a pen across the desk to her.

Fantastic.

Just how she wanted to end a perfectly horrible night, having to give a formal confession, black-and-white proof that she was wild, out of control, her mother's daughter, etc., etc.

The worst part of it all was that Chase wasn't going to want anything to do with her for a long, long time. If ever. She had seen his face as he shouted that he wanted to kill her. He didn't really mean murder, but he was mad. And mad was a foreign state of affairs for happy-go-lucky, take-what-comes, life-by-the-seat-of-his-jeans Chase.

"Do I need to get an attorney?" She'd meant for the question to have the vicious bite of sarcasm, but in her exhausted state it was simply a question.

Seth shrugged, a quick rise and fall of one shoulder. "Justin's gone fishing this week, and Harley'll be real mad if you wake him up this time of night. I suppose if you want one, we could postpone this until morning."

No sense dragging this out. She pulled the form toward her and started to write.

Half an hour later she signed her name with a flourish, dotting the *i* with a little more force than truly necessary. As she had written about seeing Chase with another woman and Manny's baseball bat and how it felt to smash in the headlights of Chase's truck, her fury mounted anew. She could feel her cheeks burning and her blood boiling as she pushed the paper across the desk toward Seth.

Then she just sat there, her breathing heavy as she watched him scan the page.

He looked up and pinned her with those knowing green eyes. "Are you sure this is how it happened?"

No, she wanted to yell. Chase had walked into the bar tonight with that bleached-blond bimbo hanging all over him, and Jessie had wanted to trash more than just his truck. But that was all it was—a fantasy. Some guy she had never seen before had beat the hell out of Chase's F-150, and she had taken the fall. Now things between them would never be the same.

She pushed the thought away before her heart broke completely in two. She couldn't remember a time when she hadn't been in love with Chase Langston. How could she not love him? He was so confident and handsome. Even though he wasn't ready to settle down, she couldn't stop her feelings for him any more than she could stop a herd of stampeding buffalo.

She propped her hands on her hips, daring him to contradict her. "Yep. Homecoming '08 all over again."

Seth looked as though he was about to wad up the paper and toss it in the trash, but he read through her words again.

"Everything was going fine, ya know. Until Chase showed

up at Manny's with little Miss Big Boobs. Now, I've put up with a lot from him over the years, but tonight I'd just had enough."

Seth scribbled notes on his own paper, not even bothering to look up as he spoke. He'd gone into that detached "cop" mode. "Is there anything else you'd like to add?"

Anything else? "Yeah, after that, I went out and kicked a few puppies—"

"Jessie." His voice was low, half pleading, half warning.

"—and burned down the orphanage."

"We don't have an orphanage."

"Not anymore, we don't."

Seconds ticked by, then turned into minutes. Long heartbeats, before Seth looked up from his work. It seemed as if he wanted to say something but was having a hard time forming the words.

"You're sure this is how it happened?" It was more question than statement.

"Positive."

Seth unfolded his length from the squeaky chair and made his way around the desk to stand in front of her.

Suddenly Jessie was aware of just how tall he was. Exactly how much taller he was than Chase.

"How 'bout this, Jessie James? You tell me the truth, or I'm going to lock you up for obstructing justice."

"What makes you think I'm not telling the truth?"

"I don't think, I know. Your neck's red. It always does that when you're lyin'."

Her hand fluttered toward the collar of her shirt, but she managed to stop it before it betrayed her. "Oh, yeah?"

"Yeah." Seth crossed his arms and stared down that well-bred cowboy nose at her.

She stared back for a full minute.

"What's it going to be, Jess?"

"I thought you already arrested me."

"Don't push me, girl. I've had a long night."

"Then I'll make it easy on you." She marched over to the cell, paused just slightly at the threshold to the human cage, then stepped inside. She turned back to face Seth. "Lock me up, Sheriff. I'm bad to the bone."

He simply looked at her for several long moments, then followed behind her to the big iron door. And locked it. *Locked it!*

She had to will her feet to stay put. She would not—*would not*—run to the bars, wrap her fingers around them, and beg Seth to hear her out. She'd be fine here. She would.

"Jessie?"

Eyes back to Seth.

"Is there something you want to tell me?"

"Of course not." She tried to rearrange her expression to hide the panic she knew was there. Sometimes she just didn't know when to keep her mouth shut.

"You sure about that?"

She lifted her chin, raised her gaze to his. "No. I mean, yes. Yes, I'm sure. I'm positive I have nothing—absolutely nothing—more to tell you."

There was a moment when Jessie wished all this had played out differently. She hadn't really thought about where they were going when they left her grandmother's house.

And whatever it was she had been thinking, it sure as heck didn't include *spending the night* in jail.

Time to accept her fate and move on. She was quite accomplished at that. Growing up as she did, it was a survival skill learned at a very young age. She might not have money. Or an education. Or a good job. Or . . . well, a lot of things. But no one could say that Jessica Elizabeth McAllen didn't have pride.

She walked over—a pretty generous description for the three regular-sized steps she took—to the cot and shook out the fitted sheet.

Although her original plan had been a good night's sleep in her own bed . . . well, she would have to take what she could get. After all, she had to work the breakfast shift at the Chuck Wagon tomorrow morning . . . if Seth let her out of jail. If not, then she would lose that job as well as the one at Manny's. And she would definitely have to dip into her savings in order to pay for the damages that Chase's truck had suffered.

She had been scrimping and scraping for years, trying to save enough money to make her escape. Then just when she was so close to getting out of town, something like this had to go and happen.

It didn't matter anyway. She didn't have enough money to strike out on her own. Not yet. But one day . . .

With a sigh, she sat down on the edge of the hard little cot and pulled off her boots. They hit the tile floor with twin thuds. Then she removed her hat and stretched her arms above her head. She needed to release the tension in her shoulders, but the motion only pointed out just how tense they really were. What a night.

She undid the buckle of her belt and slid the worn turquoise leather out of its loops, then ran her fingers across the embossed letters of her name. She loved the belt. It had been a birthday present from her mother the year she died. Careful not to scratch the decorative silver conchos, Jessie coiled it like a snake and stored it inside one boot.

She chanced a look at Seth. He sat at his desk, shuffling through papers as if his actions had no purpose, except maybe to expend built-up energy and make him look busy. His green eyes blazed. His square jaw was set. Even the dimple in his chin appeared deeper. He was upset. Most probably at her. And most probably because of the fallout that would surely arrive tomorrow.

And the next day and the next day and the next. Make one little mistake eight years ago—*eight years*—and no one ever forgot. No one in Cattle Creek, Texas, anyway.

That was why she had to leave. Even if it meant leaving Chase behind.

One day soon she would make her break and kiss Cattle Creek and Page County good-bye forever. One day soon she would head to . . . to . . .

Well, the "to" really didn't matter as long as she wasn't here.

She lay down on the cot and tucked the travel-sized pillow behind her head. She closed her eyes, crossed her ankles, and waited for the exhaustion of a long, long day to overtake her. But as much as her body was willing to fall into the abyss of sleep, her mind was spinning like an Oklahoma twister.

Mr. Jones turned over in his cot, his covers rustling as he made himself comfortable. Papers whispered against each other as Seth placed them back on his desk. His chair creaked as he stood. She heard his shoulders pop as he stretched.

Eyes still closed, she could tell when he turned out the overhead light, could hear the soft echo of his footsteps as he made his way across the room.

But instead of the door closing behind him, she heard the shuffle of pillows and the creak of worn springs. The scrape of metal against the worn tile flooring and the thud of Seth's own boots as they landed on the floor.

She opened her eyes and turned on her side, easily making out his silhouette in the dim light.

He had pulled the worn Naugahyde couch out into a bed and was now sitting on its edge, hands braced upon his knees, boots on the floor beside his bare feet. He had removed his shirt and his belt, but his jeans were still molded to his lower half like a clingy jealous lover. And though his chest was a sight to behold, it was his dark expression that captured her attention. He looked like a man with a burden, and something Jessie identified as basic human compassion made her want to go to him and comfort him.

Okay. So, that was wrong on so many levels. She was his

prisoner. She couldn't leave her cell. She was in love with his brother and . . . well, that was enough, wasn't it?

"You don't have to stay here on account of me."

His head jerked in her direction, surprise lighting his features. "I thought you were asleep."

"Nuh-uh," she said, then added, "Busy day." Wasn't that the truth?

She wasn't sure, but she thought she saw one dark brow rise at a sardonic angle.

"Well, go to sleep," he grumbled, his voice hoarse with . . . anger?

"I meant what I said. About you staying here."

He lay down on the uneven bed, propped his hands behind his head, and closed his eyes. "It's my turn."

Jessie flopped onto her back and stared up at the darkened ceiling, allowing dreams of leaving Cattle Creek to fill her head.

Sometimes her fantasies took her to New York, but she never really thought she would be happy in a big city like that. Houston maybe, but that was still in Texas. Maybe she would go to Tulsa, but Oklahoma didn't seem far enough away. Cheyenne and she would face the risk of running into Chase every July. Vegas was too flashy. Detroit too northern. Phoenix too western. Seattle too wet.

"Tell me about San Diego." Her mouth made the request before her mind had completely wrapped around the idea.

"San Diego?" he echoed as if he'd never heard of it.

"You know, West Coast. Big city."

"What do you want to know?" His voice was soft. He sounded tired, and Jessie felt bad about keeping him from his sleep. She'd ask him for the particulars of the city later. Right now there was only one thing she really wanted to know.

"Why'd you come back?" When it came her chance to leave, she wasn't ever setting foot in Cattle Creek again.

"Mama." The rich timbre of his voice wrapped around

the single word and held it in the air between them. So much went without saying, and that one word conveyed it all: if it hadn't been for his mother's illness, he would be there still.

But Evelyn Duvall Langston had been diagnosed with breast cancer, and Seth had come home to Texas.

"Do you miss it?"

"Sometimes."

"Was there someone special there?"

He waited so long she knew the answer. Tony Bennett might have left his heart in San Francisco, but Seth Langston's was a little farther south.

"You don't have to answer that," she finally said. If coming up with a response was taking him that long, then he surely didn't want to talk about it. Perhaps that California filly had broken his heart.

"Go to sleep, Jessie James."

She undid the top button of her jeans for comfort's sake and pulled her knees up. "Fine," she mumbled. "But how many times do I have to say it? Don't call me that. . . ."

It seemed as if she had just drifted off when she felt the featherlight brush against her cheek. Probably a mosquito that had found its way onto the porch through the little hole in the screen. She was going to have to fix that.

She tried to muster up the energy to brush it away, but she was just so darn tired. And it was late. Or maybe it was early. And she slept like she was in a borrowed bed.

The light touch whispered across her skin once again, and she finally gained the strength to reach up and shoo the pesky little vampire away so she could go back to sleep.

But instead of a fragile little bloodsucker, her fingers encountered . . . skin. Human skin. Most likely *male* human skin.

Her eyes flew open, her mind taking a full two minutes

of staring at the strong jean-clad thighs and uh-hum . . . other things in front of her before she finally remembered where she was and whose strong, jean-clad thighs and uh-hum . . . other things she had locked in her sights.

The night before came crashing back to her. Chase's truck, jail, and . . .

"Seth." Her voice was raspy with sleep. And fatigue. And lack of coffee.

She swung her legs over the side of the cot, belatedly remembering the top button of her jeans was undone. Even worse, the zipper had worked its way down during the night, and the bottom of her shirt had worked its way up, leaving part of her belly bare and showing the lacy edge of her yellow cotton panties. She pulled the tail of her shirt down to cover herself, then pushed her hair out of her face.

"Rise and shine, Jessie James." Seth thrust a chipped mug full of black coffee into her hands and walked to the door of her cell as if he couldn't get far enough away from her fast enough to suit him.

She didn't even bother asking him to cut it out with the nickname and instead concentrated on the strong brew and the positive effects caffeine had on her at . . .

"What time is it?" She blew across the top of the mug before taking as big a swig as she dared. What she thought had been black coffee turned out to be coffee with about half a pound of sugar in it. Really bad coffee with half a pound of sugar in it.

"A little before six."

Jeez, no wonder she was so tired.

"Chuck called and threatened to cut me off at lunch if I didn't have you to work on time."

"I hope you saved some of Darly Jo's casserole," she said, then took another restorative sip of coffee.

"Nope."

Jessie raised her gaze to his. "You're going to let me outta here?"

Seth nodded, his dark hair glistening under the lights of the office as though it was damp. He'd made coffee, obviously had a shower and shaved, and was way too awake for so early. Had the man even slept?

"I talked to Chase this morning. He said he'd drop the charges as long as you agree to pay to have his truck fixed."

She had known all along it would come to this. Just for a moment she had forgotten about the "incident" at Manny's, the state of Chase's truck, her stint in jail, and the damages she'd need to pay for. Okay, so maybe she hadn't *forgotten*, but it had slipped to the back of her mind, and now . . . well, now she was once again faced with a county full of people who always expected the worst from her, including the man she loved.

"Fine," she said, then set her coffee mug down on the floor and retrieved her belt. She laid it on the cot next to her, then pulled on her boots. At least she wouldn't lose both her jobs. Maybe Chuck would let her pick up a few more shifts until she could find something else. Then paying for Chase's truck wouldn't put such a dent in her savings. Or maybe Manny had cooled down and would regret firing her. If she was lucky—and she wasn't usually—he'd let her have her job back this afternoon. Hey, it could happen. Page County was home to only a little over three thousand people. In such a small labor force, it wasn't easy to find someone willing to take on the rowdy cowboy crowd that congregated at Manny's.

She stood and pushed the tail of her shirt back into her jeans, barely taking the time to refasten them before threading her belt through its loops. Ignoring her sleep-trodden, half-braided hair, she shoved her hat back on her head and grabbed her half-empty coffee mug before facing Seth.

He sat behind his desk, sipping his own cup of coffee. All of last night's food had been cleared away, only to be replaced with a new batch—a pan of brownies, a box of doughnuts, and a sticky caramel coffee cake that Jessie was certain was Heather Clemens's grandmother's recipe.

"Can I go now?"

He nodded once, and Jessie started for the door.

"This isn't over, you know."

"Yeah, Seth. It is."

In more ways than one.

*D*amn fool woman!
     Head bent over his notebook, Seth cut his gaze up and watched Jessie jerk open the station door. It took all his energy not to pop up from the chair like some crazed jack-in-the-box and go after her, demand that she tell the truth. Demand she forget her damned pride that kept her from defending herself against these charges in the first place.

She was going to make this hard on him. Thank heaven above Chase was on his way to New Mexico. If Seth had to deal with both of them at the same time, he'd resign.

No. He'd shoot them both, and *then* he'd resign.

"Hey, Dusty." Jessie brushed past his deputy and she was gone.

"Hey back," Dusty replied to her retreating form before the sandy-haired man turned his attention to Seth.

"What was Jessie doing here?"

"You already forget about Chase's truck?"

"No, but—"

He didn't even give the man a chance to answer, his voice sounding impatient and harsh even to his own ears. "But what?"

"I just didn't think you'd throw her in jail."

"I didn't throw her anywhere."

"But she spent the night here."

"She admitted to the damage done to Chase's truck," Seth said through clenched teeth.

"Well, now, somebody got up on the wrong side of the couch this morning."

Seth stood and slammed his hands down on his hips, his sleepless night making him as surly as that mare Jake insisted he'd keep, though no one—not even Chase—could stay on her. He still had a bad case of heartburn from Darly Jo's casserole, and he hadn't been able to do anything last night but lie awake and listen to the even rhythm of Jessie's breathing. "If you got something to say, Dusty, why don't you just come right on out and say it?"

"All right." He limped over to stand toe-to-toe with him. A couple of years younger, a few pounds heavier. Not quite as tall, but looking him square in the face and not backing down an inch. That was one of the things Seth admired most about his chief deputy.

"Why don't you stop pretending like you don't love Jessie and go for the direct approach for a change?"

Seth was so stunned he couldn't reply.

For a minute anyway.

Then he scoffed. "I don't love Jessie. Well, I mean I do . . . but more like a . . . a sister."

"Can it, Seth. I'm a cop too. Remember? Maybe I didn't train at UT or get hired on at fancy-schmancy San Diego like some people, but ASU ain't so bad. They taught me how to spot signs and clues. I know enough to see when a man's got it bad, and you, my friend, have got it bad."

"Whatever." Not quite the snappy comeback he would have liked, but Dusty had taken him by surprise. He thought he'd kept his feelings for Jessie well hidden. He'd never made an improper move toward her, never told another soul how much he wanted her for his own.

As he mulled this over, Dusty clumped over to the coffeepot and poured himself a cup. He took a tentative sip, then grimaced. "As if loving your brother's girl ain't enough."

Seth exhaled heavily, felt his nostrils flare. "I never said I loved her." And he didn't. She was the one thing he couldn't have, and for that reason and that reason alone he wanted her all the more.

"You don't have to. But don't worry. Your secret's safe with me."

Now, how could he answer that? If he said thanks, he would be admitting he did indeed have a thing for his brother's girl. And if he said he didn't have a secret that needed to be kept safe, then Dusty—with his bulldog tenacity that made him such a damn fine deputy but right now was slowly driving Seth out of his cotton-pickin' mind—would keep up the line of conversation until he found a chink in Seth's mental armor.

So he took the easy way out and just glared at him.

"You've been drinking your own coffee this morning. That's enough to make any man spoil for a fight. Whatcha say we go over to the Chuck Wagon and get us some decent joe?"

"Jessie's there."

Dusty slapped him on the shoulder like the old friend he was.

"Good," he said. "Then you can start working on that direct-approach thing I was telling you about."

"Direct approach? You mean flirting with anything in a skirt."

Dusty smiled. "Call it what you like, but keep this in mind: how's a girl gonna know you're interested unless you tell her?"

Seth shook his head. "I have work to do." He dropped back into his chair, his deputy's gaze boring through him. He did have work to do. A lot of it. He was a busy man. He had to get Johnson Jones out of there, type up the witnesses' statements from all three of last night's big happenings, and go check on the kittens Chase had left in his apartment. Not to mention, he needed to feed Sadie and let the poor pooch know that despite his brother's quest to fill Seth's life with as many animals as possible, she was still number one in his heart. Yeah, he was a busy, busy man. Much too busy to walk all the way across the street for a cup of coffee. Much, much too busy. And his reasons for not going had nothing—absolutely nothing—to do with Jessie McAllen, despite what he had said. Not to mention the fact that she was mad enough to spit nails, and he didn't want to be anywhere in range when she let loose.

"Suit yourself," Dusty replied, but instead of making his way to the door, he came up behind Seth and tapped one finger on the notebook he'd used last night when Jessie gave her statement.

All the time she had been talking, Seth hadn't been just writing, he'd been sketching too. Right smack dab in the middle of the page where the notes concerning her confession should have been was a perfect pencil drawing of Jessie's sweet face.

"Bad, my friend," Dusty said, before turning toward the door. "You got it bad."

Chapter Three

Seth slid into his favorite booth at the Chuck Wagon and tried to shake his bad mood. He had, in fact, been trying to shake his bad mood since . . . well, since yesterday. Specifically last night. Even more specifically, last night at Manny's when Jessie had requested that he handcuff her and—damn it—it might be years before he got over that one.

He was seven times a fool for coming in here. He had stuff to do. He needed to be at the station filing reports and the zillion other pieces of paper that marked the legal side of law enforcement. With Nancy on leave, the place had gone to pot. And on top of it all, he had been stuck drinking his own coffee—which was bad, but not nearly as bad as Dusty claimed it to be. And he needed to steer clear of Jessie.

But even when Seth had been at the station steering clear of Jessie, he hadn't been filing reports or the zillion other pieces of paper that marked the legal side of law enforcement. He had been brooding—plain and simple. Well, maybe not so plain and surely not so simple.

Along with the brooding, he had been watching the clock over the door, waiting to see it display the time when Jessie left her job. When two o'clock hit and she was still inside the diner, he decided he'd go over anyway. A man had to eat sometime, didn't he? Even if he was seven times a fool.

He should have just grabbed a sandwich when he went home to let Sadie out and check on the kittens Chase had dumped off. But he hadn't, because it was fried chicken day and—

Movement caught his attention, and he looked up. Jessie approached, a forced smile smeared across her face. Purple smudges cast shadows under her clear gray eyes, and fatigue weighted her steps.

Yet her chin was high and her back straight. And he couldn't help wondering how her slim shoulders carried around all that pride, day in and day out.

But one thing was certain, Seth had to be more careful where Jessie was concerned. It wouldn't take long for the proverbial dust to clear. Holding a grudge would require too much effort on Chase's part. He'd forgive Jessie in a day or two and things would go back to the way they'd always been: Seth loving Jessie, Jessie loving Chase, and Chase loving anything in Rocky Mountain jeans. Sure as the world, one day Chase would put an end to his wild streak and he would marry Jessie. Wouldn't do for everyone in town to know that Seth had a thing for his brother's *wife*.

"You here for the chicken, Sheriff?"

Her tone was falsely bright and held no clue as to what she was really thinking.

"I didn't think you'd still be here."

"Sheridan needed me to stay. She and Aaron had a meeting with someone at the college."

Seth nodded.

"You want some coffee too?"

"Now, why is everybody harping on my coffee?"

Jessie shrugged. "Truth hurts."

"Just bring me a glass of iced tea," he said, "with—"

"Lots of lemon," she finished for him, not even bothering to write his request in her order pad. Instead she plunked down his silverware and turned back toward the kitchen.

"I got the estimates from the insurance adjuster."

That stopped her in her tracks.

She turned to face him, her expression unreadable. "That was quick."

Seth shrugged. "He's a friend of mine."

That was all there was in Cattle Creek: friends and enemies and nothing in between. The lot of small-town life.

She took a deep breath before asking, "Bad?"

"Uh-huh."

"How bad?"

"Real bad."

"Three thousand dollars bad?"

He held her gaze steadily and pointed upward with one finger.

"Thirty-five hundred bad?"

Upward again.

She scrunched up her face as if she didn't want to actually say the numbers. "Four thousand?"

"Forty-two," he said.

"American dollars?"

"And change. A lot of change," he added as her proud posture started to sag. Then her shoulders caught and straightened as if she had accepted her fate and was prepared to face it. "I'll make the first payment as soon as I can."

He watched her walk to the kitchen to put in his order and had to bite his tongue to keep from calling her back.

She returned a few minutes later and slid his blue plate special in front of him. The industrial white stoneware was piled high with fried chicken, mashed potatoes and gravy, and green beans seasoned with lots of black pepper and a touch of bacon grease.

He inhaled the delicious aroma, and his mouth started to water. She filled his tea glass as he grabbed his fork. Normally he didn't eat such a big meal midday, but thanks to indigestion from his midnight snack and a certain redhead—who would remain nameless—he'd missed his breakfast. Now he was starving.

He was just savoring the first bite of the potatoes when she set the pitcher on the table then dug into the pocket of her apron. She pulled out of wad of ones, several coins bouncing off the table as she plunked the money down. "There's almost thirty dollars. It's not much, but it's a start."

"Jessie." Seth shook his head.

"No," she said. "I'll settle this debt."

She turned to walk away, but Seth abandoned his fork and grabbed her arm, stopping her. "Put that money back in your pocket."

She shook her head again, looking very close to breaking down right there on the spot, her overabundant pride the only thing stopping her. "We have an agreement."

"Screw that. Chase is just being an ass. Give him a few days to calm down and—"

She shook her head. "No."

"Quit being so damned stubborn, Jessie. You can't afford to pay for Chase's truck."

"You don't know jack sh—"

"I know that you can't afford to be prideful right now."

He used his hold on her to pull her toward him. Ignoring how good she smelled despite the fact that she had spent the night in jail, he wadded up the bills and pushed them back into her pocket.

"But—"

"No buts. I'm not going to let you do this, Jess."

A moment stretched between them, and Seth was aware of every fiber of her being. The rise and fall of her breaths, the little cinnamon dusting of freckles across her nose and forehead, the pride that seemed to roll off her in waves.

She opened her mouth and inhaled deeply, as if she was about to say something, but whatever was on her mind was lost in the shrill buzz of his phone.

He hesitated for a moment before he let go of her arm, whipped the device from his belt, and read the text message. He was only dimly aware of Jessie retreating behind the counter. It was just as well; they would have to postpone this conversation until another time.

Chester and Amos were at it again. He knew from experience that he was the only one who could calm them down enough to reach at least some facsimile of peace. At least until the next time.

He slid from the booth and stared longingly at his chicken. "Jessie, can I get my check?" He asked even though Chuck had never charged him for a meal since he'd taken up the office across the street. "I gotta go."

"Take this." She handed him a to-go cup filled to the brim with sweet tea. Through the milky plastic lid he could make out at least three pieces of lemon floating on the top. She loaded up his chicken and a biscuit into a foam box so he could eat it on the way.

"This isn't over, Jessie."

"Yes. It is." With his hands full she seized the opportunity to stuff the thirty dollars into the front pocket of his jeans.

He ignored the feel of her skin so close to his, separated only by the thin cotton of the inside of his pocket.

"No, it's not. But I have to go. We'll talk about it tomorrow." He balanced the to-go cup on the top of the container and put his hat back on his head with a small nod.

"Tomorrow?"

"At supper."

She still had that "what are you talking about?" look.

"Wesley's birthday," he prodded.

She shook her head. "I'm not going."

"Of course you're going."

"No, I'm not."

"Yes, you are."

"I've got other plans."

Such a lie. He narrowed his eyes. "What kind of plans?"

"Well, let's see. Matthew called and he's going to be in town—"

"Matthew?"

"McConaughey."

"Right."

"—and then there was the cocktail party at the governor's mansion. I'm just not sure I can fit it all in."

"I'm sure Matt will understand."

"And the governor?"

"Get a rain check."

She shifted uncomfortably from one foot to the other suddenly serious. "I don't know, Seth. Chase isn't going to be there and—"

"When has that stopped you from attending a family function?"

She had to attend the party; she was practically one of the family. She was honor-bound, duty-bound. Jessie had to be there.

"I don't think it's a good idea."

"Chicken."

"I'm not being a chicken. I really don't think it's a good idea."

"Well, I do."

"I'm not sure—"

"Well, I am. Mama will have my hide if you don't show up tomorrow."

Jessie caught her bottom lip between her teeth, worrying the tender flesh in her agitation.

Damn, he wished she wouldn't do things like that. 'Cause it made *him* want to do things like that. Made him want to do more than that. Made him want to kiss that bottom lip. And the top lip and the divot at the base of her throat, and the spot where the V of her shirt cast a shadow across the sweetly freckled skin of her breasts and . . .

"Jessie." Desire had roughened his voice, and her name came out harsher than he had intended.

She seemed to wilt ever so slightly, her backbone losing a little bit of its normal starch, before she recovered herself. She straightened and a look of determined resignation came over her sweet face. "All right." She nodded.

"I'll pick you up at three." He slapped the wad of tips back onto the table and headed out the door.

Just before three the following afternoon, Jessie dusted her cheeks with a bit of powder, then critically surveyed herself in the mirror. The magazine ad said the makeup would smooth out uneven skin tones, but from where she was standing, every one of her gabillion freckles shone like beacons.

It wasn't often that she wished she looked different—just every other week or so. She wasn't ugly. That much she knew. It was just that she was every inch the girl-next-door kinda cute in the way of puppies and baby frogs. She wasn't sexy, didn't turn heads when she walked down the street. Some throwback recessive gene had left her red-headed, and some cruel twist of fate had made her as flat-chested as a boy. But she had good qualities that had nothing to do with her looks. She was loyal, dependable, and honest. The kind of girl men married but didn't sweep off her feet. With a sigh, she smoothed some gloss over her lips and turned away from her reflection.

Today would certainly prove itself to be a long day. Why couldn't Wesley's birthday be next week or even the week after that? Anytime other than today so that the talk could die down and she wouldn't have to dodge so many accusing and inquisitive stares. But she knew she had to go.

Because despite last night's adventure and the party for Seth's five-year-old niece, there were the tragic circumstances surrounding Wesley's birth. Jake's wife, Cecelia, had died bringing her into the world. Everyone tried to make a celebration out of the day, but sometimes the sadness still managed to creep in.

Jake grieved for his wife. He never dated, rarely smiled. It broke Jessie's heart to see him like that. Jake had always been like a brother to her, steadfast, caring, and kind, just one more Langston she would miss when it came time for her to go.

She heard Seth pull up, and she grabbed her camera and her hat, dashing out of the porch bedroom she made for herself in the summertime and through the kitchen to the front room.

"That's Seth," she told her grandmother, poking her head into the parlor to check on her. "It's almost three. Don't forget to take your pills at four thirty."

Naomi harrumphed—though to Jessie it sounded suspiciously like a suppressed cough—and never wavered her eyes from the game show rerun.

"Try and use that new inhaler the doctor gave you. Maybe it'll help."

Naomi cleared her throat again.

"You have the number out at the ranch if you need anything, right?"

That did it. Or maybe it was the fact that a commercial had taken the screen from Bob Barker, so her grandmother could turn her accusing eyes on her. "What do you expect me to do, drop over dead while you're gone?"

"Of course not." But the words made Jessie's heart miss a beat. It was her greatest fear, that she couldn't be with her grandmother all the time and something would happen while she was out. She pushed that thought away. Meemaw still had a lot of life left in her.

"Don't lie to me. I've heard the doctors talking behind my back—"

"Meemaw," she sighed. "No one has been talking about you. The doctors have been very up front about everything."

"—and I know I'm not long for this world."

Jessie resisted the urge to roll her eyes. She knew what was coming. Had heard it too many times to count. It both unnerved and annoyed her that her grandmother could talk about her death like an event at the county fair.

"When I die," she continued, "make sure that you get that picture. The one of me and your mother at the river. You know the one."

She did. A framed black-and-white snapshot that hung just to the left of the door leading to the kitchen. Her mother had been about seven years old, with knobby knees and stringy blond hair. Donna had been holding her mother's hand. Naomi looked young and happy. A different lady, a different time. It was that picture that had inspired Jessie to want to take photographs of her own, capture things so easily lost.

"I don't have much," Naomi continued, "but that picture's special."

"I know, Meemaw." Jessie inched toward the door.

"I want you to keep it."

"Yes, Meemaw."

"Pass it down to your children."

"I will, Meemaw."

Naomi opened her mouth to say something more, but Jessie interrupted. As rude as it was to cut off her grandmother, Seth was waiting and once Naomi got on the subject of the picture and happier times, it might be days before she came up for a breath.

"Just take your medicine at four thirty, 'kay?"

Naomi harrumphed again and muttered something that sounded like "these young people today" as Jessie turned and made her way out the front door.

* * *

Seth was halfway to the house when Jessie came tripping down the porch, her camera swinging around her neck and a brightly wrapped package tucked under her arm. Without a word, he opened the door for her, then made his way around to the driver's side of his old red-and-white Ford.

How many times had he done this very same thing: swing by and pick up Jessie before heading out to the ranch for a Langston family function? Christmas, Easter, Jake's birthday, his mother's birthday, Grandma Esther's birthday. After all those times, all those birthdays, all those family events, why did today feel different? Why did today feel like a date?

There was only one way to get through a situation like this: keep his eyes on the road, his hands on the wheel, and an iron clamp on . . . well, an iron clamp on everything else.

Piece of cake.

Yeah, right.

Why now? he asked himself again. Why, after three years, was he having such a tough time ignoring the feelings he had for Jessie? Why was he having such a tough time ignoring *her*? Why was he so aware of every breath she pulled in, every time she exhaled? Why was he so aware of the way the air from the vents blew the wisps of her hair—those fuzzy little pieces that had escaped her braid—around her face? Her scent assaulted him and enticed him at the same time. He'd barely spared her a glance and yet every detail was burned into his brain. The exact color of her buttercup yellow button-up dress printed with tiny blue flowers and the exact way it rippled and floated around her slim frame. The worn red cowboy boots that Jake had found her over in Austin and the seen-better-days straw hat that she'd had as long as Seth could remember. The fact that the only jewelry she wore were little, dangly butterfly earrings his mother had given her when she graduated high school and the slim silver bracelet engraved with the word *dream*—also a gift from the Langston family—that she wore on her left arm in place of a watch.

Why now? He only had one answer to that question: because he was starting to want more. A real house—not just Nita Calvert's renovated garage apartment. A family of his own. A wife to come home to every night. To share a meal, share their days. A son to carry on his name. More.

He let his gaze wander to the side, just enough that he could make out Jessie's tense profile. The one big problem with wanting more was that he couldn't have the one woman he truly wanted.

It sure didn't help that his mother kept pushing Millie Evans in his face every chance she got. He hadn't had a conversation with his mother in the last two weeks without Millie's name coming up—ever since she had returned to Page County. And then there was Darly Jo . . . well, she was something else entirely. Though he had to admit she would be the most logical choice for him. She was obviously willing to enter into a relationship with him. And she knew firsthand the responsibilities of a small-town sheriff. She knew about the long hours, the spur-of-the-moment, middle-of-the-night calls. But with all things considered, he couldn't say she was what he wanted in a mate. What he wanted was sitting next to him, but belonged to someone else. And Thursday night's events just drove home what he had been denying for far too long. It was time for him to settle down and get married. Stop playing the field and—

"I don't know why you insisted that I come today."

Seth kept his gaze glued to the dusty ranch road in front of him. They had been driving for almost half an hour, not counting the side trip to the Safeway, and she hadn't said more than "Hi" and "Thanks for the ride" to him. They were almost to the Diamond and now she wanted to talk?

"You're part of the family."

"Not really." She shrugged. Not that he was actually looking at her. Not directly anyway. Just out of the corner of his eye.

"Okay. What'd you get for Christmas last year from my mother?"

"A bread machine and some underwear."

"Me too," he said, trying not to think about the whole underwear thing. "Doesn't get much more family than that. Plus, you take the best pictures."

"So you want me or my camera skills?"

Now, what was he supposed to say to that? "And your punch. Don't forget your punch."

She tried for a smile at his poor attempt at humor, but it looked more like a grimace than anything else.

"Jessie, you're an honorary Langston."

"And that's all I'll ever be."

He couldn't help himself; he turned his head and looked directly at her. "What do you mean by that?"

"Chase was real mad the other night."

"Chase doesn't stay mad for long. He did drop the charges the next morning."

Her short little braid did a small pendulum swing as she shook her head. "Chase isn't going to get over this one. No one's going to let him."

"That's not true and you know it." He peeled his gaze away from her and trained it back onto the road ahead.

He said the words, and she shrugged again, neither in agreement nor in denial. But he knew she believed what she had said. And he supposed there was a small part of it that was the truth. Small towns were cruel and unforgiving. Collectively they forgot nothing. If an individual happened to let something slip his mind, you could bet that someone in the town would be there to remind him. Unfortunately Jessie had been fodder for the gossips since the day she was born.

Of course everything would be different for her once

Chase decided to settle down. Lucky Langston was the golden boy of Page County. Hell, he'd put Cattle Creek on the map. Once Jessie hooked up—officially—with Chase, then all her worries would be over.

"You could always tell him the truth."

She made another one of those noises in response, somewhere between protest and acceptance.

They drove in silence for a few minutes; then she cocked her head to the side and asked, "Did you really get a bread machine for Christmas too?"

"Actually mine was a toaster oven."

She nodded thoughtfully as he pulled his truck to a stop in front of the big house.

Jessie had her door open before he even cut the engine. She grabbed the brightly colored present and the brown paper grocery bag that she'd brought along, then tossed a small white envelope in his direction. The fat little bundle hit his lap with a small *thwack*.

"Now we're even," she said, slamming the door shut, leaving Seth to stare at the stack of twenties nearly an inch thick.

"Jessie—" He broke off as she shook her head.

"Don't say anything, Seth. Just let me do this. I *need* to do this." Without sparing him the smallest glance, she turned on the heel of her boot and hurried toward the house.

Chapter Four

❦

Seth caught up with her, just as she reached the steps leading to the door to the ranch house.

"Wait up," he said, snagging her arm before she could escape the many, many questions he had. Like where she'd gotten that kind of money.

"Just leave it, Seth," she said without turning around, without looking at him at all. Damn. That pride had kicked in again. Her freckled shoulders were stiff, her back ramrod straight as if she had just been led in front of the firing squad.

"Jessie. You know I can't take this money."

"That was the agreement."

"You and I both know that Chase will forget about this in a day or two—"

"Well, I won't."

"Where'd you get this money, Jess?" he asked quietly.

She lifted one shoulder. Like that was any kind of an answer.

"Jessie."

"I've been saving a little here and there."

"A little? There's over four thousand dollars in this envelope," he said, smacking it against his thigh. It cracked like a whip.

She shook her head, refusing to answer.

"Jessie," he started, his quiet voice sounding overloud in the cool shade of the porch. "Why are you letting everybody think that you did it?"

She shrugged again. "Everyone expected me to do it."

He opened his mouth to respond, but she plowed on ahead.

"Let it go, Seth. It doesn't matter," she said. "Because soon, I'm gonna have all the money I need to leave this town behind forever."

Only his years of police training allowed Seth to hide his surprise. Never in his wildest dreams had he ever imagined a Cattle Creek without Jessie. To him she was as much a part of the town as the longhorn mascot of the high school football team that was painted on the water tower. Always there, true blue.

"You're leaving?"

"Did you think I was going to wait around forever?" She shrugged again. "I love him, but I'm not stupid."

He had no chance to reply, no chance to give voice to his hope.

The front door opened. Wesley stood in the threshold looking from him to Jessie and back to him again. Then in typical Wesley fashion, she turned without a word and ran back into the house yelling, "Da-ad! Nana! Aunt Jessie and Uncle Seth are here."

Jessie shot Seth one more look, then hustled up the steps and into the house.

Seth took a deep breath, trying to tamp down the beast that had risen inside him again. Aunt Jessie and Uncle Seth. Like they were a couple, as if they belonged together.

The creature under control once again, he started after Jessie and Wesley.

The heels of his boots scraped against the slate stone of the cool, broad portico as Seth crossed to the door of the big house. It wasn't the first ranch house. The original white clapboard with wraparound porch and squeaky screen door was a quarter of a mile or so down the dusty ranch road. And though it had been good enough for her parents, it was not worthy of JT Langston's bride, so he'd built her a new house with her own dowry. The Duvalls continued to live in the cozy three-bedroom, and the Langstons resided in the expansive ranch house reinforced with Oklahoma sandstone.

To Seth, it was home. He loved spacious rooms and tall, cedar-beamed ceilings. It smelled like vanilla and leather and family. There had been so many good times here, both before and after his father died. There had been lots of sad times too. Maybe that was why walking through those big oak doors was like being embraced by every good and honest thing he had ever known. He'd missed it during all his time in San Diego and had rediscovered it when he returned to Texas.

"Seth, is that you?" his mother called to him from the back of the sprawling house.

"It's me, Mama." He took off his hat and started through the spacious living room with its oversize leather furniture, cowhide throw pillows, and brightly pattered Navaho blankets.

"Did you remember the ice cream?"

"Yes, ma'am." He followed the sound of her voice and the delicious smell of sweet birthday cake to the warm, homey kitchen.

For the most part, the kitchen was open and airy with an earthy terra-cotta tile floor and all the modern conveniences that money could buy. A ristra of dark, wrinkled peppers hung in the corner between the two uncovered windows. One looked out over the ranch yard and the well-worn path to the horse barn. The other had a view of the side yard and the sparkling blue swimming pool Jake had installed as a fiftieth birthday present for their mother.

"I'm glad you're here. Millie's been asking about you."

I'm sure she has. He set his hat on the table, stowed the melting ice cream in the freezer, then kissed his mother on her proffered cheek. The combined smells of White Shoulders and prized horseflesh greeted Seth like an old friend.

Five foot four, petite, and blond, Evelyn Duvall Langston looked like a delicately aging rodeo queen instead of a devoted mother and grandmother. Dressed in a red silk blouse and dark-wash jeans, a snake-hide belt with a glittery buckle encircling her trim hips, she could have posed for *Country Living* magazine. But from the tips of her Nacoma boots to the top of her perfectly coiffed hair, she was a horsewoman at heart. There was a power in her that was almost tangible and spoke of more than just her triumph over breast cancer. She was tender and strong, the matriarch of the Diamond and the reigning queen of Page County. She had been before she married JT Langston and she remained so all these years after his death. Neighbors and friends wanted her to run for mayor of Cattle Creek, but Jake joked that the decrease in power would kill her.

"Did Jessie come through here?" Seth asked.

"She put her bag on the table and then went out back with Wesley. Tore through here like the devil was on her tail."

Chicken, Seth thought. Dump forty-three hundred dollars in his lap—literally—and then head out the back way.

"I suppose these are supplies to make her infamous punch?" Evelyn asked, fingering the edge of the brown paper grocery sack that Jessie had abandoned. "Do you think I should look and see what the secret ingredient is?"

"Not if you value your life."

"That girl is such a mess." Evelyn smiled affectionately, taking some of the sting from her words. "I guess she gets that from her daddy. Her mama was a wild one, but she wasn't so . . . so . . ."

Prideful? Hardheaded? Beautiful? Sexy?

"Feisty?" he finished.

"Mmm-hmm," his mother murmured as she casually turned her attention back to the final touches of Wesley's birthday cake. "There's a rumor going around that you arrested her night before last." The words held no more weight than the evening weather report. But Seth knew . . .

He made a great show out of unloading the bag that contained Wesley's birthday present, hoping he appeared too busy to answer.

"Did you really do that?"

He took a deep breath and braced his hands on his hips. "She confessed, Mama." There was no need going into the whole obstruction of justice thing. His mother would definitely not understand that.

She shook her head. "Well, that's no reason to go and put her in jail."

"I'm sure there are several people that would disagree with you. Chase, for one."

"That boy."

Seth didn't correct her. At twenty-five years old, Chase would be considered by most to be a man. "Was he still mad when he left?"

"Chase doesn't stay mad long," she said, then went back to the task of putting candles on the mile-wide birthday cake spread across the big wooden table. "Did she do it?"

"No."

"And you still put her in jail?"

"She confessed, Mama."

"I thought I raised you better than that. She's practically your family and the first chance you get, you go and lock her up."

He didn't know how to respond to that, so he played it safe and just kept his mouth shut. After a long silence his mother continued.

"I think she's expecting you to ask her to the Cattle Days Picnic."

He frowned. "Jessie?"

"Millie."

"And why would she think something like that?"

"Now, Seth. You're not getting any younger. Millie's a good girl from a good family. If the two of you were married—"

"Whoa, whoa, whoa," he said, not sure whether he should be annoyed or amused. "How did we get from a date to Cattle Days to marriage?"

"I'm just saying, that's all." She gave a slight shrug of one shoulder. "It's high time that we had some more grandchildren around here. And you're not getting any younger."

"I believe you've already mentioned that," Seth replied.

"Well, it's true."

And it was. But . . .

"Mama, I—" And just how did he finish that? *I love Jessie?* "I'll think about it," he managed.

She tilted her head to one side in that thoughtful pose she struck when she was meddling, but trying not to appear that she was meddling. It was a look he knew well. "I wouldn't wait too long if I were you. Ethan Davis was asking about her earlier."

"He was, huh?"

"You wouldn't want to let a fine girl like Millie slip through your fingers."

"I don't suppose I would," he said.

"But you're a grown man. Old enough to make your own decisions."

"Yes, I am."

She stared at him a moment as if she couldn't figure out why he was being so stubborn; then she went back to the fine details of the cake.

Her attention elsewhere, Seth ran one finger along the

edge of the icing for a quick taste and got a swat for his efforts.

"Seth Langston, you stay out of this cake if you know what's good for you. Grandma Esther worked all morning on it. She'll have your hide if she comes in and finds your finger tracks in it."

"Not a problem." He grinned. "I'll just blame it on Jake."

"That didn't work when you were twelve, young man. It's not going to work today."

He turned and smiled as Esther Langston entered the room. Thin and feisty, his paternal grandmother—despite her eighty-plus years—was hell on wheels on her good days and a force to be reckoned with on her not so good ones.

She pointed a gnarled finger at him. "You been in my cake?"

He plastered his best innocent look across his face. "No, ma'am."

"Don't you lie to me, boy. You know where you go for lying?"

"Houston?"

Evelyn stifled a laugh.

Grandma Esther shook her head, then turned accusing eyes to her daughter-in-law. "Too much cheek, that one. Now come over here and give your grandmother a kiss."

Seth did as he was told, bestowing a small, affectionate peck on her wrinkled forehead. Despite her sass and brass, she had a marshmallow center, and he loved the old bird with all his heart.

"Cake looks real good, Grandma."

She harrumphed and started criticizing Evelyn's candle placement. But his mother was used to her and kept right on doing as she pleased.

"Where's my brother?"

"New Mexico," Evelyn answered without missing a beat.

He didn't know whether she was being deliberately

obtuse as a joke or she was so consumed with Chase that she automatically thought of him first. He was afraid it was the latter. "My *other* brother."

She looked up from the cake, her eyes sad, her lips pressed together in a thin line. "He's in his office."

"Is he okay?"

"As well as can be expected. Each year I think it gets a little easier. But he puts on a brave face for Wesley's sake, so it's hard to say for sure."

Seth nodded. "I'll go see about him."

"That one's crooked, Evie."

"What about Millie?" his mother asked as she adjusted the candle and he headed out of the kitchen.

"I'll only be a minute."

"And then you'll go find her?"

"You need more sprinkles on this side here," Grandma said.

"It's a possibility," Seth answered.

"And ask her to the Cattle Days Picnic?" Evelyn shook more sprinkles on the left side of the cake.

"We'll see, Mama," he said, then started down the hallway to Jake's office.

He rapped twice on the thick wooden door, then stepped inside at his brother's distracted-sounding summons to enter.

If there was nothing like coming home, then surely there was nothing at all like entering the enormous office that had once been JT Langston's and now belonged to his second eldest son. Aside from Jake's framed diplomas that hung on the wall to the left and a snapshot of Wesley that sat on the large mahogany desk, Seth would bet that nothing had changed since his father's death nearly fifteen years ago. Stepping inside was like stepping back in time. But in a good way.

Not that the ranch was running the same as it had been in his father's day. No, Jake had taken the Diamond into the twenty-first century and beyond. He worked long and hard—probably too long and too hard, given the fact that it was his daughter's fifth birthday celebration, and he was chained to his desk.

Except Jake wasn't working. At least he didn't *appear* to be. Unless there was some New Age ranching technique that required a cowboy to sit at his desk, his elbows braced on its surface, his head buried in his hands.

He didn't move as Seth approached. Not good. A squatty glass of amber-colored liquid sat near, and Seth was afraid that the heartbreaking memories of the day were more than Jake could handle.

"Tell Sonny I'll be there in a minute," Jake said his voice muffled, tired.

"You'd better come now. The clown canceled, and you're the only one who can wear the suit."

Jake jerked up at the sound of Seth's voice, rising out of his seat as if he had been caught doing something he wasn't supposed to. Like maybe brooding. Or drinking.

"When'd you get here?" he asked, walking around the desk.

Jake was the tallest of the Langston boys, topping Seth and Ty by at least an inch and Chase by several. He had the same green eyes and dark, dark hair inherited from their father. But what Seth noticed most in his brother's face the most were the brackets at the side of his mouth, the product of stress and grief. The light salting of gray at his temples and the tiny little lines that fanned out from his Langston eyes, memories of days in the sun and long-ago laughter. But Jake seldom laughed anymore—only for Wesley. He rarely smiled anymore—only for Wesley. And Seth had to wonder at the irony of the one thing that brought his brother joy was the one thing that had taken it all away . . . Wesley.

Seth looked at the tumbler. "A few minutes ago."

Jake caught the direction of his stare. "It's iced tea."

"I knew that."

The eldest Langston shook his head and smiled a sad

little smile that barely touched his lips. There was no hope of the movement ever reaching his eyes. "No, you didn't. You thought I'd fallen off the wagon."

Seth feigned innocence. "Who, me?"

"Don't even try to lie. You were checking up on me, and I love you for it."

"Good, because I've got a favor to ask."

Jake didn't comment, just raised a dark brow and waited.

"I need to put this in the safe until the party's over." Seth held out the bank envelope Jessie had given him.

Jake whistled under his breath. "Is that what I think it is?"

"No, it's not a payoff. I told you when I took this job I'd be honest and trustworthy."

Jake chuckled, then shot a pointed look at the stack of twenties. "That sure ain't lunch money."

Seth crossed to the wall safe and pretended preoccupation in getting the combination correct so that he didn't have to answer. At least not right away. He just wasn't sure how much to tell Jake. He set the money inside, shut the door, then turned back to face his brother. "It's the money to fix Chase's truck."

"And you have it why?"

Seth took a minute to answer, unsure of whether he was ready for the fallout from the truth, yet unwilling to lie all the same. "Jessie gave it to me."

"Is it true you made her spend the night in jail?"

Seth pinched the bridge of his nose and wished that he hadn't left his hat on the kitchen table. If anything he could throw it at Jake—for old times' sake. Instead he took a deep breath and counted to ten. "She confessed."

"But did she do it?"

"You know, there I was. Chase was screamin', half the town was watchin', and Jessie was confessin' . . ."

"Did she do it?"

"And then there's the whole Homecoming '08 thing. . . ."

"Yeah, but did she do it?"

Seth looked his brother square in the face and expelled a pent-up breath. "No."

"And you made your brother's girl spend the night in jail. For a crime she didn't commit. That's cold. Even for you."

"I was hoping she would break down and tell the truth."

"You're talking about Jessie McAllen, right? 'Bout this tall, red hair. Kind of impulsive."

"I know, I know. But it seemed like a good idea at the time."

Jake nodded and a long brotherly silence stretched between them.

"I'm glad you're here," Jake finally said.

"Did you think I wouldn't show?"

His brother shook his head, a wistful smile barely curving up the corners of his mouth. "Nah, I'm just glad."

"You're just hoping to get out of this whole clown thing," Seth said as he led the way to the door.

"About that," Jake returned, following him and turning off the office light on the way out. "Not a good joke. The clown is the only entertainment we have."

Chapter Five

❧❖❧

Langston family get-togethers usually included the entire ranch and half of the town. Wesley's party was no exception. Aside from the traditional clown that Evelyn hired every year, Jake had arranged for "pony" rides on a gentle old mare named Ginger for the younger children and a heavy plastic dummy bull had been dragged from the barn into the yard to entertain the others. The older boys were practicing their throws while the adults finished up the last of the cake and watched from the large green tent that had been set up for the occasion. Seth knew that it wouldn't be long before a few innings of softball or a not so friendly game of powder-puff football broke out.

"Uncle Seth, watch me!"

Seth smiled and waved to prove he was doing just that as Wesley tried her hand at roping the plastic bull. Wesley was all Langston, though she was the spittin' image of her mother. With her blond hair and enormous brown eyes, the only things she seemed to have gotten from her father were the slashing dimples on either side of her bow-shaped mouth. Dressed in a red T-shirt, cutoff Wranglers, and once-shiny-but-now-covered-in-dust brown ropers, she looked every inch the tomboy she had been raised to be.

As Seth watched she settled the rope easily around the bull's head and turned back to smile at him under the brim of her straw hat.

Seth gave her two thumbs-ups just as a pixie in purple denim shorts and a pink T-shirt with a smear of chocolate icing on the front came screaming into view. Seth prided himself on knowing his community, but he had never seen this child before. Though with the current oil boom, the county was filling up with families that he had yet to meet. Her dark hair was curly and tangled, the sparkly tiara perched on top, glittering in afternoon sun. Her chocolate brown eyes were vaguely familiar. She couldn't have been more than four, her feet in their scuffed red cowboy boots pumping furiously as she ran from Denny Anderson, one of the ranch hands' boys. Denny carried a small grass snake in one hand, a wicked smile on his little-boy face.

"You stay away from me or I'll . . . I'll . . ."

"You'll what?" Denny leered at her.

"She'll sic the sheriff on you," Seth drawled.

Denny stopped, his grin instantly falling from his face.

"Hi, Sheriff Langston," he said sullenly, dropping the snake to the ground, where it slithered off harmlessly.

The pixie, knowing an ally when she found one, slipped behind Seth, wrapping her chubby little arms around his legs.

"Go on back to the party, Denny."

"I was just playin'."

"Go on."

"It wasn't poisonous," he added as he dragged his feet and returned to the group of boys taking turns "riding" the oil barrel that had been rigged between two trees.

"Layla?" a voice called. "Where are you?"

"Mommy," the imp behind Seth cried. But instead of letting him go, she clutched him even tighter.

That need for a family of his own reared its ugly head once again. Was there such a thing as a male biological time clock? If so, his was currently gonging like Big Ben. Given half a chance, the pint-size cowgirl princess would have his heart for her very own. Seth looked up to greet her mother and instead found . . .

Millie Evans.

"Hi, Seth."

The years had been good to her. Seth couldn't see much difference in the Millie he had known then and the one who faced him now. Oh, she had a few little creases at the corners of her deep brown eyes and they were filled with the wisdom that only age can bring. She was a tad curvier than he remembered, but all in all, she was the same girl he'd known practically his whole life. "I heard you were back."

She nodded, the moment between them familiar and yet uncomfortable. Nostalgia urged him to lean in and kiss her cheek, to take her hands into his own, but too many years had passed and he stopped himself from acting on the impulse. "Layla and I got into town a couple of weeks ago."

"She's yours?" He remembered now hearing through the grapevine that Millie had a daughter.

"Most days," she answered with a smile, the wind stirring the ends of her dark brown hair as she twisted the obviously Layla-made macaroni necklace around the fingers of her right hand.

"I'm sorry to hear about you and . . ."

"Travis."

Seth nodded.

Millie shrugged and let go of the necklace. It fell with a slight rustling noise against the soft cotton of her faded green T-shirt. "People get divorced all the time. Your mama tell you about that?"

"Of course."

Millie shook her head. "She's found a reason to drive out to the ranch every day this week."

Seth smiled. "She means well."

"She's a great lady."

Seth could only nod.

"I heard that you made Jessie McAllen spend the night in jail."

"Good news travels fast."

"So does bad news," she murmured. "Did she do it? Did she really trash Chase's truck?"

Seth looked over to where Jessie had retreated behind the lens of her camera, snapping off frame after frame of the day's festivities. Sissy Callahan stood nearby, and judging from the tense line of Jessie's shoulders, the conversation between them was anything but friendly. "Does it matter?"

Before she could answer, a cloyingly sweet voice drifted between them.

"There you are. I swear, Seth, I've been lookin' all over the place for you."

"Hi, Darly Jo." Seth hoped the smile on his face was welcoming, or at the very least not too close to the grimace it really felt like. "You remember Millie Evans."

"Actually it's Sawyer."

Of course she'd keep her married name. Divorced or not, she had a child with Travis . . . Sawyer. But to him she'd always be just Millie Evans.

There had been a time when Seth had thought that he and Millie would get married. They dated all through high school, started at UT together, but then she had decided during their senior year that ranch life wasn't for her after all. She'd broken up with him the week before finals and eloped with a baseball player the day after commencement. Seth had thought his heart would never be the same. He'd accepted the job offer in California. Buried himself in every beach babe he could find. He had gotten over Millie. Proof positive that he'd get over Jessie too.

But more than that . . . maybe it was time to try to forget

about Jessie. Try to get a life. Maybe even get married, have babies. No doubt with a little time he could learn to love someone else. No doubt about it.

"Of course," Darly Jo said, echoing Seth's thoughts as she nodded, then slipped her arm through his. "I've been lookin' all over the place for you."

"So you've said."

She sidled up close to him, as close as humanly possible, and Seth resisted the instinct to push her away even though he could feel Millie's questioning gaze on the two of them. Apparently Darly Jo was in an unusually possessive mood today. Just what he needed. His mother shoving Millie at him, Darly Jo tugging on him, and—

Just then Seth felt a pull at his legs and looked down to see Layla staring up at him, a mulish expression on her pixie face as she did her best to push him and Darly Jo apart. Darly Jo looked a bit startled, but seeing as she didn't have any children of her own, she wasn't sure how to react to the situation. She opened her mouth to speak—more likely protest—then thought better of it and instead decided to go for the "ignore it and maybe it will go away" approach.

Seth tried to hide his amusement as she tottered on the thick wedge heels of her sandals and took a step back, as Layla the Princess did everything in her little girl powers to put even more distance between them.

Note to self: give this kid anything she wants for saving me.

"Well, I came over to see if you could give me a ride to Cattle Days next weekend," Darly Jo said, her beauty queen smile never wavering despite Layla's efforts.

Seth tried to look chagrined and disappointed at the same time. "I'd really love to, but Millie just asked if I'd escort her." He slipped an arm around Millie to pull her close and felt her stiffen under his unexpected touch. "For old times' sake and all."

Darly Jo's pink-shellacked lips formed a surprised "Oh."

Seth silently prayed that Millie wouldn't contradict him. And she didn't. She just stood there, rigid under his embrace as she looked from him to Darly Jo.

Darly Jo looked from Millie to him and back again. "I see," she said, though her tone was not the least bit understanding. "Well, maybe some other time, then." She allowed Layla one more small shove; then she waggled her fingers at them in farewell and headed off toward the buffet table still laden with the remnants of birthday cake and the last dregs of Jessie's famous punch.

The minute she turned, Millie stepped out from under his arm and glared at him. "What was that all about?"

Seth eyed her sheepishly. "Uh-hum, Darly Jo has a tendency to be a little—"

"I noticed," Millie said without waiting for him to finish.

"Sorry. I shouldn't have used you that way. I'll make it up to you."

"How's that?"

"By actually escorting you and the lovely Miss Layla here to the Cattle Days Picnic."

But Millie was shaking her head before he could even finish.

"Why not?"

"I don't think that's a good idea."

"I think it's a great idea."

"I love picnics," Layla chimed in from behind him.

"Seth, I—" Millie shook her head.

"If you go with me, it'll get my mother off your back." At that he saw her resolve start to crumble.

"And there are rides."

"I love rides," Layla hollered, her boots stomping as she danced in place.

"I won't take no for an answer," he pushed.

"Please, Mama, please, please, please."

"How can you say no to that?" Seth teased.

"Fine," Millie said, her tone grudging. "But you're buying."

* * *

Jessie clicked off another snap and tried not to stare.
Everyone knew that Seth Langston and Millie Sawyer
had had a thing . . . once upon a time . . . when she was
still Millie Evans. But the possessive way Seth snaked his
arm around her and pulled her close had Jessie wondering
how quickly the spark of that old flame could be brought
back to life.

Like she cared. She blew her hair out of her face and
checked the film in her camera. In the age of digital pho-
tography, she found a thrill in taking a picture and then
having to wait to see the finished product. Wait to see
whether she had captured the moment or missed. Wait to
see if the lighting was right on film or just in the present.
It was important to make sure that the film was correct and
she still had enough in the old camera to keep taking pictures. Wouldn't do to run out. And it gave her something
to look at besides Seth . . . and Millie . . . and Darly Jo.

Why had she never noticed that Seth was such a chick
magnet?

He even had Layla, Millie's four-year-old daughter,
hanging on to his every word. And his legs.

Was she surprised because she had just never thought
about him that way? Or was there something different
about him today? She cut her eyes up from changing the
film to chance a look at him. She didn't lift her head,
wouldn't want to start a load of gossip.

He smiled at something one of the adoring females said,
a quick flash of even white teeth and slashing dimples.

Nope, he looked the same. So what was different?

She tossed that thought away and turned back to taking
pictures. On the other side of the horse corral, what looked
to be a softball game was beginning to form. She snapped
off a couple of shots. Wouldn't be long before Sissy Callahan Murphy made her move and said something like

"What a shame! Coach Edwards would be soooo disappointed to know that malicious destruction of private property is all that the hours of batting practice has netted his favorite high school softball player."

Jessie turned away and pretended not to hear, but she could feel the heat rising in her chest all the way to the tips of her ears.

Thankfully Sissy had used up all her cattiness for the day and flounced off to join the game.

Jessie had known that showing her face at Wesley's party wouldn't be a cakewalk, but she'd no idea how hard it really would end up being. She endured the not so veiled jokes and barbs, the whispers behind the hand—as if she didn't know that they were all talking about her. She just put on her game face and cowboyed up. She smiled, pretended not to hear, and kept right on serving up plates of the chocolate cake with a side of blue bubble gum ice cream. She played with the kids, took pictures, and otherwise pretended to have the most wonderful time she'd ever had at a birthday party. But enough was enough.

Jessie went to find Seth and see if he was ready to go.

Damn, it was hard to hold her head up in this town. Sometimes she felt as if her neck would break under the strain.

She managed to retain her composure until she found him. And she even kept herself together as she said her good-byes to the Langstons, gave Wesley a big squeeze, and gathered up her things for the trip back to town.

Only when Seth pulled the truck out of the yard and started back toward town did she allow her guard to slip.

She laid her head against the seat back, the motion tipping her hat over her eyes.

"You okay?"

She could tell by his voice that he had turned to face her. "Yeah," she said, though they both knew it was far from the truth.

She sighed and tried to push all the negativity out with

the air. They weren't at the party anymore. She didn't have to keep her guard up or a fake smile plastered across her face.

The thought had a real smile curving her lips at the corners.

"There it is."

At his words, tears stung the back of her eyes. Why was it that Seth had always been there for her?

She pushed herself up straight. "Do you know why I did that to Sissy Callahan's 'Vette?"

"I have an idea."

"It was the water tower."

"Huh?"

"That day, Chase had painted 'Sissy and Chase' on the water tower." She shrugged as if it didn't still hurt. "I was jealous."

It had been the beginning of the end for them. She could see that now. But at the time, all she could think about was that Chase had performed this grand gesture for Sissy Callahan when she, Jessie McAllen, was supposed to have been Chase's girl. So why couldn't he paint the water tower for her? Even then, she never should have taken it out on Sissy or that poor unsuspecting car, but it was easier than getting mad at Chase. Even when he had come in with yellow paint under his nails swearing that he had nothing to do with it, she'd believed him and instead went after Sissy.

"He just wanted to get into her cheerleading skirt."

"I'm sure he succeeded too." The thought made her stomach sink, even after all these years.

"You're probably right."

She leaned her head against the seat back and closed her eyes, trying to keep the memories at bay and not succeeding.

"Give it a couple of days, Jess."

She nodded but knew deep down it was going to take more than a couple of days for this storm to blow over.

* * *

Seth chanced a quick look at Jessie. She looked dead on her feet. Carrying around all that pride had to be exhausting. But what choice did she have?

Cattle Creek was the greatest place on earth, but it wasn't always the easiest place to live.

Small towns were like that, like one big family. And everyone knew what a pain family could be.

He just wished that Jessie didn't have to suffer further at the hands of Chase. She had enough of her own problems to deal with before his brother piled even more on top.

Would she really leave Cattle Creek? If she could hand him thousands of dollars to fix Chase's truck, how much more did she have squirreled away?

Even more important, what would he do without her around?

Chapter Six

❦

"Damn it! Of all the luck."

Jessie opened her eyes and sat up straight. "What's going on?" She blinked a couple of times, trying to wash the sleep from her eyes. Had she fallen asleep? She shook her head to clear away the wispy cobwebs of fatigue. These days it seemed that she was more tired than she had ever been. Seeing as how she wasn't working at Manny's any longer, she could only blame her exhaustion on the fact that she had been working like crazy trying to build up her escape fund and her body was in sore need of rest.

Big billowing clouds of white smoke poured out from under the hood as Seth eased the truck toward the side of the road.

"The truck overheated," he said, putting it in park and killing the motor.

"Ya don't say." Jessie tried to keep her face impassive, but her lips twitched just the same. She pushed her hair back and half turned to face him.

Seth pointed through the windshield without removing

his hand from the steering wheel. "I'm pretty sure, yeah," he said with a nod. "Hopefully it won't take long for it to cool down, but—" He peered out the windshield at the cloudless Texas sky. Today's high was supposed to be near one hundred. "In this heat it might take a little longer."

"How convenient." Jessie sat back and crossed her arms.

"What's that supposed to mean?"

"Nothing really." She shrugged. "It's just that when a boy—"

He cleared his throat.

"—*man* runs out of gas—"

"I didn't run out of gas. The truck overheated."

"—it's usually," she continued as if he hadn't spoken, "just a way to be alone with the girl he has in the poor old broken-down truck."

"It's a great truck."

"In 1973 maybe." She couldn't help teasing him.

"Those are fighting words," he growled. "If you insult a man's truck, then you need to be aware of the consequences."

"Oh, yeah? Like what?"

"Like—" He leaned toward her, but then seemed to think better of it, or maybe he remembered who he was with. He shrugged, turning to face the front.

Jessie stared at him, perplexed by this sudden change. For once she felt as if she were seeing the real Seth, the man behind the badge. The man behind the mask. She hadn't been aware that he wore a mask until he let it slip, and now that it was firmly back in place, she was curious—no, more than curious—about who Seth became when it was gone.

"Did you do this with Millie?"

"Hmmm?" He turned back to face her, but his eyes were focused on a point just above her left ear.

"Millie. Did you ever tell Millie that you had run out of gas just so you could, uh . . ."

Seth nodded, then ducked his head looking almost chagrined. Almost.

"Men are skunks," she said with a laugh.

"Not all of us." He chuckled.

"Might as well be." She sat back in her seat as smoke continued to roll out from under the hood.

But instead of thinking about the trickery of men, she remembered the time she had accidentally run across Seth kissing Millie in the game room at the ranch. She couldn't have been more than ten, but she could tell that it was a good kiss, like the kind in the R-rated movie she had snuck in to see. They had thought they were alone, and Jessie had been nearly paralyzed with something she couldn't name as she watched them. Now she knew it was merely curiosity, but that kiss had stayed with her all these years.

Did he kiss the same now? Did he cup his hands around the girl's face, treasure her as he had Millie? Would Millie be the next girl he kissed?

Why did she even care?

Suddenly she wanted to know what it felt like to be kissed that way, with that all-consuming need. Cherished, desired, loved.

She scooted across the seat toward Seth, not giving a second thought to anything but him. And that kiss.

He didn't speak as she tipped back his hat and pressed her lips to his.

He was on fire.

Or maybe he was dreaming.

How else could he explain the fact that he had Jessie next to him? Sweet Jessie with her lips hovering over his. Their breath mingling. She wet her lips with the tip of her tongue.

Seth groaned and pulled her to him again.

Never before. Only in his wildest fantasies had he imagined that Jessie would come to him like this. She smelled like sunscreen and strawberries and tasted like the last hot day of summer. She tasted so good and yet he was mad at her for the way she made him feel, the way she made him forget all about the fact that she had been with Chase first. Mad about the fact that despite everything, he still wanted her.

Not so gently he ran his fingers into her hair, knocking her hat off her head. His mouth devoured hers, the kiss turning from sweet to fierce in mere seconds.

He wanted her. And yet he hated himself for wanting her. He should stop kissing her. He should let her go. But he couldn't. He had held himself in check for so long that once the dam had broken, there was no going back.

He would have her, if only this one time, and maybe then he could get her out of his system. His desire burned like hot coals doused with gasoline. He wanted her, and he wanted her now. The lines between truth and reality blurred as she responded to his plundering kiss.

How could she make him want her so badly? What type of sorcery did she employ that could make him forget everything else but the need to possess her?

She whimpered as he nipped her bottom lip. He wanted to punish her for making him want her despite all else. And yet he couldn't stop kissing her. Loving her was like a runaway freight train with no engineer.

He hated her. He wanted her. He had to have her.

But this was not how he wanted her. He wanted to bare every inch of her, kiss every smooth centimeter, taste every silky millimeter. Instead he was sitting inside his busted truck, burning up with desire and anger. He pushed a hand between them even as his mouth continued to plunder hers. She gave as much as he offered, meeting him violent kiss for violent kiss.

He freed himself, barely registering that Jessie had raised herself up on her knees, straddling him, giving him complete access to whisk her panties to one side.

He buried his face in the side of her neck, taking a bite

here and there. He wanted to make sure she knew that this time was different. This time she was with him.

Her breath caught as he entered her. She was tight. So tight. Not "gee, it's been a long time" tight, but "never done this before" tight. And that just couldn't be.

He pushed a little farther. Met with more resistance and the barrier of her innocence, but that meant . . .

Goddamn it.

He pulled away. "Jessie."

Her head was down, her hair shading her expression from his searching gaze.

"Jessie, look at me."

She did, and Seth felt a thousand emotions hit him at once. Gentleness and a touch of anger. Not with her, but with himself. Up until now he'd been thinking about her being with his brother, not knowing that she never had been. He had been fueled by anger and a desire he couldn't contain. He hadn't been gentle.

She had a bite mark on the side of her neck. Her lips were red and swollen from the force of his kisses.

Damn it.

They were both still nearly completely dressed. And it was her first time. It never should have been like this.

He swore again. He had to stop. Now. He placed his hands on her hips, intending to put an end to this madness.

"Seth?"

"We can't do this, Jessie."

"Please don't stop."

Maybe it was the urgency in her voice. Or maybe the fact that he couldn't deny her anything. He didn't know. Why did she want him? He could ask, but it wasn't time for talking.

He pulled her lips to his once again, taking his time. Soft, sweet kisses even as he settled her lower into his lap. This was how it should have been from the start. He couldn't undo that. He could only make it right from here.

He laved the red mark on her neck, gave it a kiss to heal the sting. But even as he wanted to take it slow, that outrageous desire reared its head, demanding to be assuaged. She squirmed against him, unable to complete their joining as long as he was holding back.

"Seth?" Her voice was soft and filled with questions, her eyes closed.

"This may hurt a bit." He hated to cause her pain. Yet he needed to love her completely, fully.

She opened her eyes, those gray depths, raging with a desire all her own.

He swore, then covered her mouth with his once again.

She gasped as he broke through, but he swallowed the sound, vowing to make this right. Love her as she deserved to be loved.

Even if they were in the front seat of his pickup.

He eased a hand between them. This time his touch was gentle, meant to bring her pleasure. She made a mewing noise as he found that sweet spot, brushed it with the pad of his thumb.

But even as he wanted to take it slow, Jessie was having none of it. She rocked against him, pushing him too close too soon.

"Jessie," he groaned.

"Love me, Seth." She pushed to her knees once more, then lowered herself, sheathing him completely.

She gasped, her muscles tightening around him as she found her release, the motion pulling him over the edge of ecstasy.

It was over almost as quickly as it had begun, and though she had found pleasure in Seth's embrace, she felt strangely unsatisfied.

He set her from him and got out of the truck, only putting his clothes back to rights once the door was between them. He crammed his hat onto his head, effectively hiding his expression from her searching gaze.

What did a person say in a situation like this? Her mother had died when Jessie was too young for such advice, and her grandmother had never been any help in that department. Jessie had been sort of an outcast in school, always on the fringes of the cliques and unable to fit in even with the misfits. She had no girlfriends to pass on pithy remarks or classy "pillow talk" as they called it. So she just watched as Seth lifted the hood. She had seen him walk around to the bed of the truck and retrieve a rag and a recycled milk jug full of water. At least now the smoke had dwindled down to a small curl.

Any moment now he could slam down the hood. The truck would start, and she still hadn't thought of anything to say.

Given the look on his face, "I'm sorry" seemed the most appropriate, but she wasn't sorry. Not in the least.

In fact, she was glad that he had been her first. She was thankful to have shared something so intimate with him, though she had never dreamed it could happen. When she had pressed her lips to his, suddenly waiting until she was married hadn't seemed so important any longer. And neither had Chase.

Good Lord, what would she tell Chase?

Her heart pounded at the thought. Then she took a deep breath. She wouldn't tell Chase anything. He didn't need to know. Everyone in town might believe that one day they would get married, but she knew the score. As much as she loved him, he didn't love her enough to give up his tomcat ways. And by the time he grew up enough to see he needed to change, she would be long gone.

Seth slammed down the hood, his hat still pulled low over his brow. Jessie scooted over to his side of the truck, laying one arm in the open window as he approached.

"Why do I get the feeling you're mad at me?"

"Why am I—" He scoffed and with a shake of his head, braced his hands on his hips.

"Did I do something wrong?" She had thought it had been good, that Seth had, well, *liked* it. But she didn't know for sure. How did a person tell those sorts of things?

"You didn't do anything wrong, Jess. Now scoot over."

She retreated to her side of the truck as Seth climbed into the cab. But he didn't say a word the rest of the way back to town.

He was thinking. She had known him long enough to realize that. But that angry look still hovered around his eyes.

He pulled into her driveway without a word. Jessie slid from the cab and slammed the door behind her before racing up the steps and into the house.

Seth nearly crumpled with relief as he let himself into his garage apartment.

Sadie met him at the door, her silky stump of a tail wagging like crazy. He scooped her up into his arms and received a rain of doggy kisses for his trouble.

From the kitchen came the meows of the kittens that Chase had dropped off just a few days before. Seth had been too busy to find them homes yet, but if nothing else, he would run them out to the ranch tomorrow. Jake could always use a few more mousers in the barns.

He planted a quick kiss on the top of the Yorkie's head, then set her back on the floor. "Give me just a minute, girl, and I'll get us both something to eat." *All of us,* he silently amended as the mews intensified. Yep, tomorrow he was taking the kittens to the Diamond.

Sadie trotted along behind him as he made his way toward his bedroom door. There weren't many dividers in the apartment. Just the walls that blocked off the kitchen from the living room, the living room from the bedroom, and the tiny bathroom from everything else.

He made his way to the shower, stripping down as he went. He needed to clean himself up, but he was loath to wash the scent of her from his clothes. To say that he had handled the situation badly was an understatement. He hadn't even said anything to her on the way home.

But what was there to say? Nothing at all. More than he could voice.

He stepped beneath the cool spray and let the water run over him as it warmed. He needed time, time to think, time to get a handle on everything. His anger, his confusion, and the many questions he wanted to ask her but was afraid of the answers.

It had been her first time.

How could that be?

He had been so caught up in the thoughts that his brother had been there first, and yet he still wanted her more than his next breath. Then to find out that she had never been with Chase.

He scrubbed his hands over his face and did his best to wash away the hurt and longing.

Just because she didn't belong to Chase didn't mean that she was Seth's. He had taken something precious from her. A girl didn't "accidentally" stay a virgin until twenty-five in this day and age. And Seth had snatched it away with the snap of his fingers.

He turned off the water and stepped from the shower, wrapping a towel around his middle even as his hair dripped down his back.

Tomorrow, he promised as he made his way to the kitchen, a second towel slung across his shoulder. Tonight he would get his thoughts in order, give Jessie time to let everything sink in, and tomorrow he would head over to her house and they would talk this out, face-to-face.

He dumped the contents of the can of cat food onto a saucer as the baby felines braced their paws on his bare legs. Their claws were like needles as he gently shook them loose in order to put their food on the plastic place mat next to the fridge. Tomorrow, he promised. Right after he took the cats out to the Diamond.

B y Monday at lunch, Jessie knew Seth had to be avoiding her. And she'd be damned before she would go to him. A girl had to have her pride.

But having off all day Sunday and waiting for him to call or come by had been nothing short of hell.

"Jessie."

She knew he was there the second before he spoke. She whirled around, a rolled bundle of silverware in her hand. "Hi, Seth." Talk about awkward. But she didn't want it to be. Why did it have to be?

"Can we talk?"

It was two o'clock and the Chuck Wagon had definitely slowed down from the lunch crowd. Only a couple of diners still hung around, finishing up the last of their meals.

"Please?" he asked. "I wanted to come by yesterday, but Amos and Chester were at it again and . . ."

She wanted to tell him no, make him sweat it a bit, but Sheridan came out of the back and ruined any ready excuse she had about not being able to leave the restaurant.

"Hey, Sheriff."

"Sheridan, do you mind if Jessie takes a break? I need to talk to her a minute."

"Sure thing." Her dark brown gaze fell on first one of them and then the other as if somehow she could tell that things had changed between them. But had they?

"I really shouldn't leave," Jessie started. She didn't want to have this conversation. Why couldn't things go back to the way they were before she had kissed Seth?

"Too bad." He wrapped his fingers around her upper arm and steered her from the Chuck Wagon. Once on the street, he looked one way, then the other, as if unsure as to where they should go. In the end, he led her into the small alley between the restaurant and the dry cleaner next door.

Once they were alone, she pulled away from his grasp and crossed her arms. "What's this about, Seth?"

He stared blankly at her. "You know damn well what this is about."

She lifted her chin and met his gaze. His eyes were darker than Chase's, more like the pastures that surrounded the ranch just after a spring rain. So much alike and yet so different. In Seth's eyes she could see some of the life that he had lived. Eight years away from his home and family. She steeled her heart and her resolve. "And?"

He looked from side to side as if making sure that they were well and truly alone. "Saturday . . ." He shook his head. "I didn't use any protection and—"

"Don't worry about it."

His questioning gaze swung back to her. "Does that mean you are on the pill?"

Was that what this was all about?

What did you think, dummy? That he was going to declare his undying love for you?

"It's all taken care of," she muttered.

"What?"

"Don't worry about it," she said, lifting her chin from its resting place on her chest. "It's all taken care of."

He mulled over her words for a minute, then gave a quick nod. "Listen, Jess, I'm—"

She punched him on the arm. "I swear, Seth Langston, so help me God, if you say you're sorry . . ." She didn't have the words to continue, but "sorry" was the one thing she couldn't bear to hear.

Without finishing, she pushed past him and back down the alley. She listened for his footsteps to sound behind her, but all was quiet except the purr of an engine as a truck rolled past.

All she could think about was how Seth made her feel.

He made her . . . *burn.* Chase had never done that. All these years she had saved herself. Saved herself for the man she would one day marry. But once she'd had Seth's lips on hers, that whole "saving herself for marriage" thing didn't seem quite so important any longer. All she could think about was more. More kissing, more touching . . . *more.*

But that was something she would never have. Not if he was sorry.

Without looking behind her, Jessie opened the door to the Chuck Wagon and ducked inside.

Chapter Seven

Somehow Jessie managed to avoid Seth for the rest of the week. Everywhere she went, people were still whispering about her. It was ridiculous to think that they knew what had happened between her and Seth, but it felt as if they did, all the same.

She went to the store to pick up a few things to cook for supper at home, and the cashier stared at her as if she could read all Jessie's secrets. The trip to the drugstore to pick up Meemaw's medication rendered the same results. She needed out of this town, if only for the day, but that wasn't happening.

Thursday came with no break in sight. It was opening day at Cattle Days, and Chuck had scheduled her to work in the food tent. She didn't mind, not really. She needed the money to make up for all that she had spent on Chase's truck.

Still, cooking hamburgers over an open flame in late June in Texas was not a pleasant place to be. She wiped her forehead on the wet towel she had hanging around her neck. It had been nice and cool when she placed it there, but after the first hour the thing was letting off steam.

"Jessie?"

She whirled around at the sound of her name. "Seth," she breathed, pressing one hand to her heart. "What are you doing here?"

He smiled and glanced around the small blue tent. "I believe it's a law that everyone in Page County has to attend Cattle Days."

Despite the nearly one hundred degree temperatures and the fact that she had been cooking hamburgers for nearly six hours straight, she felt the heat rise from her neck to the roots of her hair.

She had managed the entire week without seeing Seth. Now to run into him when she was dripping with sweat and smelling like grease was more than she wanted to contemplate.

Not that she cared. She wasn't out here to impress Seth. And even if she wanted to, it wasn't like she was hanging around Cattle Creek for long. As soon as she had the money, she was gone. Maybe even as early as next year . . .

But she hated that she looked like a chambermaid while he looked like the quintessential Texas man. Faded jeans, well worn and hip hugging; cowboy boots, broken in and a bit dusty from the lack of rain; burnt orange Texas Longhorns shirt, stretched out at the neck and around the tail, but still a fine shirt; and straw cowboy hat, molded to fit the man underneath.

Not that she had been looking or anything.

"Where's Millie?" she asked. "Didn't you bring her here?"

He studied her for a moment. "Why? Are you jealous?

Jessie scoffed. "Of course not."

He gave her another hard look as if he were trying to see past all her defenses. And that was something she couldn't have.

She turned back to her grill as Seth finally answered, "She and Layla went home with Mr. Evans."

"Sounds like you were a great date." She hated the sharp tone of her words. If he noticed it too, she didn't know. She mopped her face again and flipped a couple more of the burgers.

"It wasn't a date."

Jessie might have been stuck in the food tent most of the day, but she knew a date when she saw one. Seth and Millie had walked by with sweet little Layla at least five times that she had noticed. Once Seth had even swung the little girl into his arms the way a good father would do. From her place in the tent it looked like more than a date. It looked like a perfect little family.

But what did she care? She was leaving soon, and she would do well to remember that.

"Uh-huh."

Seth just shook his head. "Are you almost done here?"

"I can't leave until Debbie Ann comes in. That's when my shift is over." And since Manny never called to offer her job back, then her evening was free—but she wasn't going to tell him that. "Why?"

"I thought I might buy you a pronto pup. Maybe we can talk."

"There's nothing to talk about," she said, her heart pumping heavily in her chest.

"I think there might be."

She braced her hands on her hips and shot him the hardest stink eye she could muster. "I disagree."

"Fine, then you can eat and I'll talk."

"It may be a while. You know how Debbie Ann is." And with any luck Debbie Ann would be her late-as-usual self.

He nodded.

"Maybe we should postpone this until later." *Coward.*

"I've got time." He crossed his arms in front of that broad chest. Jessie ignored the way his biceps bulged with the motion. Well, she *tried* to ignore it, but she could still feel the warmth of his skin and the firmness of his muscles beneath her fingers. The memory was intoxicating. She needed to keep as far away from Seth Langston as she could, regardless that every atom in her body wanted to run to him.

She opened her mouth to protest, but Debbie Ann came rushing in. Today she was only ten minutes late instead of fifteen, so Jessie considered that an improvement. Jessie hadn't come into work late a day in her life, but since Debbie Ann was Chuck's niece, there was nothing anyone but him could say on the matter.

"Sorry, Jessie," Debbie Ann gushed. "Let me get an apron and you can get out of here."

Five minutes later, Jessie was out of excuses as to why she couldn't grab a quick bite with Seth.

But that didn't mean she was done trying. "I—" she started.

He shook his head. "This is a pronto pup we're talking about. You won't have another chance for one until fall. Are you really going to pass this up?"

"Fine." She relented and allowed him to walk her over to the football boosters' food truck.

"You sure you don't want any fries to go with that?" Seth nodded toward the golden brown corn dog she held in one hand.

All the stands had their own strengths, and while Chuck's had the best hamburgers, no one could beat the football team's pronto pups.

"This is enough." She had done nothing but cook all day. She wasn't even all that hungry.

They took their food over to one of the picnic tables set up in the empty lot at the corner of Main and Tenth. The spot had been a car lot once upon a time, but the business had moved out closer to the highway, leaving the lot empty for years.

Jessie took a bite of her corn dog, licking the excess

mustard from the corner of her mouth. Working behind the grill all day and smelling the burgers as they cooked had curbed her appetite. But now that she was away from all that, she discovered that she was starving. Maybe she should have gotten those fries after all.

"What did you want to talk about?" she asked between bites. Best get this over with as soon as possible, even if she wanted to just sit and enjoy her food.

"I think we should date."

"Are you kidding?" She swung her gaze back to his, but his green eyes were serious and steady. "I can't date you."

"If this is about Chase, I'll talk to him. We'll figure something out."

Jessie shook her head. "This has nothing to do with Chase." And it didn't. She would talk to Chase when the time came. Or maybe not. With the rate at which he came home when the circuit was in full swing, she might not see him again until after the finals in November. And by then she hoped she could forget all about her and Seth and what had happened in the cab of his truck on one hot summer day.

"Then let's go out."

"No." Dating Seth Langston was something she could not do. He was too honorable, too noble to want to date her for any other reason. The last thing she wanted to be was his charity case.

God, she had made such a fool of herself over Chase. She would not do the same thing with Seth.

"You feel guilty, don't you?" She didn't need his pity.

He ducked his head closer to her so that no one else could hear. "You were a virgin, and I took that from you."

Jessie straightened, pride stiffening her backbone. "Listen, cowboy, you didn't *take* anything. I *gave* it to you—willingly, knowingly. Big difference."

"But—" he started.

She shook her head.

"Do you have to work tomorrow?" he asked.

She wanted to lie and tell him yes, but he would surely be at Cattle Days the entire weekend. He would know if she was absent. "No."

"Then come walk around here with me. The pie-eating contest is tomorrow. And the talent show. It'll be fun."

She shook her head, sorely tempted by his offer. But she wasn't about to be any man's pity date. She pushed to her feet. "Thanks for the offer, Seth, but I'm not ready to date again. And I don't know if I ever will be."

Saturday rolled around. The last day of the Cattle Days celebration. Even though the house was blocks from Main Street, Jessie could hear the music from the bandstand. The talent show was the best part of Cattle Days, aside from the Restaurant Wars, which was the highlight and pinnacle of the three-day celebration. The four main restaurant owners competed against each other every year, cooking a specified dish and serving it to the town on Saturday night. Everyone in attendance cast one vote for their favorite restaurant. Winner got a check for a thousand dollars and a plaque, but even more important, bragging rights for the next year.

Jessie managed to avoid the festivities all day Friday, but by Saturday she couldn't keep away any longer.

"I'll be back in a little while, Meemaw," she said, around three in the afternoon. "Do you want me to bring you back anything? They're cooking chili."

Her grandmother scoffed. "It's a hundred and hell outside, and they're cooking up hot peppers."

Jessie shrugged. It was Texas after all. "I'll take that as a no." She plopped her hat on her head. "You have everything you need before I leave?"

"Get on, girl. You're messing up my stories."

Jessie rolled her eyes, careful not to let Meemaw see. "I'll be back around nine."

Meemaw harrumphed, and Jessie started for the door.

She was shutting it behind her when her grandmother hollered, "Bring me some of Kora Mae's chili. Last time I ate at the Chuck Wagon, it about killed me."

Jessie smiled and didn't bother to mention that it'd been fifteen years ago.

"Sure thing," she said. Grin still in place, she made her way down the porch steps and into town.

As she walked through the crowd, Jessie enjoyed her time doing nothing. With so many people milling around, she didn't feel that everyone in town was looking and pointing quite so much. Well, they might have been, but they weren't looking and pointing at her. There were too many other sights at Cattle Days to see than the town's number-one troublemaker.

Tomorrow the cleanup would begin. Tonight was just about fun.

"I knew you couldn't stay away."

Jessie turned to see Seth lounging against one of the thick metal poles holding up one of the voting tents.

He looked delicious in his crisp jeans and black polo shirt embroidered with the official crest of Page County.

"No date?"

He flashed her a quick smile. "You had your chance yesterday, remember?"

"Puh-lease." She went to turn away, only to have him fall in step with her. "Are you here in an official capacity?"

"Don't say anything, but word around town is Kora Mae claims that Manny may have tried to steal her secret recipe, and she's gunning to sabotage his entry this year."

"Sabotage how?"

Seth shrugged. "Who knows? But that's why I'm here."

Jessie shook her head. "You don't really think . . ."

"No, but if I'm not here and Manny beats Kora Mae, or even the other way around, then things might get ugly."

"Small towns." Jessie sighed.

"What's wrong with small towns?"

"How long do you have?" she asked.

"Cattle Creek's not that bad. In fact, Cattle Creek is just about the best. Where else can you walk around on a Saturday night, shooting the bull with the sheriff and eating homemade chili out of foam coffee cups?" He handed her a cup of Kora Mae's special recipe.

"Thanks," she said.

"I'd sure appreciate your vote, Sheriff," Kora Mae called. She gave him a big wave.

He took a bite and gave her a thumbs-up. "You got it."

She smiled and up-patted the back of her hair. "Thanks, hon."

"How does she keep her hair like that?" Jessie wondered aloud. Kora Mae had moved to Cattle Creek aeons ago from Maryland. As far as Jessie knew, she was the only Texas "hon" ever to exist.

"Word at the drugstore is they order Aqua Net by the case just for her."

Jessie laughed and took a bite of the chili. "It's good," she said, then coughed as it scorched the back of her throat. "But hot. Hot. Hot." She fanned her mouth as if that alone could take away the burn.

Seth grabbed her a shot of milk from one of the drink tables. Jessie downed it in a quick gulp but had a feeling her esophagus would never be the same.

Side by side they walked through the people all milling around, eating chili, and drinking beer. Lots of other people were gulping milk when the peppers got too hot.

"You ready to try Manny's?" Seth asked.

"I've had Manny's chili. Many times."

"Yeah, but I heard that he was trying something new for this competition."

"Like Kora Mae's recipe?"

He laughed. "Some exotic pepper. Though he won't tell anyone what it is until after the judging."

"Competition is rough this year."

"Don't you know it?" He grabbed them each a cup of Manny's chili. They tasted it and looked at each other.

"Is it just me or does this taste just like—"

"Kora Mae's." Seth nodded. "It's going to be a long night."

"*Hola*, Sheriff." Manny stepped out from behind his table and offered Seth a hand to shake. "How is it?" The honky-tonk owner asked.

"Good. Good," Seth replied as Jessie reached for the milk to calm the heat of the peppers.

Manny winked and nudged Seth in the side. "I hope I can count on your vote this year."

Seth gave him a quick nod and a smile. "Of course."

Jessie whipped her head around to see if he was serious. Didn't he just tell Kora Mae that he would vote for her?

"*Gracias.*" Manny clasped Seth's hand and shook it some more. "I really appreciate you, Sheriff."

Jessie waited until they had walked out of Manny's earshot before turning to Seth. "Did I just hear you say that you were voting for Manny's chili?"

"Yep." Seth tipped his hat to a passing couple.

"And before that you told Kora Mae that you would vote for her entry?"

"I did."

She stopped so suddenly he was ten feet away before he realized she wasn't next to him.

He backtracked to her side. "Is there a problem?"

"You can't vote for both of them."

He nodded. "And I don't. I vote for all of them," he said. "It's the only way to keep the peace."

He grinned and continued on to Chuck's tent.

Jessie shook her head and tagged along, feeling as if she had learned more about Seth in this last hour than she had her entire life.

Seth accepted the cups of chili from Chuck and handed one to Jessie.

"So, what about Kora Mae and Manny?"

Seth smiled, and she melted like chocolate in the summertime. "I'm hoping that it was just a coincidence and praying that one of the others wins."

She laughed. The man was too charming by far.

He took a bite of the chili and looked over to where Chuck waited expectantly. "I think we have a winner."

Chuck beamed as only an overweight middle-aged man in a dirty apron could.

"You are bad, Seth Langston."

"No, I'm good."

She almost choked on the bite of chili.

Seth pounded her on the back until she managed to recover.

"Nothing like a little self-confidence."

He just grinned, and they moved on to the last booth.

Juan Garcia was owner and chef at the Cantina and current reigning champion of the Restaurant Wars.

Seth got them both a cup of chili and promised to vote for Juan.

"I'm going to laugh if you get caught stuffing the ballot box."

"It's okay. I know the sheriff."

"Very funny."

"So, who gets your vote?" Seth asked.

Jessie scraped the last of the chili from the cup and raised it in salute. "Juan, definitely."

She took her ballot and marked it for Juan, then stuffed it in the nearest collection box.

Sometime tonight, after everyone went home, the mayor and his crew would tally the votes, and tomorrow after church, the winner would be announced in the town square.

"We can only hope that the name of the winner doesn't leak like last year," Seth said. "With all the talk of stealing recipes and secret peppers, there may be riots."

Jessie shook her head but chuckled all the same.

She enjoyed the night, just walking next to Seth doing nothing more than eating chili and making small talk. It was almost as if they were back to where they had started from before that hot afternoon. Well, almost. They were back to themselves with a new, sexy charge in the air. But getting involved with Seth was an even worse idea than staying involved with Chase. She was breaking ties with this town, and she could hardly wait until she saw the last of it. But tonight she had seen it from Seth's point of view. All the little eccentricities that made Cattle Creek what it was.

When she heard him talk about the town, she wondered why she ever wanted to leave.

"You ready to head home?" Seth asked. Night had fallen while they ambled around the cook-off. The strings of mini-bulbs lit the area, looking like tiny lightning bugs in flight.

"I guess I better. I told Meemaw I'd be home by nine."

He looked up at the indigo sky. "I think you're already late. Do you want a ride?"

"Thanks, but I'll walk." The last thing she needed to do was to get into a car with him.

"Suit yourself," he said, but fell into step next to her.

"You don't have to walk me home."

"I think my mother would disagree with that. But I also want to."

As much as she wanted to, she couldn't tell him no. It didn't help that she wanted tonight to go on forever. She shrugged. "Suit yourself," she said, echoing his earlier sentiment.

Together they started toward Larkspur Lane. The farther they got from Main, the quieter the streets became. The lights and sounds of the Cattle Day celebration faded to almost nothing.

"Well, here we are," Seth said.

"I had a good time tonight," she said, only then realizing that the words were part of date conversation and this wasn't a date. "Thanks for walking me home." She spun around and started toward the porch.

Seth measured her stride for stride.

She made it to the door before she turned to face him. "Seth?"

He hooked one finger under her chin and lifted her mouth to his.

His kiss was sweet, but controlled. His hands trembled as he held her in place. It was a shadow of the kiss they had shared the afternoon of the kiss that had started it all. But it held promise, as if to say "there's more where that came from." And she wanted more. Heaven help her, she did.

But for how long? Until she saved enough money to get out of town? That could be months, and if she kept kissing Seth Langston, she might be completely in love with him by then. She would be brokenhearted and Seth would move on to the next one of his casserole groupies.

She stepped back away from him, when she wanted nothing less than to melt into him completely.

"Good night, Seth." She turned away to let herself into the house, but Seth stopped her, planting one last kiss on her lips.

"Good night," he said, and then he was gone.

Chapter Eight

꧁ ✦ ꧂

Jessie!" her grandmother called. "That Langston boy is out front."

Jessie came out of her darkroom, coaching herself not to run to the doorway. "Seth?" she asked as she peeked out the front window.

All day Sunday she had relived their kiss from the night before. And the last little peck he gave her, as if to tell her that she wasn't running the relationship, he was.

But it wasn't Seth. Chase stood in her driveway having just got out of his newly repaired pickup truck.

It was Monday afternoon. Another week had passed. Another week of avoiding Seth, which was proving to be impossible, counting and recounting her escape fund, and making sure that her grandmother took her medication.

Nothing had changed. Not really. He'd kissed her and walked with her at Cattle Days. Nothing overly special. So why did her life feel so complicated?

Normally she would have run down the porch steps and

flung herself into Chase's arms, but not today. Not after the past few weeks.

The screen door slammed behind her as she came out to greet him. "Does this mean you're talking to me again?"

"Hey to you too, Jessie. The truck does look nice. Bill does a good job."

She shoved her hands into her front pockets, more than uncomfortable with the situation.

He smiled that devil-may-care, crooked grin that had melted her heart since day one. "Aren't you going to come give me a kiss?"

She shrugged. "That depends."

"On?"

"Whether or not you still want to kill me."

"Oh, Jessie, you know how it is."

She dipped her chin and made her way to his side.

He wrapped one arm around her and pulled her close, planting a quick kiss on the top of her head.

"I thought we might catch a show."

"You're staying?" She craned her head back to look at him.

"Just for a while. I've got to be in Denver tomorrow night."

"Oh."

"So, you up for a movie?"

She shook her head. "Can we just go someplace and talk?"

The shadow of a frown crossed his face, but just as quickly as it came it disappeared again. "Sure."

"Let me get my hat."

Chase smiled. "That's my girl."

His girl? Jessie ran back into the house to get her knock-off Stetson as Chase waited outside. Was she Chase's girl? Dang, she was confused.

"Meemaw," she called as she let herself in. "I'm going out for a bit."

A fit of coughing was her only response.

"Meemaw?" Jessie grabbed her hat and made her way into the parlor. Her grandmother's cough grew worse with each passing day. Jessie knew the prognosis was bleak, but if her grandmother would take her medicine, she would at least be more comfortable. And maybe then her cough wouldn't rack her frail frame until Jessie herself wondered how her grandmother could stand such torture.

Meemaw was doubled over in her chair, her breath heaving, as Drew Carey asked for bids in the *Showcase Showdown*.

Jessie grabbed the bottle of pills and a glass of water, then knelt at her grandmother's side.

"I'm not dead, you know," she said without sitting up.

Only worry kept Jessie from rolling her eyes. "I know that, Meemaw. Now take your pills."

Her grandmother slowly pushed herself upright and took the medication that Jessie offered. "What was that you said?"

"I'm going out for a bit." Maybe she shouldn't go. Her grandmother's color wasn't good. Maybe she should tell Chase they would have to postpone their talk until later.

Or maybe she was just being a coward.

"I'll be home in a little while, okay?"

"Fine, fine," she groused. "I'm a grown woman, Jessica Elizabeth. I think I can manage by myself for a couple of hours."

"Yes, Meemaw." Jessie donned her hat and started for the door, pausing for a moment to look back at her grandmother before heading out to Chase's truck.

"Is Manny's okay?" Chase asked as she climbed into the cab next to him.

"Sure." Jessie would have preferred to eat at the Chuck Wagon, but she knew that it was too far in town for Chase. He seemed to stay on the fringes, frequent the places closest to the highway so he would have the quickest means of escape.

How many times had she ridden next to Chase in his shiny red truck? Countless. How many times had he kissed her? She couldn't recall. But it had been a while. Funny, but as much as she was Chase's girl, he seemed to be keeping her at a distance these days.

She leaned toward him, across the console, pointing to something out the driver's-side window as an excuse to get closer. Chase leaned to the opposite side.

But did that prove anything?

How many times had they gone out in the last few months? How many times had he asked her?

She had asked him to the Sadie Hawkins Dance. But that was sort of the point. And she had asked him to go to last year's Cattle Days Picnic. He had asked her to the movies a couple of times, but it seemed that more and more their relationship had become increasing platonic.

She was so confused! She couldn't remember a time in her life when she wasn't in love with Chase Langston. So why did she keep thinking about Seth? And what did it all mean?

With a sigh, she shifted back to her original position, all too aware that once she moved, Chase eased into place as well.

She thought about trying her theory again and moving closer to Chase, but decided against it. She was confused enough as it was. And a few minutes later they pulled into the graveled parking lot at Manny's.

She did her best not to be hyperaware of Chase as they walked toward the entrance. Like most small-town Texas honky-tonks, Manny's served just enough food to keep people coming in at all hours. They opened their doors at lunch and closed them at two a.m., serving hot wings and cold beer every day but Sunday.

How could she be so conscious of Chase when he wasn't even touching her? Or maybe it was because of that lack of contact that she was so aware. Seth would hold her arm, place his hand on her back, cup her elbow in his palm. Chase walked behind her. Just there. Not touching, not helping or guiding. Had it always been like that? She couldn't remember.

"Hey, look who's here." Chase pointed across the empty dance floor.

Seth and Millie were seated on the opposite side of the place, their heads bent close together as they talked over the pulsing beat of the jukebox.

What were they doing here? And why did she care that they were together? They had a history, but she and Seth had . . .

"Let's sit over here." She slid into a booth farthest from the pair. How was she supposed to talk to Chase about everything with Seth just across from them?

"Sure."

A waitress Jessie had never met came over and Chase ordered them a couple of soft drinks and a basket of wings. *She must have been the one who took my job.*

"So, what do you want to talk about?" Chase asked as their server moved away to turn their order in to the kitchen.

Jessie took a steadying breath, but all the words that she had practiced on the way over left her in an instant "I thought you were never going to talk to me again."

He shot her a rueful smile. "You know how it is. I can't stay mad at my best girl."

"That's just it," Jessie said, nervously shredding the top napkin from the stack the waitress had left for the earlier patrons, "if I'm your girl, why did you bring the blonde here the other night?"

"I didn't bring her—"

"Please don't tell me she followed you."

"But she did."

Jessie shook her head. He just couldn't see it. "Whether

she followed you or not, that didn't mean you had to . . . to . . ." She waved a hand in the air, searching for the best word to describe Chase's behavior. She came up short.

"Is that what this is all about? Angela?"

"That was her name?"

Chase frowned. "I think so."

"Yeah," Jessie said, but her gaze was drawn back to Millie and Seth. What were the two doing together? "I guess you could say that."

"You don't really think she meant anything to me." It was half question, half statement.

"What am I supposed to think?" she asked as Seth looked up and caught her gaze. Even with the entire width of the dance floor between them, she could see the flash of hurt and anger in his green eyes. What call did he have to be upset with her? He was the one who asked her to date him, then showed up with another girl just days later.

The memory of his desk the night he arrested her surfaced in her mind. There had been casserole pans stacked on top of cake pans on top of muffin tins and more.

No doubt Seth Langston was one of Cattle Creek's most eligible bachelors, and there he was, sitting across the bar with his onetime girlfriend. It just went to prove it.

She wondered if Darly Jo had come by the office to pick up her good Pyrex pan. And if anything else happened.

White-hot frustration flooded her. That was all it was. Just aggravation over falling victim to the charms of Seth Langston.

A new record dropped in the jukebox and a soft ballad started. Jessie grabbed Chase's hand and stood, tugging him to his feet. "Dance with me."

"What? Now?"

"Yes, now." She pulled on him until he stood and took her into his arms.

"The wings will be ready soon."

"They can wait." She didn't know what possessed her,

but she wanted to show Seth that she could move on. Or maybe she wanted to show him that their afternoon together didn't mean any more to her than it did to him.

She stepped a little closer to Chase, glancing over to see if Seth was watching. He was and somehow she managed to curb her smirk of triumph. She had slept with him willingly, but she would not be his pity date.

Chase twirled her around just in time to see a glaring Seth stride toward them.

"Sorry, brother—I'm cutting in."

Chase looked as if he might protest, but then he released her and bowed out. Jessie had one last look at him approaching the table where Millie sat before Seth tugged her close.

"What are you trying to prove, Jessie?" A smile still pulled at his lips, but it didn't reach his eyes.

"I'm not trying to prove anything." She tossed back her head as Dustin Lynch continued to sing about cowboys and angels. It was far better to concentrate on the song's lyrics instead of how it felt to be in Seth's arms once again. Right. That was how it felt. But how could that be?

She was vaguely aware of Chase leading Millie out onto the dance floor. At three o'clock in the afternoon they were the only people in Manny's and certainly the only ones dancing.

"Then why are you here with him?" Seth asked.

"Why are you here with her?"

"I asked her to meet me here to talk about coming to work at the jailhouse."

"Did you fire Nancy?"

"I don't think she's coming back, but until she does, there's still a lot to do."

"So the two of you came all the way out here?"

Seth chuckled. He had pulled her close enough that she felt the sound vibrate and rumble out of his chest. "Why, Jessie, you sound almost jealous."

She squarely met his clouded gaze. "Why would I be jealous?"

"I was about to ask you the same thing."

"Whatever." Not the pithy remark that she would have liked, but it would have to do on short notice.

"Your turn," he said.

"He came by the house today. I thought it would be as good a time as any to tell him about . . . you know." The heat that filled her face could have toasted bread. But she wasn't sure what to call that afternoon in Seth's truck.

"And?"

She tossed back her head so she could see him better from under the brim of her hat. "It hasn't come up yet."

He made some sort of derisive noise, but Jessie decided to let it slide. He was entitled to his opinion.

But one thing was certain: she would never tell Chase as long as she was dancing in the warmth of Seth's embrace. She stepped away from him and surprisingly he let her go.

Without a backward glance she tapped Millie on the shoulder. "I believe this dance is mine."

What was that all about?" Millie asked.

Seth shrugged and led her back to their table. He hated leaving Jessie with Chase. But hadn't it always been that way? "Oh, you know Jessie."

"Yeah, but I've never seen her act that way around . . . you." She slid back into the booth and pinned him with that deep brown, knowing gaze. "Does this have anything to do with the other night and Chase's truck?"

"No," he answered truthfully.

"Then what's going on between the two of you?"

"You know Jessie," he repeated with a dismissive flick on one hand. It took every ounce of willpower he had not to look over to where Chase and Jessie danced. He didn't succeed. They were dancing close. Real close and though he wanted to get up and snatch a couple of feet between them, he managed to keep his seat. Whatever the game she was playing, he wasn't going to fall for it.

"Yeah," she said. "I do and I also know you."

"What's that supposed to mean?"

She gave him that mysterious smile he knew so well. "You're a smart man. You'll figure it out. Now, when do I start?"

So you're heading to Denver?" Jessie asked an hour and a half later as Chase walked her to the front porch. She tried not to compare the way Chase walked her to the door to the way Seth did. They were two different days, two different dates, two different men.

Seth had the obvious advantage. It had been dark, romantic, and he had taken charge and kissed her like he meant it. Maybe he even did.

"Big ride tomorrow." Chase gave her that trademark smile that had charmed her all these years. Today it just made her wish she had danced more with Seth at Manny's.

Jessie nodded. She never had a chance to talk to Chase about Seth. She wasn't even sure Chase would care. "Be careful," she said.

"You know it. Oh, I almost forgot." He pulled an envelope from his back pocket. "Here's your money back."

She frowned. "Money from what?"

He shifted from side to side as if suddenly uncomfortable. "My truck. Seth had the bat dusted and found out that some guy from Amarillo trashed it."

She looked at the envelope, thumbed through the contents. It was the same money that she had given Seth not so long ago.

"Seems this guy has a friend riding in the competition. I guess they wanted to keep me out of the game."

"I suppose," Jessie murmured.

He shoved his hands into his front pockets and stared at the ground. "Sorry I accused you and everything."

"It's okay," she said, a bit numb with shock. Chase had thought her guilty, while Seth had done everything in his power to make her confess the truth. Not only that. He was so confident in her innocence that he had squirreled the money away until he had proof.

Chase bussed her cheek and loped back down the steps.

Jessie watched as he swung himself up into his truck. The whole town thought she was guilty. Yet Seth knew she wasn't. He was the only one. Her champion. She waved to Chase. Seth had believed in her. Really and truly believed in her.

Chase gave her a little salute in return and backed out onto Larkspur Lane.

With a sigh, Jessie tucked the money into her purse, then let herself in the house.

"Meemaw, I'm home." She put her hat on the stand by the front door and dropped her bag next to it. "Meemaw?"

Only the hum of the window unit Jessie had set up in the parlor greeted her. Not even one of her grandmother's answering coughs.

She must be asleep. Jessie eased into the parlor, careful not to wake her.

Her grandmother was slumped in her chair, her neck at an uncomfortable angle. A glass lay on the floor at her feet, a large water stain surrounding it.

"Meemaw?" she whispered, even as the truth penetrated her veil of denial. "Oh, Meemaw." Jessie collapsed onto her knees, taking her grandmother's gnarled hands into her own. Tears burned her eyes as she pressed a kiss onto the backs of her fingers. Jessie laid her head in her grandmother's lap as her tears started to fall.

She had been afraid this would happen. Her Meemaw had died without anyone around. Jessie hadn't even gotten to say good-bye. Now the regrets piled on her one by one.

If only she hadn't gone out. If only she had checked her grandmother's medication. If only, if only, if only . . .

She allowed herself a few minutes to sink into her sorrow. There was so much to do that she couldn't give herself the luxury of a good long cry. She had calls to make, people to contact. So many things to do. But first she needed help.

She picked up the phone and called Seth.

Chapter Nine

❧ ✸ ❧

They buried Naomi McAllen on the first rainy day they'd had in nearly six weeks.

Seth stood under the tent next to Jessie as they lowered her grandmother into the ground. The rain tapped out a soft rhythm as they stood side by side, though not touching. Jessie's posture was brittle as if she was barely holding herself together.

But somehow she managed as everyone filed back to her house to eat the casseroles, corn bread, and pie.

Other than her father whom nobody had ever seen, Naomi was Jessie's last family. Seth had no idea what it would feel like to be all alone in the world. He couldn't imagine. Though he did remember the sense of abandonment he had when his own father had died. Seeing as how he had four brothers, a mother, and three grandparents living at the time, he could only imagine how alone Jessie felt.

"Thank you for coming," Jessie said as she walked Seth's mother and grandmother to the door. They were among the last to leave the wake, which left only Seth.

His mother shot him a look behind Jessie's back, one of concern and love.

Seth replied with a silent nod and watched as Jessie shut the door behind them.

She leaned back against it and closed her eyes. She held her shoulders at a tired angle, but somehow he knew she wouldn't break down. Not now. Not yet.

"Are you going to be okay?"

Her eyes snapped open as if she had forgotten for a moment that she wasn't alone. With a sigh, she pushed herself off the door. "I guess I better clean up this mess."

She produced a ponytail holder from who knew where and scooped her strawberry blond curls into a high spout on the top of her head. Then she brushed past him into the kitchen. Her steps quickened as if somehow she could run from whatever was dogging her heels.

Seth followed, finding her tying a worn apron over her gray dress. He knew for a fact that his mother had taken her on the shopping trip to buy the clothes she was wearing. And even with its elegant lines, Jessie had paired it with her black cowboy boots. She'd shed those as soon as they walked into the door after the funeral. Now she stood with her bare feet on the worn linoleum. Her toenails were painted bright pink and snagged his attention. How many times had he seen her feet? Countless, if he factored in all the hours they had spent as almost-family members swimming in the pool at the ranch house or down at the lake, but he never remembered her having pink toenails. Nor did he ever remember really seeing them. He'd made love to her and he hadn't even seen her feet?

"You don't have to do this now, Jess."

There wasn't a mess. The ladies' auxiliary from the Baptist church had seen to that. All the food had been put away, the trash taken out, and the dishes washed. All that was left to do was dry and put them away.

"It's okay. It won't take but a minute." She whirled

around to face the sink and flipped on the water with one deft flick of her wrist.

"I think you should sit down for a little bit," he said, even though he understood. If Jessie sat down she'd have way too much time to think, but he had to know she was going to be okay before he left. If he left.

"Linda Sue did the dishes." She made a face. "I used to work with her at the Chuck Wagon. Not the neatest person."

He came up behind her and turned off the water, so aware that he had trapped her between himself and the cabinet. How easy it would be to spin her around and take her into his arms and kiss her as he should have the other day. Kiss her and cherish her the way she should be kissed and cherished.

She looked up at him, her eyes stormy and confused. "I don't want to sit down," she admitted. Her voice cracked on the last bit. "She's gone, and I can't just sit down."

The tears that she had held in all day rose into her eyes. She blinked them away, but more took their place.

He hated to see her cry. He hated to see her in pain. Especially when he could do nothing to ease that ache in her heart. He wrapped his arms around her and pulled her close. She was warm and sweet and sobbing.

"Shhh," he murmured. "It'll be okay."

Her arms snaked around his back and fisted in his shirt as if to hold him close and never let him go. "I can't believe she's gone."

"She's in a better place, Jessie."

"I know," she sobbed. "That's why it's so wrong of me to wish she was here."

He smoothed a hand over her hair, loving the feel of the springy curls against his fingers. "It's not wrong of you. It's only natural. I think it would be wrong if you didn't feel that way."

With her hands still tangled in the back of his shirt, she

lifted her head from his chest, her gaze locking with his. "You do?"

"I do."

In a flash, the moment of grief turned into a moment of intimacy. He smoothed her hair back from her face, fighting with every fiber of his being not to lean in and kiss her lips. It was a short battle.

He lowered his head slowly to give her plenty of time to tell him no, push him away, but instead she reached up on her tiptoes and met him halfway.

Unlike the kiss from that day in the truck, this one was soft and sweet. With his lips he tried to tell her how sorry he was, how much he loved her, and how he would always be there for her. He wasn't sure if she got the message. Those were words he couldn't say out loud. He could only hope that somehow her mind interpreted what he longed to say.

Seth lifted his head, knowing that if he stayed much longer, it wouldn't stop with kissing. Now was not the time or the place. She was too vulnerable, too filled with grief. He couldn't take advantage of her again. He stepped back, but she pulled him close once again.

"Seth," she breathed. Her head was tilted back, her eyes half-closed. She looked wondrous and lovely, and Seth wanted nothing more than to sweep her into his arms and find some soft place to lay her down. "Stay here tonight."

It was the invitation he'd been waiting for half his life. But it was also the one he couldn't accept.

He set her from him, jarring that desirous look from her face. She didn't know what she was asking. He couldn't be the one to take advantage. "I don't think you should be alone tonight, Jessie. But I can't stay here. Why don't you go out to the ranch and spend the night?"

Her expression snapped back to attention as if she had realized where she was, who she was with, and all the events of the last few days. She shook her head. "No, that was silly of me to ask." She scoffed, letting out a sad little laugh that was more derisive than anything else. "I'll be fine. Really." She turned away from him and faced the sink once again, flipping on the water as if the last moments between them had never happened.

"I'd feel better if you went to the ranch, Jessie. That way, you'll be there if you need anything."

She didn't bother to turn back around as she answered, "I won't need anything, Seth."

"Jessie, I—" He was always messing up where she was concerned.

"I said I'll be all right." She scraped all the previously washed silverware into the sink and tipped in a dollop of dish soap.

As far as he could tell, it looked clean, and he couldn't imagine the ladies' auxiliary leaving her anything to do. But he knew how she felt. If she sat down the memories would come. It was always that way.

Her back was stiff, her posture brittle. Only her pride kept her upright. And if there was one thing she had, it was pride.

"Jessie," he started again.

"Hmmm?" She didn't turn around to face him.

"What are you going to do?"

"I told you, Seth. I'm going to do these dishes, then take a nice long bath."

"No. What are you going to *do*?"

She stopped washing the silverware but didn't turn to face him. "Meemaw had a reverse mortgage. The bank will take over the house and I'm going . . . somewhere."

He moved closer so he could see her face, possibly read her expression. "Where?"

She shrugged and continued washing dishes, sparing him only the briefest of glances. "Somewhere. I don't know."

"So you're still leaving town?"

"There's nothing for me here."

I am, he wanted to shout, but he couldn't say those words. He understood her reasons for leaving even if he hated them.

"If you change your mind about going out to the ranch, let me know. I'll drive you."

She nodded but didn't turn around.

"And if you need anything, you know where to find me." He reached out to her but stopped short of making contact. She wouldn't change her mind. And she wouldn't call.

Not quite Chase's girl. Not his either.

Seth exhaled the remaining tension in his body, then blew a kiss toward her back and let himself out of the house.

Two weeks passed in something of a daze. Jessie went through all the motions: work, home, shower, repeat. Seth came by the diner every day to check on her. Every day she lied and said she was fine. Well, it wasn't really a lie. She would be fine one day, real soon.

She finished applying a touch of mascara and gave her reflection one last critical look. One day at a time, wasn't that what they said? She scooped her hair back into a pony-tail and left the bathroom. She had twenty minutes to get to her shift at the Chuck Wagon.

One day at a time and one day real soon. Her mantra. For now she would live one day at a time. Then one day real soon she was going to pack up everything she deemed worthy and head out. She still hadn't figured out where she was going. Away from Cattle Creek. And for now that was enough.

Away from Seth.

Her heart gave a painful thump. The worst part of leaving Texas would be leaving him behind. He had started to mean so much to her. He came by every day to check on her, to see her, make sure she was all right. Oh, how she would miss that. Miss him.

She wasn't sure exactly when the shift occurred, when her feelings for Chase had become something less than romantic. Or had she ever really loved him like that at all? Maybe she had simply been in love with the idea of Chase. He was larger-than-life, an American hero, a legend in his own time. Yet one day it just seemed as if all she could think about was Seth. Where he was, what he was doing. Instead of being strange, it felt as natural as the sunshine on her face. Since the funeral he had been her rock, her solid, the one person she knew she could depend on. The last two weeks had been eye-opening. When had Seth become so important to her? But the answer to that was always. He had always been there, always watched over her. Always. But only recently had that become clear.

She turned toward the calendar, as if checking to make sure it had only been fourteen days, but what she saw instead was the little flower reminder sticker she used to mark when her period was supposed to start. She gasped. She was late. Not for work. Late late. For her period.

Her stomach fell.

Probably end up pregnant. Wasn't that what Meemaw had said?

Jessie closed her eyes, thankful that her grandmother wasn't around to see this.

Wait. Just because she was late didn't mean she was pregnant. Lots of things caused women to skip periods. Stress, pressures, unprotected sex with cowboys in the cabs of their trucks.

Her eyes flew open. She had to be wrong. This couldn't be happening. Just when she was so close to getting out of this town. This couldn't be her fate.

She refused to believe that she was pregnant. Only one way to find out. She grabbed her purse and started for the door.

* * *

Jessie walked into the drugstore with her chin high. *Act natural.* But her knees wanted to lock up on her and her hands trembled. Maybe she'd be better off going to the clinic and taking her chances with Shirley. The front desk receptionist wouldn't know patient confidentiality if it bit her on the behind. No, she was better off here.

She turned down the aisle of unmentionables. There was a chance if anyone saw her that they would think she was buying tampons. Best grab what she needed and get on out of Dodge. She snatched up the first pregnancy test she saw. The longer she stayed, the greater the chance that someone would spot her and say—

"Hey, Jessie."

She whirled around as Millie Evans neared. It took all her self-restraint not to shove the box behind her back. How was that for suspicious behavior?

"I thought I saw you come in. How are you?" Concern filled Millie's voice.

Even though two weeks had passed since Meemaw's funeral, Jessie still had to endure all the looks of pity and sympathy. It was tough enough to know that she was alone in the world, but to be constantly reminded of it was more than one person should have to suffer.

"I'm fine. Thanks. Seth treating you okay at the jail?"

"I couldn't ask to work for a nicer man." Her gaze dropped to the box Jessie held. She could only hope that her fingers were wrapped around it in such a way that Millie couldn't read it, but the size and shape ruled out anything other than what it really was. Maybe Millie was looking at something else. It wasn't like Jessie could ask her.

"Well, I guess I should be getting back." Millie held up her sack with the receipt stapled on the outside. "Have a good afternoon."

"Yeah," Jessie murmured. "You too."

She watched as Millie walked away, wondering if she'd been better off taking her chances with Shirley.

S eth."
     He took his feet off his desk and sat up straight as Millie came rushing into the jailhouse. "What's wrong?"

She looked from him to Dusty, then over to the holding cells. Johnson Jones hadn't managed to wake up yet and find his way home even though it was after two o'clock in the afternoon. She slid into Dusty's chair and rolled close, her knees bumping Seth's as she swung near. "I just saw Jessie at the drugstore."

He nodded coolly even though his heart gave a hard pound. "Did she look okay?" He'd been doing his best to give her some time. He called nearly every day to check on her and made sure that on her off days, either his mother or his grandmother paid her a visit. He wanted to have her at his side, but he knew that her goal was to leave Cattle Creek. As much as the thought saddened him, he knew he couldn't make her stay.

"You could say that."

"Quit talking in riddles, Millie," Dusty groused. Though Seth thought he was more upset about her sitting in his chair than her manner of speech.

Millie glanced over to Jones, then eased in a bit closer. "She was buying a pregnancy test."

"You don't say." Dusty took off his hat and slapped it against one thigh.

"It didn't take you long to get back into the swing of small-town life." Seth said the words even as his heart jumped into his throat. A pregnancy test? But that would mean . . .

"Is that all you have to say?" Millie asked.

"She told me she was on the pill," he whispered.

But she hadn't. Jessie never said those four little words. Just dodged the issue. And he had let her.

Millie shot him a gentle smile. "So was I."

He looked from one of them to the other, realizing in that moment that they both knew he was responsible.

A pregnancy test!

The words sank in. "Jessie's pregnant?" He was on his feet in an instant. "I need to get over there and—"

Millie's hand on his arm stopped him in his tracks. "Hold on, cowboy. First of all, you don't know that she's having a baby, only that she bought a test."

"But—" If she bought a test, she had to suspect she was pregnant. And if she was pregnant . . .

"There are a number of things that can cause a woman to miss her cycle." She rolled her eyes. "Gawd, I can't believe that I'm talking to you about this." She shook her head and continued. "Just look at all the stress she's been under. That alone would be enough to throw her off schedule. And second of all, you wouldn't be so careless as to not use protection . . ." She stopped and turned questioning eyes to him.

He cleared his throat, a surer sign of his guilt he couldn't imagine, unless it was the heat he felt rising up to his hairline.

"She'll tell you when she's ready," Millie quietly continued. "If you go over there now, like this—" She waved a hand in front of him. He was poised for flight, every muscle in his body tense and ready to move. His jaw was clenched, his fists tight. "You're only going to make it worse."

"But—" He turned to Dusty for help, but his chief deputy only shrugged.

Millie placed one hand on his chest and gave a little shove. Seth fell back into his seat. "Give her some time," she suggested. "A week, maybe two."

"She's got three days."

"Seth," Millie started in protest.

"Three days," he repeated. That was plenty enough time to take the test and come tell him what she had found out.

And plenty enough time for him to go out of his mind wondering if he was about to be a dad.

It was the longest three days of his life. Aside from the fact that he had to be patient, Jessie had stopped taking his calls. She didn't have a cell phone, so he had left messages at the house, but not once had she picked up or returned his call.

"I'm going over there." Seth crammed his hat on his head and started for the door.

"You could at least wait until she gets off work," Millie said. She had her back to him as she filed papers and cleaned through the mess of a system he had devised when Nancy went on leave.

He checked his watch, as if he hadn't already done that twenty or so times today. Jessie didn't get off work for another half an hour and he didn't think he could wait until then.

"Seth." Millie's voice was ripe with caution.

"I'm going over there," he said again, and pushed his way out of the station before she could convince him to wait. Or physically make him.

The heat greeted him like a slap in the face, the rain from two weeks ago a distant memory now. He waited for two cars to pass, then crossed the street to the Chuck Wagon.

"Hey, Sheriff," Sheridan said as he walked through the door.

"Where's Jessie?" he asked, then caught himself. "I mean, hi, Sheridan. Is Jessie around?"

The fortysomething blonde shook her head. "Chuck let her go home early."

Worry filled him. "Was she feeling okay?"

"I think so. She said something about an appointment at the bank."

"Right." He gave a nod. "What time did she leave?"

"About an hour ago."

Which would give her plenty of time to take care of her appointment and get back home.

"Can I get you something to eat?" she asked.

"Nah, thanks anyway." He tipped his hat and headed out into the sunshine.

Seth loped back across the street and popped into the office long enough to grab the keys to his service vehicle and tell Millie and Dusty that he'd be out for the rest of the afternoon. Then he started toward Jessie's house.

Damn, it was hot. He turned the air up a notch and thought about Jessie walking home in this heat. And pregnant. Possibly pregnant, he corrected. But somehow he knew. The question was if she bought the test three days ago, then why hadn't she been by to tell him the good news?

There were only two possible answers. One, she didn't think it was good news and had no intention of telling him. Or two, there was no news to tell. But he knew that wasn't the case. She should have talked to him by now.

His anger mounting by the second, he pulled the truck to a stop and got out. The house looked the same as it always did, run-down and sad. But Jessie was never going to fix it up. She was leaving town.

Leaving without telling him that she was having his baby.

Steam fairly billowed out his ears as he took the porch steps two at a time and knocked on the door with more force than necessary. "Jessie," he hollered, propping his hands on his hips. "I know you're in there."

He raised his fist again but didn't connect with wood.

Jessie wrenched the door open, her expression as annoyed as he felt. "What's wrong with you?"

He pushed past her into the house and took a deep breath to control his emotions. She was pregnant. He had to remember that. Feeling marginally in control, he rounded on her. "When were you going to tell me?"

She shook her head. "Tell you what?"

"About the baby."

She blanched. "How did you know?"

"Millie."

"Of course." Jessie eased down onto the hard-backed chair next to the front door. "I don't know," she finally said.

Seth resisted the urge to scoop her into his arms and kiss away all that hurt and confusion. It was better by far if he stayed angry, at least for now. "You don't know when you were going to tell me?"

She shook her head. "I chickened out."

"What?"

"I didn't take the test," she said, louder this time. "I got nervous and couldn't go through with it."

"Where is it now?" he asked.

"In the bathroom."

He gave a quick nod and hauled her to her feet. "Let's go."

"Go where?"

"To the bathroom. It's time to find out if we're going to be parents."

Dumbfounded, Jessie allowed him to lead her through the house. He pushed his way into the small powder room that she used. The incriminating box was sitting on the counter, the test nestled inside, just waiting to show her how stupid and irresponsible she had been.

Seth picked up the box and handed it to her. She snatched it away from him, her fingers trembling so bad she couldn't get the darn thing open.

"Give it." Seth took it from her, but she noticed his fingers were shaking even more than hers. Finally he ripped open the box and the bag inside. "Here." He handed her the wand and started reading the instructions. "You need to, uh . . . pee on that and we wait two minutes to see if a pink line appears." He looked up and pinned her to the spot. "Well?"

"I hope you don't think I'm going to pee with you in here."

"Jessie, I—"

"Out." She planted her hands on his back and somehow managed to get him on the other side of the bathroom door. With a decisive click, she turned the lock and caught a glimpse of herself in the mirror above the sink. Once she took the test, there was no going back. And once she found out the truth, then everything would change.

Blowing her hair out of her face, she told herself to quit stalling.

She jumped as Seth knocked on the door. "You okay in there?"

"Fine." At least the anger had leached from his voice.

With a sigh she moved to the toilet to take care of business.

"Are you finished? I heard the toilet flush."

"Almost." It hadn't been the easiest thing, peeing with Seth just outside the door, but she'd managed. Now the last thing she wanted was him standing over her while she waited for the results. *They* waited for the results. Like it or not, they were in this together. At least until she outlined her plans for him.

"Almost, hell. Open the door, Jess."

She glanced into the wand's little plastic window. It hadn't been thirty seconds and already the line was visible. Maybe Seth read the directions wrong. She opened the door and Seth barreled inside.

"Are you sure a pink line means a baby?" She swallowed hard.

"It's positive, isn't it?" He looked over to the wand and paled under his tan.

One thing was certain, nothing would ever be the same again.

Chapter Ten

❧✦❧

A baby," he whispered, picking up the little plastic device and staring at it as if it contained all the mysteries in the world.

She supposed that in a way it did.

"Nothing has to change for you, Seth."

"I don't see how."

"This baby—" Dear God, she was having a baby. The thought sent a shiver through her. She was excited and filled with dread at the same time. A baby to love and cherish.

"I'm not going to have such an important discussion in the bathroom." He took her by the hand and dragged her into the living room. "We have some plans to make."

Jessie shook her head. "I've made my plans. I'm leaving Cattle Creek."

"Where are you going?" Seth asked. His expression gave nothing away.

She had been planning to escape for so long, yet she still didn't have the answer to that one. She was still dealing too much with her grandmother's death to focus on her dreams.

She hadn't been able to leave Cattle Creek when Naomi was alive. Now that she was gone, Jessie was having a hard time not feeling a little bit guilty, as if she had caused her grandmother's death by her own dreams. It was dumb, but the feelings were there all the same. She shrugged but didn't meet his gaze. "I'll let you know where I decide to go."

"You'll let me know." The words were lethal.

"Yes." Her breath stuttered in her lungs, but she managed to continue. "I'll contact an attorney, and he can draw up the papers."

"Papers?"

"You know, papers." She gave what she hoped was an encouraging nod.

Seth's eyes blazed green fire. "Are you asking me to sign away my rights as a father?"

"Be reasonable, Seth. This isn't what you want."

"How do you know what I want? Did you ever think about asking me?"

"Once I get settled, I'll contact an attorney. He can handle it all. I don't want to keep the baby from you."

"Damn right, you won't." His nostrils flared as his breath heaved in and out of his chest.

"But you don't owe me anything." It wasn't as if Seth was in love with her. Marriage was out of the question. She saw no need to bind them together that way. Just like her mama before her, she would raise the baby on her own. She might not have a college education or many job skills, but she had her camera. Maybe she could work for a photographer until she could open a studio of her own. She would do what she had to do to take care of her child.

She'd lost every blood relative she ever had. This baby was her future, her family, and she didn't want to share her with anyone.

"So you've got it all figured out."

"It's better this way." Now more than ever, she had to go. Having the baby here, in Cattle Creek, would totally upset the dynamics of the family. Once word got out, there wouldn't be a Langston who would look at her the same again. And that was something she couldn't stomach.

"Better for who, Jessie?"

He watched the emotions and answers flash across her face.

"I want a fresh start in a new place. And I surely don't want to raise my child in Cattle Creek where no one will ever forget that I got knocked up by Seth Langston."

"Well, too bad, because you did get knocked up by Seth Langston and now you're going to marry him." He didn't know why he was yelling. Well, maybe he did.

"I'm not marrying you."

"What did you expect, Jessie? That you wouldn't tell me and just move away and take the baby? *My* baby." Despite his anger his heart lurched at the thought of his child.

"I told you."

"Big of you." He braced his hands on his hips.

She opened her mouth to say something, but he never knew what.

"Just what were you planning on doing, Jess? What are you going to tell him when he asks about his father?"

"*She'll* be fine without a father."

"Just like you."

"That was mean."

It was, but he didn't care. He felt mean. Mean and ill and hateful and happy and nauseous all at the same time. "Make no mistake, Jessie. I will be a part of this child's life, whether you want me to or not."

She tucked her chin to her chest and put her hands over her ears. "It's not like that," she whispered.

"Like what?" he demanded, though he had lowered his voice to be a better match to hers.

"It's not that I don't want you to be a part of the baby's life. I don't want you to feel like you have to be. We're not in love or anything. What kind of life is that?"

The heartbreak in her words was his undoing. He wrapped his arms around her and pulled her close. Lord, he could get used to the feel of her in his arms, soft and pliant. How would she feel in a few months when she was round and showing? The thought filled him with excitement. "We may not be in love, Jessie." At least she wasn't. "But we can be good together. We'll make a fine home for a baby. I know it." He kissed the top of her head even as her tears wet the front of his shirt. Her arms came around him and he nearly groaned out loud from the feel of her innocent touch.

All he needed was a little time and he could show her what love was about. They had known each other for a lifetime, had practically grown up together.

"What about Chase?" She had to ask the one question that he wouldn't allow himself to even think.

"This has nothing to do with Chase. This is about you and me. And our baby."

She took a deep shuddering breath, as if pulling herself back in control.

"If you don't agree, I'm going to get Grandma Esther and you know what will happen then."

Jessie laughed and took a step back, wiping her tears away with the backs of her hands. "Just give me a little time to absorb all this, okay?"

"I'm not giving up until you say yes."

Her smile wavered just a bit. "I expected nothing less."

Seth's footfalls *thunked* against the slate porch as he climbed the steps leading to the big house. He had been putting this moment off for three days, but it could wait no longer. He let himself into the house. "Mama?" he called, taking his hat off as he stepped into the large family room. His whole apartment would fit into the one room, but with the wooden beams, hardwood floors, and leather furniture, the space projected a cozy air.

The large painting above the fireplace caught his attention. His mother had had it commissioned from a photograph taken of Chase a few years back. He was on a bucking bull and was wearing chaps that depicted the Texas state flag. One hand was wrapped in his rope, the other high in the air. It was a beautiful painting, but today it was the last thing he wanted to see.

"I thought I heard you call." The heels of his mother's boots clicked against the hardwood floors as she stepped out of her office. She leaned in and gave him a kiss on the cheek. "What brings you out today?"

He glanced from the portrait of Chase back to his mother. "I need to talk to you about something. Is Jake around?"

"He took Wesley out to ride fences." She shook her head. "That girl. I'll never make a lady out of her the way he lets her run wild. Come on in here and have a seat." She led the way back into her office.

Seth collapsed into the horseshoe-shaped leather chair in front of her desk and waited for her to take a seat behind it.

"What's on your mind today?" she asked, once she had settled into her chair.

Seth crossed his legs, ankle over knee, and tapped his fingers against the heel of one boot. Suddenly he was sixteen again and having to fess up to the biggest mistake of his life. "Jessie's pregnant."

He watched the emotions flit across his mother's face— surprise, understanding, then resignation. "I see." She sat back in her chair, her demeanor calm and collected, but he knew inside her head the thoughts were going ninety to nothing. "What do you propose to do?"

"I'm going to marry her."

She seemed to mull it over, then shook her head. "That's

very noble of you, Seth. But I don't think it's your place. Obviously we need to talk to Chase. Does he know?"

"I need to call and talk to him, but . . ." He trailed off. He needed plans in place before he told the news to his baby brother.

She reached for the phone sitting to her left. "We need to call him," she said, pressing buttons as she spoke. "He needs to get back here and take care of his responsibility."

"It's mine."

She couldn't hide her shock. Her eyes wide, she stopped mid-dial and returned the phone to its cradle. "I see."

He stood, unable to bear the confusion on her face.

Naturally she thought the baby was Chase's. After all, Jessie had been Chase's girl from day one. Or at least that was what everybody in town thought.

Now his mother knew that Seth had slept with his brother's girl. Not only had he breached the brotherly trust issue, but he did it with a lasting, living, breathing memory.

"Are you sure?" she asked.

"I am."

She gave a thoughtful nod. "And your plans are?"

"I'm going to marry her."

"I see." His mother stood as well. "I guess we have a wedding to plan."

Seth shook his head. "We'll just have a quick civil service. Maybe drive over to San Angelo." That would stop the wagging tongues for a while, but soon enough, word would get out that he and Jessie were having a baby.

"Unacceptable," his mother said. "You need to do it right, son. Langstons only get married once."

Seth pulled his service truck to a stop and then leaned over to open the passenger-side door. "Get in."

Jessie warily eyed him. He hated when she gave him that look—part frightened deer, part stubborn mule. "Why?"

"We have a few things to talk about."

She glanced down the sidewalk toward the turn off to Larkspur Lane, then back to him.

She was on her way home from the Chuck Wagon. He had tried to make it over there before she got off work, but Chester Gibson decided that Amos Carver had stolen all the coolant from his air conditioner and had called Seth. After calling in a repairman and taking a quick look at service records, Seth figured it was time to fill the thing up again. Without apology to his neighbor, Chester paid the repairman and Seth was free to go. But now he was chasing Jessie down the streets of Cattle Creek instead of picking her up from work as had been his original plan.

"What if I don't want to talk?" She sounded plumb wore-out, but some things couldn't wait until she was ready.

"Get in, Jessie James."

She flounced over to his truck and slid into the cab next to him. "Fine," she said. "But don't call me that."

He didn't say a word as he started the truck down the road once again.

"I thought you were taking me home," she said as they passed by the turnoff to her house.

Seth shook his head. "I thought we might go down to the lake."

"Are you going with me to watch the fireworks tonight?"

"Are you asking?"

"Maybe."

"We have a lot we need to talk about."

"Fine." She crossed her arms and slumped back into her seat.

She rode that way the entire short trip to the ranch.

"This isn't the lake," she said as he stopped the truck at the entrance to the horse pasture.

"There's a lake here."

She nodded.

They had all been fishing down here too many times

to count. He knew it as well as he knew the big lake on the other side of the highway. But that lake would be filled with teenagers and families alike, trying their best to enjoy the summer break from school. Add in the fact that it was the Fourth of July and everyone in Page County would be splashing around in water. He needed to be alone with her, have some peace and quiet. Someplace where they could talk and get things worked out before they got married.

She slid from the cab without him asking and opened the gate. He drove through and she shut it behind him before swinging back into the truck once more.

He had already instructed Millie and Dusty to handle everything they could until he texted them to say that he was available again. He needed no distractions. This was too important to have to deal with petty crimes and high school pranks. Dusty was plenty capable, and Seth had more important fish to fry. But he'd said an added prayer that the town's good nature would last at least long enough for him to straighten out a few things with Jessie.

He pulled the truck to a stop under the shade of a large oak. Family legend stated that it had been planted by William Travis himself, but Seth suspected that it had been William Langston, his great-grandfather, who had done the deed.

He got out of the truck, then looked over to his sullen passenger. "It's too hot to sit in the truck all afternoon."

"It's too hot to be in Texas," she groused, but she got out and came around the front of the truck.

"You want to go somewhere else? Name your place."

"How about the Arctic Circle?" she asked.

"I don't think they'll have fireworks there tonight."

"Don't care."

"Then I'm in, but only if you bring your bikini."

Her expression remained tense as she stared out over the placid water.

"That was a joke," he explained.

She didn't respond.

"Jessie, this marriage will never work if you keep acting like it's a prison sentence."

"Isn't it?"

"No."

"You actually *want* to marry me?"

He opened his mouth to respond, but she cut in before he could get the first word out.

"I'm not a fool, Seth. You're marrying me because you have to. I'm marrying you because you're making me. What I want to know is how long we're going to pretend to be happy after the baby comes before we go see Harley for a quickie divorce."

"How about forever?"

Her eyes widened, then narrowed as if she wasn't sure whether to be surprised or wary. "Forever?"

"You have a problem with that?" His mother talked about Langstons marrying forever, but Seth had been in love with Jessie for so long. He wanted to be married to her, love her daily. Forever.

He went around to the back of his patrol vehicle and pulled out the quilt he kept there for emergencies. He had taken to carrying it ever since he rescued a preschooler from a tidal pool. The poor child had been shivering uncontrollably. Seth had wrapped her in his jacket to keep her warm, all the while wishing he had something bigger and softer to do the job.

He spread the quilt underneath the tree and sat down. His weapon was poking a hole in his side and he was pretty sure his handcuffs might puncture a kidney, but he was doing this for Jessie. He patted the space next to him. "Come sit with me."

She looked as if she was about to tell him no; then she exhaled heavily and plopped down next to him. "We should have brought some fishing poles."

We. He liked the sound of that. "Next time," he promised.

Her shoulders lost that defensive slant and that little muscle in her jaw quit jumping. Those had to be good signs.

"Why'd you bring me out here, Seth?"

"I wanted to talk to you."

"We could have talked in town."

He nodded. "But here no one is going to bother us. And everyone in town isn't a part of this."

"Someone needs to tell them that."

He laughed. "We'd probably have to get a law passed."

She picked up a stick and tossed it into the water. "This isn't going to be easy, is it?"

"Nothing ever worth it is. At least, that's what Grandma Esther always says." But Jessie'd had more than her share of hard times. That was the first thing he wanted to change.

"I've always loved coming out here," she said, finding another stick and tossing it. "It's like being in another world."

"It is."

Cattle Creek was small. Not even two thousand people lived in the town, so there wasn't that many big-city sounds. But here it was so quiet he swore he could hear the grass grow.

"When we all used to come out here, I used to pretend that I was really part of the family. Not just a friend."

"Does that mean you pretended that I was your brother? Because that has a pretty big ick factor for me."

She laughed. "It wasn't about that. It was about . . . belonging. I wanted so much to be a part of what y'all had."

Seth nodded. But that was before Mav left and Ty went to war. It was before Jake married Cecelia and Seth had stolen his brother's girl. It was before a lot of things.

"Is that crazy?" she asked.

"No, it's not crazy at all." He used his free hand to tilt her chin up, then swooped in to capture her lips with his own.

He couldn't tell her his feelings. It was too early. He knew she needed time. But he wanted her to know that he loved her. If only on this level.

He wanted to lay her back on this quilt, strip her down, and have his way with her until she begged for him to marry her. But not today.

She sighed as he raised his head.

"You are a Langston, Jessie. And from now on you always will be."

"If you keep saying that, I might just start believing it."

"That's my plan." Seth smiled and bussed her lips once more. They would be just fine. It might take a bit with all the obstacles they had to overcome, but soon—real soon— she would know how much he loved and cherished her and the child she carried.

He released her, loving the dazed look in her eyes. Yep. The good Lord willing, they would be just fine.

Jessie watched Seth beneath half-closed lids and tried her best to pull herself back together. His kiss held some magical quality that made her forget where she was, who she was, and everything she was supposed to be doing. Once his lips touched hers, he was all she could think about. And she wanted the kiss to last forever.

She managed to scrape together the shreds of her self-control and turned back toward the water. It was better by far if she didn't look at him. Every time she did she relived that afternoon in the truck and wondered how different it might have been if Seth had known that she had never been with Chase.

Or was that even important to him?

"I should be going through Meemaw's things," she said. Though wading through the remains of her grandmother's life was the last thing she wanted to be doing, it beat reliving that afternoon for the umpteenth time in only a couple of weeks.

It was difficult enough to know that she was gone, but to have to sort through the keepers and the throwaways . . .

well, it was hard. Getting rid of even the basics, her liniment and ashtrays, was proof that Naomi McAllen was never coming back.

"Relax a while, Jess. I'll help you with all that."

She shook her head. "It's not your job."

"I'm your future husband, and I say it is."

Husband. Marrying Seth was one thing, but she had never even thought about the fact that he would be her husband. Someone to share all the good times and the bad. She had lost her family a couple of weeks ago. Yet in another odd twist of fate she had gained a new one. Seth and the baby, living with her as a family.

"About that," she started. "I still haven't said yes."

"Well, get on with it, because I'm not taking no for an answer."

Because he was too noble to allow his child to be born out of wedlock. As old-fashioned as it was, Jessie knew that was the reason. What else could it be? "I guess we should pick a date. You know, before—"

"Before you start getting fat." He shot her a mischievous grin. So cute and crooked she had to pretend to be upset with his comment.

"Seth Langston! What a thing to say."

"I'm just playing."

Jessie returned his smile. "I know."

"So you are going to marry me?"

Like he had any doubt. "Yes." Like she had any choice.

"Two weeks from today."

"T-two weeks," she sputtered.

"The quicker we become a couple, the quicker everyone will start to accept us as a couple, and the quicker we can really become a couple."

He wanted to be a couple with her? The thought warmed her from the inside out. Or maybe that was just the lingering aftereffects of his kiss.

"Marrying me means staying in Cattle Creek."

She nodded.

"Forever."

"I know." It was both the worst and the best part of their arrangement. She'd had it in her head that she was getting out as soon as she could, but the thought of staying there—with Seth—put it in a different perspective. With one major problem.

"What about Chase?"

"I'll call him this week." His mouth turned down in a serious line.

"Maybe I should call. I mean, after all, this was my fault."

He shook his head. "It takes two, Jessie."

"But—"

"We're in this together."

"Then maybe we should call him together."

He unclipped his phone from his belt and handed it to her. "I get pretty decent reception out here."

She took it from him as if it were a snake about to strike. She could do this. She *had* to do this. She thumbed her way through the contact list until she came to Chase's name. She punched the call button and bit her lip as it started to ring.

From the other end of the line, the phone picked up. She took a breath, not sure what she was going to say, and then his recorded voice came on, telling her in that Chase way of his to leave a message and he'd call back.

"Chase, it's Jessie." Could she sound any more nervous? How about stupid? Of course it was her. What other female would be calling him from his brother's phone? "I need to talk to you. Can you call me back? Thanks." She hung up, knowing that it was the worst message ever left, but she couldn't tell him over the phone that she was pregnant with someone else's child and she was marrying that man in two weeks. *Oh, and by the by, it's your brother Seth.*

Nope, that was almost as bad as the action itself.

"He didn't answer."

"I gathered."

"He's probably out celebrating." She wondered if his party companion was a blonde or a brunette. Crazy enough, the thought didn't fill her with heartache and pain.

Probably because she had so many other things on her mind. But she supposed that was to be expected when she was having a baby and had two weeks to plan a wedding acceptable for the Langston family.

Jessie handed him back the phone. So much was going on inside her head she thought she might explode.

"Where are we going to live?" she blurted. It might not be the most pressing question, but it was the one that jumped to the forefront first.

"I've talked to Jake and he said we could move out to the ranch house."

Jessie shook her head. Moving in with the prying eyes of his family was the last thing she wanted. "I can't move in there with your mother."

"The original ranch house." He shot her a smile as if he had come up with the best plan ever.

The small white house sat off the road and far enough away from the big house that no one would just walk over. It would afford them a bit of privacy as well as keep them close to the family. As much as she hated to admit it, she loved the idea. Plus, with her grandmother's reverse mortgage she only had a few more weeks to stay in the house before it was put on the market.

"Okay."

Seth studied her expression, though what he was looking for was beyond her. "That's another reason why we need the two weeks. Are you up to getting it ready? I know Mama and Jake will help. Of course, I'll be there when I can."

"I have to work." She might only have the one job now, but it was important to her. How was she supposed to get the money to leave if she—

Her thoughts skidded to an abrupt halt. She wasn't leaving town. She was staying, marrying Seth, and dealing with the consequences of her actions.

"You don't have to work anymore. In fact, I don't want you to work at all."

Her hackles were up in an instant. Somehow she managed to control her fighting side. Seth was just looking out for her. *For the baby.* "What if I want to work?"

He sighed. "For once will you just let me take care of you? Is that so hard?"

It was impossible, but she could try. She *would* try. She was only making things harder for them. But it was all she had known. She had struggled to fit in, struggled to make ends meet, struggled to be a part. Now she would have all that and more as Seth's wife. "Okay."

"Good, because I already called Chuck and told him you wouldn't be coming back."

She was on her feet in a heartbeat. "You what?"

He wrapped his hand around her wrist and pulled her back into her seat. "Calm down, Jess. I was thinking of you at the time."

"I can see that."

He shook his head. "I thought you were going to let me take care of you."

"That was before I knew you had already gone behind my back and resigned me from my job."

His handsome face pulled into a frown. "You lost me."

Tears rose into her eyes. "Everything's happening so fast." Way too fast. All her plans had changed. Everything. She was staying in Cattle Creek, getting married, having a baby. Her life was no longer her own.

"Shhh . . ." He pulled her to him. "You shouldn't be working that hard. You're pregnant, remember?"

She sniffed. "How can I forget?"

"It's okay," he murmured. "It's all going to be okay. I just don't want you to have to worry about anything. You can understand that, right?"

He gently rocked her back and forth. She loved the feel of his hand as he smoothed her hair. More than anything she wanted it to be okay. But her life had spun out of her control. First her grandmother. Now this. Early on in her life she'd had to learn what was within her control and what wasn't. She couldn't stop the vicious rumors and all the talk about her family. That was one thing that got to her from time to time, but that she had learned to largely ignore.

But her job, where she was going to live, and who she was going to marry had all been things she used to identify as her own. Now all that had been taken from her as well.

Yet she had lost her desire to fight it all. Or maybe she was just tired.

"Yes." She sniffed.

He pulled away and wiped the pad of his thumb against her cheek, capturing the last lingering tear. "Let me worry about providing for us and where we're going to live and you just worry about getting together a wedding and growing a baby. Deal?"

She nodded even as fresh tears stung her eyes.

"Don't cry, Jessie. We'll get through this. Together. I promise."

She wanted to believe his sweet words, but she knew that Seth would make the best of the situation he had been presented, whatever that situation might be. And she would have to do the same. But she was under no illusion that he loved her. He had gotten her pregnant and he would make it right.

Chapter Eleven

❦✳❦

"There is, uh . . . one thing," Seth said as he drove through town. Their afternoon together had been wonderful. More amazing than she could have imagined. But she couldn't read anything into it. That was just Seth, an all-around good guy.

Why couldn't she have fallen in love with him long ago instead of Chase? It would have made things a whole lot easier, but then, when had her life ever been simple? Never, that's when.

"What is that?" she asked as he pulled in front of Nita Calvert's.

Seth cut the engine and gave her a rueful look. "Come on," he said, sliding from the seat. "I have someone I want you to meet."

"The fireworks are going to start soon," she said, looking through the windshield at the quickly darkening sky. They had heard a couple of rounds of firecrackers go off as they drove past the park. The only place anyone was allowed to set them off was on the asphalt basketball court to keep down the fire hazard. In order to help keep the code easy to follow, the City Council set up a huge fireworks show every year.

"We have time," Seth countered. "Now come on."

Jessie got out of the truck and went around the front to stand next to him. "I've already met Nita."

He shook his head. "Just come on." He led her around back to the doorway that led into his apartment.

She tried to remember a time when she had come here with Seth, but she couldn't think of any. Strange she felt so close to him yet she had never seen where he lived. Or maybe it was that she had always pictured his home as the Diamond.

Seth took out his key and unlocked the door. From inside the apartment, a dog started to bark.

He shot her one more unreadable grin, then stepped inside. "Sadie," he called, then crouched down as the dog answered his summons.

"Jessie. I'd like for you to meet Sadie. Sadie, Jessie."

"Pleasure," Jessie said, only briefly remembering that she was addressing a pooch. A four-pound pooch judging from the size of her.

It was the tiniest dog she had ever seen. Or maybe it only looked that small because of the way Seth cradled it in his big hands. "Is that a . . ."

He nodded, looking only mildly embarrassed. "Yorkie, yes."

Despite all the seriousness of the last couple of weeks, Jessie's lips started to twitch. "And how exactly did you come to have such a sweet little puppy?"

To her amazement, Seth planted a quick kiss on the top of Sadie's tiny head. "Chase brought her home last year. I never found her a home, so I ended up just keeping her."

Jessie nodded. "And how is it that I'm just now seeing her?"

He shrugged and placed the dog on the floor between them. "No reason."

"Dogs like Sadie have to be groomed, you know." Evidently he did. Sadie had a tiny pink bow tied between her ears. Surely he didn't . . .

"Yeah," he admitted. He propped his hands on his hips, clearly a defensive gesture if she had ever seen one.

She mimicked his pose and continued. "I've never seen you take her into Wag the Dog." Cattle Creek's only pet groomer sat two doors down from the Chuck Wagon on the opposite side of the sheriff's office. He would have to be sneaking the dog in for her not to have seen him carry Sadie to the groomer's. Unless . . .

A slow grin worked its way across her face. "So that's how Wanda keeps getting out of those parking tickets."

"Let's just say that Wanda and I have come to an agreement."

Jessie cocked her head to one side. "Huh," she said. "I would have never guessed that you would compromise your police integrity in order to get your sissy dog groomed."

"Hey," he protested. "Sadie and I find that comment unnecessary and offensive."

"But true." She laughed.

Seth scooped Sadie back into his arms. "Sadie, sic 'em." He held the dog close to her and Jessie got a lick on the nose.

She took the dog from Seth and scratched her behind one ear. Sadie let out a doggy sigh of pleasure.

"That's right," Jessie crooned. "We girls gotta stick together. But"—she turned her gaze back to Seth—"one false move on your part and I'll tell the whole town you own a girlie dog."

Seth threw back his head and laughed. "Fine," he said. "As long as you don't tell them I carry her around in a designer bag."

Jessie snuggled Sadie close and surveyed the man she was marrying in two weeks. "Okay, cowboy, but that will cost extra."

* * *

"Come on or we'll miss the fireworks," Seth said. He parked his service vehicle and got out.

"We're going to miss it anyway if we're here." Jessie stopped on the sidewalk outside the sheriff's office and held her ground.

"Don't you trust me?" His words were a challenge, he knew, but he couldn't do this alone. It took two to make a marriage and he needed her by his side, not pulling away every chance she got.

"Yes," she said.

The one word shouldn't have filled him with so much joy, but it did. "Then come on."

He led the way around the back of the two-story brick building to the side entrance. Once upon a time, the building had been a library and the entrance was for deliveries and such. Now it was just one more door to make sure was locked.

"Did I know this was here?" she asked, peering in the entrance.

"I don't know. It's not like something we talk about a lot." He turned on his flashlight app and shone it up the concrete staircase off to their right.

"Are you sure you're not bringing me someplace dark and secluded so you can take advantage of me?"

"Is that a possibility?"

Jessie didn't respond. One minute she was playful and the next she was putting her guard up. He was beyond ready for her to trust him with all the faces of Jessie McAllen. The real ones.

"Be patient," he said. "You'll see." He started up the stairs, careful to shine the light where she could see as well. He couldn't have her falling.

"Is this it?" Jessie asked, looking around at all the stacked boxes and cobwebs. He really needed to get someone in here to clean.

"Nope. This is." He opened the door with a flourish and gestured toward the flat roof.

Jessie gasped.

Down in the direction of the river, the first explosion of fireworks burst into the sky. He couldn't have timed it better if he'd tried.

"Come on," he said, taking her arm to lead her over to the lawn chairs he'd set up.

Their chairs faced the show and since they were up a little higher, it seemed as if the fireworks were going off right in front of them.

Seth alternated his attention between Jessie and the actual fireworks celebration. Her expression of awe and appreciation was more beautiful to him than the actual show.

"Would you like a lemonade?" He opened the cooler between the chairs and offered her the drink.

For a moment she took her eyes from the spark-filled nighttime sky to focus on him. "Thanks, Seth."

He wanted to lean in and steal a kiss, but years of holding himself in check kept him in place. "You're welcome, Jessie."

She turned back to the fireworks, and somehow Seth knew. Things were changing between them. The circumstances surrounding their evolving relationship might be a little unusual, but they had a chance.

They just might make it after all.

Hey." Jake stepped back to allow Seth room to enter. "What brings you out today?"

Seth removed his hat and moved past his brother farther into the house. "Oh, you know. I was out this way."

"Mama's not here," Jake said.

"I know. She took Jessie to San Angelo to buy a wedding dress."

Jake stopped and eyed him in a way only older brothers can.

"I thought I would stop by and call Chase," Seth finally said.

Jake gave a knowing dip of his chin. "I see."

"I've called twice, but he hasn't returned my calls."

"You leave a message?"

Seth shot his brother a look.

Jake chuckled. "I guess not."

"I thought maybe if I called from here . . ."

"He would think it was Mama and pick up?"

"Something like that."

"You want to use her office phone?"

"Does it matter?"

Jake turned and led them down the hallway that led to the Langston home offices. "I guess not." He opened the door to his own and stepped inside, flipping on the light as he went.

"Where's Wesley?" Seth asked, flopping down in the seat in front of Jake's desk.

"She's out at the pool with Grandma Esther." Suddenly Seth wished more than ever that he could join them.

Chicken.

It was time to get this over with. He picked up the phone and dialed Chase's number.

"You got a recording." Chase's voice reached across the line. "You know what to do."

"Chase, I need to talk to you. It's . . . important. Call me ASAP." Seth hung up the phone and eyed his brother from across the desk. "He needs to know."

"I agree, but you can only do what you can do."

Seth shook his head.

"You want to talk about it?"

"What's there to talk about?"

"Oh, I don't know . . ." Jake mockingly tapped a finger

to his chin. "How about how you ended up in such a compromising situation with your brother's girl?"

"She was never Chase's." The words sprang from his lips before he could stop them.

An understanding light dawned in Jake's eyes. "So it is true. The baby's really yours?"

Seth nodded, then shifted under Jake's steady gaze.

"You're in love with her." The airy words were filled with wonder.

Seth was so accustomed to denying it that he opened his mouth to do just that. "Yeah," he said instead. His shoulders slumped as the weight that had been placed there released.

"Does she know?"

"No," he whispered.

"And I assume Chase doesn't either."

"Nope." Seth sighed. "I've loved her for so long," he admitted. "Since we buried her mother."

Jake's dark brows disappeared under the dark flop of hair covering his forehead. "Really? So what are you going to do about it?"

Seth shot him a grim smile. "I'm going to do everything in my power to make her love me back."

It's awfully expensive," Jessie protested as Evelyn pulled yet another gorgeous dress from the rack. She couldn't afford such a garment, especially not for just one day.

"It's your wedding day and it should be special," Evelyn said simply.

Jessie bit back a sigh. She'd made such a mess of things. And it had all started with one little kiss. Now she had trapped Seth into marriage, Chase wasn't taking her phone calls, and their mother looked at her as if she should be voted Tramp of the Year.

"I'll do my very best to make him happy," she said, finally accepting the hanger from Evelyn. "Seth, that is."

Evelyn's face softened. "I know you will, dear. It's not Seth I'm worried about."

Jessie could only nod.

It was Chase. With Evelyn it was always about Chase. She had one son in a war zone and one who had walked out one night and never returned, but it was her youngest son who took up the majority of her thoughts and prayers.

Not that Jessie believed for a minute that Evelyn was aware of her favoritism. The fact remained that everyone else in the family was aware of it. Accepted it even as just part of life as a Langston.

"Chase will be fine, Evelyn. I can promise you that." Visions of his blond buckle bunny from a few weeks ago flashed through her thoughts. There was one in every town at every rodeo. Sometimes a brunette, sometimes a blonde. Maybe even a redhead thrown in for good measure. She had known all along that he wasn't faithful to her. How could he care about her as he claimed if he was running all over the country with other women? No, he only thought he loved her and once he knew that they could no longer be, he would pick up his life and continue on in the only way Lucky Langston could. One woman at a time. Maybe two.

Evelyn nodded and handed her another hanger holding a beautiful lace dress. "Go try these on, dear. Come on out when you're ready. I want to see them." She tried for a smile and Jessie couldn't help noticing that it didn't reach her eyes.

She retreated to the dressing rooms and shut the door, thankful to have even a small reprieve from Seth's mother. Evelyn meant well, and she was a wonderful lady. But the strain of her constant surveillance and her probing questions were taking their toll.

She sat down on the little square bench in the corner

and pulled out her new cell phone. Seth had presented it to her yesterday when he finally took her back home from the ranch lake. She had protested at first, but as usual, he had worn her down and she had accepted the gift. Now she was thankful to have it as she dialed Seth's number.

She hadn't used the thing until now and she was a little nervous as the phone rang on the other end.

"Jessie?" He sounded happy to hear from her.

"Tell me again how everything's going to be okay."

"Is my mother driving you crazy?"

"Tell me."

"Everything is going to be okay. What's she got you worried about?"

"Chase."

Once again his name hung between them. How could they go on with his brother constantly hovering around?

"Chase is a big boy, and he'll get over it."

"Do you really believe that?" she asked.

"He made his choices." Seth's voice came across the phone lines like the growl of a bear.

"Let's just run to the justice of the peace and get married," she suggested. "This wedding planning is nerve-racking."

Seth chuckled. "You know Mama is not going to let us get away with that."

She pulled at a loose thread on her jeans and glanced at the dresses hanging next to her in the stall. "I know."

"Just hang in there. Just two more weeks and it'll all be over."

"Jessie? Are you in here?" Evelyn called from the hall between the dressing rooms.

"I gotta go." She jumped to her feet as if she'd been caught with her hand in the proverbial cookie jar.

"Jessie," he protested but she hung up without answering.

"Just a minute," she hollered toward the sound of Evelyn's voice. But she needed more than a minute. A lot more.

* * *

In the end, Jessie bought the most beautiful dress she had ever owned. Creamy white silk and lace with pearl buttons and tiny little hooks and eyes that she was certain she wouldn't be able to fasten before she walked down the aisle toward the altar and Seth. The purchase put quite a dent in her dwindling savings, but she couldn't allow Seth's mother to buy her dress.

But Evelyn had drawn the line at the boot store and paid for the navy blue Tony Lamas with the cream-colored inlaid roses with tan stitching.

"Consider it your something blue, my dear," Seth's mother said as she whipped out her American Express and handed it to the man behind the counter.

Before Jessie could utter a second protest, the boots were hers and they were whisking out the door once again.

"Now," Evelyn said, turning on her blinker and changing lanes. "We need a cake, flowers, invitations . . ."

"That seems like a lot," Jessie protested weakly.

"And your hair." Evelyn cast her a quick glance, then turned back to face the San Angelo rush-hour traffic. "Who's going to do your hair?"

She reached up a tentative hand and lightly fingered her messy curls. Her hair did what it wanted when it wanted to do it. "No one's doing my hair."

Evelyn sighed. "Jessica, this is your wedding day. Now's not the time to be worried about money and such. I know this isn't something you and Seth planned, but you still deserve to be the most beautiful bride Cattle Creek has ever seen."

Jessie blinked back tears. Stupid hormones. They had her crying like a baby at the drop of a hat. Or maybe it was the overwhelming situation she found herself in. Or maybe it was simply time to take back some control over her life.

She pushed herself up a little straighter in the truck seat and faced her future mother-in-law head-on. "I don't want to have anyone do my hair. I think a simple bun is just fine for an afternoon at-home wedding. As far as the cake goes, I would like Grandma Esther to make it. She makes the best cakes in three counties as it is. I don't need it to be fancy, but I would like it to taste good. And for napkins and that sort of thing, let's run by the Dollar Tree and see what they have. I think it's ridiculous to spend ten dollars a package for something that people are going to wipe their mouth on and then throw away."

Evelyn reached the next stoplight and turned to face her as they idled waiting for it to turn green once again. "If that's how you feel about it," she said quietly.

Jessie nodded, the spinning in her head stopping for the first time in days. "It is." She nodded to add emphasis.

Evelyn checked the light and put the truck into motion once again. "Then Dollar Tree, here we come."

Jessie eyed the front door of the ranch house, unable to deny the charm of the old place. She had come out here a couple of times with Seth and the other Langston boys as they visited with their grandma Duvall, but Jessie had forgotten how quaint the little house was.

"What if there are spiders?" she asked. That would be just what she needed to completely blow the sweet fantasy of ranch life now blooming in her head.

Seth chuckled from behind her and moved to unlock the door. "Oh, there are spiders. I can promise you that."

Jessie shook her head. "I'm not going in. Not unless you fumigate and have it inspected." She shuddered. "I don't do spiders."

Seth held open the door and Jessie could see even from the distance where she was standing that dust and cobwebs liberally accented the old rooms. No, thank you.

"If you don't want to help me clean this up, I suppose you're okay with moving into Nita's garage apartment with me?"

"Unfair, Seth," Jessie said as she loped up the steps and into the house.

The heels of her boots *thunked* against the heavy-planked floor. Although a layer of dust covered the wood, Jessie could see that it was a rich, dark brown. She had a vision of it cleaned and glowing, vibrant rugs scattered throughout.

"Jake said he'd have the power turned on by tomorrow afternoon. And I've arranged for all the appliances to arrive later in the week." Seth walked across the front room and poked his head through the doorway leading to the kitchen. "We've got four bedrooms—three of which are really small—a dining room, and this room here, but we can add on if need be."

"It's perfect just the way it is." She spun around in a circle, trying to take it all in. Suddenly the spiders weren't such a concern.

Between the two of them, they had enough furniture to fill the place. It just needed a good scrubbing, maybe some curtains.

He motioned for her to follow him. He took the entry-way opposite the one that led to the kitchen. She sneezed as she trailed behind him down a narrow hallway.

"Bless you," he said as he stepped into a large airy room nearly the size of the front room. A large bay window jutted out from the house with two more flanking it. "This is the master room. Our room."

She could well imagine the polished floors, sheer, gauzy curtains, and her wrought-iron bed pushed up close to the windows that would let in the morning light from an eastern sun.

"I hired Johnny Garcia and his crew to paint. You'll need to pick out the colors and get that to him as soon as possible. The quicker he has that, the quicker he can get started."

"You've thought of everything," she whispered.

He shrugged, but she noticed a faint flush of red creeping into his cheeks. He turned and motioned for her to follow him once again. Back up the hallway to the door they had passed earlier.

The door creaked as he pushed it open. "And this will be the nursery."

The room was tiny, perfect for the new addition they were expecting. Jessie could imagine the crib pushed next to the window, dancing beams of sun stealing into the room. A swing, a changing table, and tons of stuffed animals to fill the space.

She turned to Seth tears blurring her vision. "Thank you," she whispered, wrapping her arms around him.

A beautiful sense of peace stole over her as he wrapped her in his arms. His heart thumped under her ear, its rhythm steady and comforting.

"Don't thank me yet." A chuckle rumbled up from his chest. "We still have a lot of work to do."

A lot of work or not, she knew that somehow, some way, everything was going to be just fine.

Chapter Twelve

❧ ✵ ❧

Everything is going to be okay. Everything is going to be okay, Jessie chanted as she took one last look in the mirror. Her sense of ease from the day she'd stood in the ranch house, wrapped in Seth's strong embrace, had long since vanished.

They had turned Evelyn's office into a makeshift dressing area for her. And though she had managed to secure some time to herself, this was one of those occasions when she could have used a mother's or sister's advice.

This morning it had hit her smack in the face. She was marrying Seth Langston. Tonight he would drive them over to the ranch house and they would spend their wedding night in the tiny four-bedroom where they had decided to raise their family.

She took a deep breath and pressed a trembling hand to her fluttering stomach. It was way too early for the baby to be moving, which meant nerves were responsible for its current upheaval.

Maybe she would feel better if they had gotten in touch

with Chase. Everyone had tried to call him, including Evelyn, but it seemed that Chase had more important matters to attend. Jessie couldn't help wondering if she was a brunette or a blonde.

Still, she wished she'd had the chance to explain things to him, to bring full closure to their relationship. Most of what was between them must have been in her head, but Jessie would feel better if she told him what was happening before it actually happened. Knowing Chase, he'd call tonight after they had all gone home and be pissed that no one had bothered to tell him.

Home. Tonight she and Seth would go back to their new place and pretend to be happily married. They had been acting like a real couple for the last two weeks, picking out paint colors and baby furniture, checking on the progress of the house. He had resigned her from her job to help get the place ready, then forbade her to do any actual work. He didn't want her painting or moving furniture. She supposed that was for the best, yet she felt a little like a diva, instructing others in what to do while she stood off to one side and supervised.

But she hadn't protested. She told herself that was because she had too much work to do at the house to argue every little point with Seth, but the truth was she was scared. Of Seth and how he made her feel. Of the town and the rumors she knew had to be flying around like crazed bats. Were people talking more about her, Seth, and the baby or the fact that the staid and true sheriff was marrying Cattle Creek's resident wild child? She didn't want to know. So she had holed up in the old ranch house and pretended that paint colors and furniture polish were the most pressing matters she had.

She took one last look in the mirror to check her makeup and smoothed her hands down the front of her dress. She must have lost a couple of pounds in the last two weeks, since it fit a little bigger today than it had when she bought it. She hadn't had any morning sickness, so she knew her nerves were the culprit.

A knock sounded on the door and she whirled around as Seth eased inside.

"Are you ready?"

She shook her head. "I mean, yes."

He beamed an indulgent smile at her. "Everyone's waiting on us."

She looked down at herself, one last double check to make sure she was ready.

"Mama said you might need this." He handed her a penny, a small frown on his brow. "For your thoughts?" he asked.

"From the poem. Something old, something new; something borrowed, something blue." She had a new dress, her old bracelet, borrowed pearls, and blue boots. She slipped the coin down the shaft of the left one. "Put a penny in your shoe."

Seth smiled as he watched her. "They need to rewrite that for cowgirls," he teased, then held his arm for her to take. She lifted her small white rose bouquet from its box and hooked her arm through his.

They had agreed to walk down the aisle together. It had been Seth's idea and Jessie had jumped at the plan. Jake was the only male who might possibly stand in and walk her down the aisle, since neither of them had a father, but Seth had said they were in this together, starting with their first walk to the altar together. It only seemed right.

Pastor Stanley from the Methodist church waited next to the fireplace. Jessie used all her energy to walk next to Seth without tripping and all her willpower to remain upright and conscious. Were all brides this nervous? Or just pregnant ones who were mismatched to handsome cowboy sheriffs? He smiled at them and Jessie wondered if he knew their secret. How many people in Cattle Creek knew that Seth was marrying her because they were having a baby?

And of those, how many were betting that the baby actually belonged to Chase? The thought made her nauseous.

"Dearly beloved, we are gathered here today . . . ," Pastor Stanley started as a loud hum began to ring in Jessie's ears. This was really happening.

How many constituted "dearly beloved"? Only Evelyn, Grandma Esther, Jake, and Wesley were there to witness the event, yet the man talked as if there were two hundred guests crammed into the Langston ranch house.

Jessie mentally shook her head to clear her thoughts and did her best to concentrate on what the preacher was saying.

"Repeat after me. I, Jessica Elizabeth McAllen, take thee, Seth Daniel Langston, to be my lawfully wedded husband."

She trembled.

Seth gently squeezed her fingers, spurring her into speech.

Her voice sounded squeaky and high-pitched as she repeated her vows to love, honor, and cherish him until death. Seth's voice rang with confidence and affection as he made his promises to her.

Was he really planning on staying married to her forever? Could they make it with everything stacked against them? Did she want them to?

Wesley stepped up next to her and tugged on her dress. Jessie turned as the young girl flashed her snaggletooth smile and handed her a plain gold band.

Jessie took it, shooting her own trembling smile to Wesley and turned to Seth. "With this ring, I thee wed," she said as she slid it on his finger.

Then he reached into his pocket and pulled out a matching band and pledged the same to her.

"I now pronounce you man and wife. Seth, you may kiss your bride."

He stepped closer to her and tilted her chin with one hand.

Jessie's eyes fluttered closed as his lips met hers only briefly. Still, the touch was explosive, like every other kiss they had shared. Yet this one held a promise of more, of a lifetime, of the child nestled between them.

He lifted his head, his fiery green eyes blazing into hers. For the first time in the two weeks since they had been planning this wedding, she thought about tonight. She and Seth all alone in the house they had planned to share. Alone in her full-size bed. It was the only one in the house as of yet. A couple couldn't sleep in a bed that size without brushing against each other with every breath. And if Seth meant to make a real go of their marriage, then . . .

She continued to stare at him, his eyes promising the world, a world she so desperately wanted for her own.

"Well, well, well."

The moment was broken.

Jessie turned, only vaguely aware that everyone else did the same.

Chase stood just inside the great room, his duffel bag in one hand, the other wrapped in a blue cast from fingertip to wrist. A yapping puppy danced around his feet, his pink tongue lolling out one side of his mouth. The poor pooch was completely unaware of the rising tensions in the room.

The bag hit the floor with a thud. The puppy danced backward, then let out a shrill bark.

"What have we here?" Chase drawled looking from her to his brother.

Seth took a step forward. "We tried to call you. Several times, in fact."

Chase shrugged. "Had to get a new number. Crazy girl," he said, his gaze landing on Jessie. "You know how it is."

Jessie trembled under his scrutiny.

"Would someone like to tell me what's going on or am I just supposed to guess why my brother is marrying my girl?"

"Chase, I—" Jessie started forward, but Seth stepped in front of her.

"This is our wedding day," he stated, his voice steady and deep. "We can talk about this later."

Chase shot his brother that trademark grin of his, but it didn't reach his eyes. "I think we need to talk about this now."

Everyone opened their mouth to explain, but it was as if no one knew exactly what to say. Or maybe it was where to start.

Finally Jake took a couple of steps toward his brother. "Seth and Jessie are going to have a baby in a few months. Getting married is the natural thing for them to do."

For a moment she thought she saw pain flash in Chase's eyes, but it was gone almost as quickly as it came.

"I see." His gaze flicked over her, then landed on Seth. "There's no accounting for taste, I guess."

"Watch yourself," Seth snarled.

Jessie had never heard him use that tone of voice before. Ever-cool, levelheaded Seth sounded as if he had been pushed to the edge.

"What?" Chase asked, his stance belligerent. "Is it my fault one Langston wasn't enough for her?"

Like a flash Seth moved toward his brother. Jessie didn't have time to utter more than a strangled cry as Seth grabbed Chase by the collar and forced him back against the nearest wall. Pictures rattled as Seth slammed Chase's head against the wood. Evelyn cried out.

"Take it back." Seth's voice was low and dangerous. Jessie was rooted to the spot, as was everyone else in the family. Wesley moved behind her nana as Jake sprang into action.

He pushed between his brothers, doing his best to keep the situation from escalating beyond control.

Jessie clamped a hand over her own mouth to keep her cries at bay. She was the cause of this. Her and her impulsive ways. She would never do anything to upset anyone in the Langston family, and yet in one afternoon she had managed to hurt them all, a lasting, bone-deep wound that might not ever heal.

"Let him go, Seth," Jake said. "It's not worth it."

"Yeah, Seth," Chase snarled. "She's not worth it." He pulled away, yet remained close enough for a brawl.

Seth started after his brother once again, but Jake blocked his path.

"Get out, Chase," Jake said, not bothering to look at his youngest sibling.

Chase wiped his uninjured hand across his mouth, the action leaving a telltale trail of blood. Somehow in the scuffle his lip had been busted. "Yeah," he said with an angry sniff. "I think I will."

He stopped long enough to scoop up his duffel bag and headed for the door, his legs stiff.

A few heartbeats later the front door slammed behind him.

"I'll just . . . ," Evelyn started, then turned and ran after Chase.

Jessie wanted nothing more than to crumple to the floor in a sobbing heap of regret. What had she done? How could any of them ever forgive her?

Instead she stiffened her spine and blinked away her tears. All of her life had been building to this moment. Her grandmother was right. She was no better than her mother—in fact, she might be worse. But she was going to do everything in her power to make it right.

Seth took the plate of cake from his mother, who insisted that the two of them follow as many wedding traditions as possible. He had thought about this moment a couple of times in the last two weeks. He was supposed to feed his bride a bite of cake and she was supposed to do the same for him. He had imagined smashing it on her face and then kissing away the frosting, not caring that his family was keeping a watchful eye.

But since Chase had walked in the door, the mood had been ruined. Seth wasn't up for silly cake play. He wanted to whisk Jessie home and show her, in ways that Chase never had, how much he loved her and how he couldn't live without her. But even that was now impossible. He couldn't bring himself to brand her to him until she loved him in return. It might be naive of him, but he wanted that in return. Needed it. She was his, damn it, whether she knew it or not.

He jumped as a door slammed somewhere in the house, but he still managed to feed Jessie a bite of their wedding cake without incident.

After Chase had stormed out, their mother went after him and convinced him to stay. Seth supposed that it probably took some convincing. Chase never did like to be told what to do. He'd come back in, but he was prowling through the room like a caged animal.

Seth was more than ready to go home.

He accepted the bite of cake that Jessie fed him. It seemed as if she wasn't in for playful feedings either.

His mother clapped as if cake eating was the most spectacular thing, then called for Jake to start the music.

Seth turned to Jessie. "Do you want me to tell her that we can't do this right now?"

She bit her lip and shook her head. He wasn't sure if she wanted that first dance with her husband or if she wasn't willing to battle his mother over the lost tradition.

He gave her a quick nod and led her from behind the table to the small patch of floor that had been cleared of furniture for this one occasion.

As naturally as breathing, he pulled her into his arms, realizing he had been waiting years for this very moment. Her dress appeared to be made of nothing but lace, and her hair curled around her face like a woodland sprite's. If he'd thought his world had been set on its ear when she told him she was pregnant, it was nothing compared to realizing that he couldn't live his life without her. He had loved her for so long, but his love was different now. It had been consummated. It was real and tangible and it had produced a child, another life to carry on, another Langston.

"You look wonderful. Did Mama help you pick out your dress?"

She frowned at him. "She was there." Her voice held a sharp tone. Everyone was on edge thanks to Chase. "I'm perfectly capable of picking out my own dress." She shook back her hair, the curls brushing his fingers as she did.

"That's not what I meant. It just looks expensive, is all." And that was something he shouldn't have brought up either. "I mean, I don't want you to spend your money on things like that. You should have—" He stopped. There was no way she would have let him pay for her trousseau. "You look beautiful," he murmured.

She didn't respond, and the tension didn't leave her shoulders.

"It's going to be okay, Jess."

She turned those incredible gray eyes onto him. "Will it, Seth?"

From somewhere in the house another door slammed.

Seth bit back a sigh. He could only pray that it would.

Jessie sucked in a calming breath. It was over. There should be some solace in the fact. She twisted the unfamiliar gold band with her thumb and told herself to take it one day at a time. Wasn't that the best way to get through whatever a person faced?

One day at a time. Tomorrow, who knew?

Soon she and Seth would head over to the old ranch house and start their life together. Until then, she had gone out onto the patio to escape from it all.

The pool twinkled like a turquoise jewel. The sun reflected off the water, sending diamondlike sparks dancing around. She longed to strip down and dive into the water, forgetting her troubles. But as with anything, she would eventually have to get out, dry off, and face life.

She drew in another breath and straightened her shoulders. She'd never had things easy. Why should this be any different? That was her lot in life. Jessie McAllen, wild child. It didn't matter that she hadn't done anything to deserve it. Well, aside from Homecoming '08. It had always been that way and Cattle Creek was too small for any of that to change now. And the baby she carried was just fodder for the gossip mill. Never mind that the father was the brother of the man she had always thought she'd marry. That only made it worse.

"Jessie?"

She whirled around as Chase came out of the house. Had he been looking for her or had he simply come out here by chance? "Hi, Chase. I—" But she had no words to finish that sentence. *I'm sorry. I can explain. I'm sorry that I can't explain. Maybe we were never meant to be together all along.*

But she had seen the betrayal that had flashed in his eyes when he saw her and Seth together. Whether or not she and Chase were destined to be a couple was not the issue. She had broken their understanding. And with his brother, no less. Words couldn't make up for that kind of pain.

"Don't say it," he demanded, his voice husky from an emotion she couldn't discern. "Just . . . don't." He took another step toward her and held out a small white card. "This is my phone number."

She stared at the card, unwilling to touch it as if it were somehow poison. "I already have your number in my phone."

"That's the old number. This is the new one."

She shook her head, unsure of what to say. Chase's emotions seemed to be on a runaway roller-coaster ride.

One minute he was snide and hateful. The next concerned and caring. And she wasn't sure where she fit into his highs and lows.

"Just take it." He pressed the card into her palm. "That way you'll always have it."

His hand was warm in hers, the card a little bent at the edges as if he had been walking around with it awhile before actually giving it to her.

"If he ever . . . if he *ever* treats you bad, you call me. Anytime, Jessie. I mean it. Day or night and I'll come. I'll always be there for you."

She searched his face for some hint of his true feelings. Did he really think Seth would treat her poorly? He couldn't. Yet maybe this was Chase's way of apologizing for never being there for her all these years.

Swallowing hard, she gave a little nod.

"Ahem."

Jessie started and turned toward the patio door.

Seth looked from her to Chase and back again. "Am I interrupting something?"

How much had he overheard? His thundercloud expression was the same one he'd been wearing all week, so it was anybody's guess. He couldn't have heard much or else he'd have Chase against the wall again. Or maybe—even worse—maybe Seth didn't care that his brother had just questioned his integrity in front of his wife of two hours. His pregnant wife.

She had made such a mess of things.

Jessie shook her head and slipped the card into the bodice of her dress when Seth wasn't looking. She hadn't brought a purse to the ceremony. It wasn't as though she needed one at the house, but she didn't want Seth to see what Chase had given her if he hadn't already.

"Not at all, big brother." Chase's tone dripped pure acid. He gave Jessie one last fleeting look, then pushed past Seth and back into the house.

Seth turned to her, but she had no words. "He . . . uh, he just wanted to wish us the best of luck."

His nostrils flared and a muscle in his jaw jumped as he clamped his teeth together, but to his credit he didn't call her a liar outright.

But what did it say about her that she was willing to lie to him mere hours after the ceremony?

Nothing good, that was for sure.

Seth gave a stern nod, then reached his hand out to her. "Come on," he said. "The pastor is leaving. I think it's time for us to go as well."

Chapter Thirteen

❧ ✷ ❧

Seth pulled his truck into the dirt space to the right of the front porch and got out. He couldn't say it was an actual driveway, just a rutted dirt road with a strip of grass down the middle. He should have gotten Fred out here to grate it smooth before the wedding, but there just hadn't been time. Now he was bringing his bride home to a house he loved, on a road as rough as a cob.

His bride. He went around to the passenger's side and opened the door.

He had been so shocked and hurt that Jessie kept that damned card with Chase's new phone number. Just the fact that she hadn't crumpled it up and thrown it back in his face spoke volumes. She was still in love with Chase.

What did you expect? You get her pregnant and she just forgets about the brother that she really loves? Fool didn't begin to cover it.

"Here." She handed him the plastic container holding the top layer of their cake.

Grandma Esther had insisted that they bring it home

and put it in the freezer to keep as part of their one-year wedding celebration. It might be nothing more than a silly wedding tradition, but he vowed to do everything in his power to make sure they got to eat that cake. He owed Jessie that much.

He stepped back as Jessie slid from the truck. She had barely said two words to him since Chase stormed out of the big house. And he knew that she was blaming herself. Then to find them together on the patio was almost more than he could stand.

They hadn't been close, but he could tell that a secret lingered between them. Was Jessie feeling guilty about marrying him? Had Chase convinced her that she was somehow less of a person for falling victim to Seth's advances?

"It's not your fault," he wanted to yell, but he knew it would do no good. Jessie needed to see Chase's shortcomings for herself, not have Seth point them out to her. Until that moment, he'd keep his opinion concerning his brother to himself.

Without a word he followed her to the porch.

She stopped at the door, her hands full with food and the bottle of nonalcoholic grape juice his mother had bought for them to toast with.

Unfortunately, after Chase's little exhibition, no one had felt much like celebrating. They'd cut the cake so that Wesley could have a piece. His mother had insisted that they have a first dance. After that, they had stood around for about half an hour chatting with the pastor and trying to pretend that everything was as it should be. Jessie had stepped out onto the patio and Seth had started loading everything into his truck for the short ride over to the old ranch house.

He skidded to a halt behind Jessie, suddenly so very aware of the intimacy of their situation. They were married, about to enter the house they would share for . . . well, forever if he had anything to say about it.

He cleared his throat and moved to set the cake container on the old church pew that sat to the right of the front door. On the far left side, the chains suspending the porch swing from the roof creaked as the wind pushed against it.

"I guess this is where I carry you over the threshold?" He hadn't meant for the words to come out like a question.

What was it about Jessie McAllen that had him stumbling over himself like a greenhorn?

"I don't think that's necessary." She shifted from one foot to the other as she waited for him to let her into the house.

"Jessie . . ."

She shook her head. "Don't, Seth. It's better if we don't pretend our marriage is normal. Meemaw used to always say 'only a fool fools himself.'"

He wanted to protest, tell her their marriage could be anything they wanted it to be. They had formed something of a bond during the two weeks that led up to today. True, Chase had come back and ruined that for all of them, but only they could allow Chase to destroy what they had. All they had to do was believe. Seth knew that, as certain as he knew his name. Yet something in the set of her jaw had him biting back his words and opening the door for her to precede him inside.

The place had changed a lot in the fourteen days since they visited. Seth knew that Jessie had been spending almost all her free time getting the house ready for this moment.

He looked around, impressed with the feat she had pulled off. Of course, he had hired painters, movers, and cleaners to move the process along. After all, he didn't want her breathing in paint fumes or overexerting herself. Still, he knew that she needed some sort of vested interest in the place. Nesting, wasn't that what all the books called it? She had done a wonderful job pulling the house together in fourteen short days all the while planning a wedding that his mother would approve of.

The walls were painted a dove gray, which gently contrasted with the dark wood floors and pristine white trim. Sheer white curtains covered the windows, letting in light while adding an airy feel to the place. His whiskey-colored leather sofa sat against one wall with the matching armchair across from the fireplace.

Sadie caught one look at them and barked out her welcome.

Seth scooped her up into his arms as Jessie moved past him and into the kitchen with the juice and cake.

Sadie whined as she watched Jessie pass. He knew the feeling. He almost had her there, had almost convinced Jessie that everything was going to be fine between them, and then Chase had to step in.

The worst part of all was that he couldn't stop wondering, if she weren't pregnant, if he hadn't forced her to marry him, would Jessie have gone off with Chase?

Chances were that if Seth hadn't gotten Jessie pregnant and hadn't forced her to marry him, then Chase would have never even thought about asking Jessie to go off with him. But that was really beside the point now, wasn't it?

Damn it all to hell! He set Sadie on the floor and ran his hands through his hair. How was he supposed to prove to his wife that he loved her and cared for her if every time he turned around everyone was telling them how they shouldn't be together?

Okay, so maybe he was being a little dramatic, but he and Jessie would never make it if something didn't give. He had made mistakes and was doing everything in his power to make them right. All he wanted was to be married to Jess, raise their child, and somehow convince her that he loved her above all else.

Was that so much to ask?

He looked to Sadie, who only wagged her tail in response.

"It's up to me, is that what you're saying?"

She barked, then let her pink tongue loll out of one side of her mouth. Sounded like an agreement to him.

Without another thought, he headed for the kitchen.

It, like the rest of the house, smelled of fresh paint and wood polish.

Jessie was standing at the window looking out over what could liberally be called a backyard.

"Hey," he greeted her, hoping not to startle her from her thoughts. She seemed a million miles away as she stared into the falling dusk. Soon it would be completely dark and after that, time for bed. And that was something they hadn't talked about since she agreed to marry him. No, sir, because paint colors and whether to buy a stainless steel or white enamel refrigerator were much more pressing matters. Now here they stood, married, acting like strangers, unsure of the next move.

"Hey." She turned away from the window but leaned her backside against the edge of the sink.

He flashed her what he hoped was his most charming smile. "Why don't you get us a couple of wineglasses full of that grape juice and we go out on the porch and watch the sun set?"

An emotion he couldn't name flashed through her storm gray eyes. "Seth, I . . ." She stopped, but she didn't need to say any more for him to know.

"Forever is going to feel like more than eternity if you don't give this a try."

She shook her head. "Can we start again tomorrow?"

He should have said yes and walked away, but something in him wouldn't let this lie. He took her by the shoulders and turned her to face him. "Listen, Jess, I love him too. He's my brother and I would give almost anything to go back and—" He stopped. "Just give me a chance," he asked. "Just give *us* a chance."

She studied him quietly for what seemed like days but

could have been only a few seconds. "Okay," she said on a sigh.

Relief flooded him.

He pulled her close, intending on wrapping her in a warm embrace. He wanted a new start. He just wanted to hold her close.

But as always when she was near, his good intentions seemed to fly out the window.

"Jessie." He groaned her name as he tilted her face to hers.

The touch of his lips to hers was explosive. How had this happened? He deepened the kiss, pulling her closer to him, so close there wasn't room for a breath between them. And yet it wasn't enough. He wanted more. He needed more. He had to make sure that she knew how much he loved her and that their life together could be— *would* be—more than she could ever imagine.

She had asked for tonight. And he should give that to her. He released her as quickly as he had taken her into his arms.

She grabbed the edge of the sink as if she needed the support.

He shoved his hands into his trouser pockets as much to hide his reaction to her as to keep from reaching for her again.

"I've got to go," he said. He had thought he could do this. He thought he could spend tonight simply being with her, being at her side, and that would be enough, but one kiss and he knew that he needed more. He would always need more where she was concerned. But he needed to take this slow. Slower than his libido demanded. She might be pregnant with his child, but they had skipped so many steps. Important steps that drew one person to another. He wanted a relationship with her, not just a bed partner. So for now . . . "I . . . I'll be at the station."

He didn't wait for her answer. He spun on his heel and beat a path for the door.

* * *

Jessie watched, unable to utter a word, as Seth walked out of their house.

Their house. That thought alone was enough to send her heart pounding. How had it come to this?

She jumped as the front door slammed behind Seth. The sound of his truck starting singed her ears. But no headlights cut through the window as he swung his truck around. No gravel spun as he started for town.

He wasn't supposed to have to work tonight. Yet he was on his way to do just that. After asking for a do-over with her that could only mean that he had changed his mind.

Jessie pressed her fingers to her temples and made her way from the kitchen to the bedroom. Sadie trotted along behind her and jumped onto the bed as Jessie started to undress.

The look on Chase's face.

She shook her head. This wasn't about Chase and yet it was. She had never meant to hurt him. And now it seemed that she had hurt Seth as well.

The beautiful lace dress dropped into a pool at her feet. She picked it up and hung it in the closet next to the rest of her clothes, her jeans and secondhand shirts. Without a doubt it was the most beautiful garment that she had ever worn. She trailed her fingers down one short sleeve, then sat on the edge of the bed and pulled off the gorgeous blue boots. Such special clothes for such a special day. Such a special day that had so quickly turned into a disaster.

What did you expect?

You slept with your boyfriend's brother, got pregnant, and then married him. How did you expect Chase to act?

That was the problem. Chase acted just the way she would have expected him to. It was Seth who was confusing her. One minute asking her for a second chance, the next one kissing her, but then walking out the door with her lips still tingling from wanting.

He hadn't gotten a call. He'd merely left. For some reason he needed to be separated from her. And that was the hardest part of all. How could he ask for a second chance then leave her to go to work? And on their wedding night.

Just how long was this going to last? Certainly not forever, regardless of all Seth's sweet words. She could only hope that they made it until the baby was born, but who knew?

One thing she did know: Seth was an honorable man. He'd stand beside her and the baby until . . . forever. He'd already said that. But Jessie knew she wouldn't be able to live with him like this forever. She wanted more from him than his honor. All she could do was her best. She would take each day as it came. Give each day all that she had and hope for the best. When the time came and it was over, she'd move on just as she had always planned.

It seemed as if forever was going to be a long time in coming.

Seth wasn't sure how long he sat in his truck in the drive. Just sat there. Everyone always told him that he didn't talk enough. Didn't explain, didn't ask enough questions. Not when it really mattered. And what did he do tonight? He had walked out on the woman he loved more than life on their wedding night. That was wrong on so many levels. If they were going to have a chance—the same chance he just asked for from her—then he needed to stop holding in his feelings. He needed to get in there and *talk* to his wife.

He cut the engine and slid from the Tahoe. He could do this. Too much was at stake. He stalked up the porch steps and into the house.

Jessie whirled around as he entered. Her short blue robe brushing midthigh. She pressed a hand to her heart. "Seth, you scared me."

Unsure of his next move, he took his hat from his head

and twirled it in his hands. "I'm not very good at this. I mean everyone fusses at me about not saying what's on my mind and not expressing myself. I'm not a good talker. I know I'm not. I try, but the words . . ." He broke off and shook his head. "I don't want to go anywhere tonight, Jessie. But I don't know if we're ready for all this." He waved a hand in the air, hoping she understood. Wild sex in the front seat of a pickup was completely different from setting up house with a person. "I care about you so much. And I—"

"Shut up and just hold me."

He stopped. "What?"

"Shut up and hold me," she repeated. She looked as fragile as a china doll. No wonder, she had been through the wringer these past few weeks. She didn't need sex right now, she needed comfort. "You think you could do that?"

He swallowed hard, suddenly realizing this was the very beginning of what would hopefully be a lasting marriage. "Yes," he croaked.

He pulled her into his arms and didn't let her go until morning.

Midmorning the next day, Seth drove home, then loped up the porch steps and into the house. He had been loath to leave her that morning, but duty had called and he had crawled out of bed, leaving her warm embrace behind.

Their marriage had been so hasty that he hadn't been able to take too much time off. But he had vowed to come home every chance he got. How else was he going to court his wife? And that was exactly what he was going to do. He was going to court his wife and show her how great things could be between them. He was going to take it slow, and when they made love again, it wouldn't be in the cab of a truck, but in a nice, soft bed. And he was going to love her all night long.

"Jessie," he called, not giving himself time to relish that she would be there, at the home that they shared. That had to be a good sign, right?

Sometime between last night and lying with her in his arms and this morning, he realized that he had been going about this all wrong. Everything between him and Jessie was backward. They shared one explosive kiss that had led to an unplanned pregnancy. Now they were married and they hadn't even been on a date. How could he expect them to have a shot at forever if they didn't have the same opportunities as other couples? How could he expect her to fall in love if she had no reason to? But those were things that he could correct. And that was exactly what he was going to do. Starting right now.

It was time to woo his wife.

"Jessie," he called again, making his way from the living room into the kitchen.

She straightened from the box she was unpacking when he entered and clutched one hand over her heart. Pulling the buds from her ears, she shot him a relieved look. "You scared me to death. What are you doing here?"

He grinned. "I live here."

"What are you doing here *now*?" she corrected.

"I have somewhere I want to take you." He shifted from one foot to the other, suddenly as nervous as a teenager on a first date. But this was more important than any date he'd been on in his life. This one counted.

"Take me?" She set the mixing bowl she had just unpacked onto the counter and stared at him as if he had suddenly grown another head.

He was making a mess of things. Scratch that. He had already made a mess of things. Now it was cleanup time. "I'm sorry about last night," he said, figuring an apology was the best way to start. "But I need you to put on some shoes and come with me."

To her credit she did just that. She disappeared into

their bedroom, returning a minute later with her worn boots on her feet.

He swallowed hard and forced this crazy desire for her back into its safe box. With her cutoff jeans and distressed Dallas Cowboys T-shirt, she shouldn't have looked quite so sexy, but to him . . .

"Where are we going?"

He smiled. "It's a surprise."

She raised a brow in his direction, but he wasn't budging. "You'll just have to wait until we get there to find out."

For a minute he thought she might protest but then she shook her head and preceded him out the door.

Jessie watched warily as Seth slid behind the wheel of his old Ford truck. "We're taking that?"

"Of course." He cranked the glass all the way down and braced one arm in the window. "You have something against my truck?"

She shifted, unwilling to say the reasons out loud.

But from the look on Seth's face, he understood. The last time she had ridden in Seth's truck was that fateful day of Wesley's birthday party.

"Nah." She shook her head and swung into the cab next to him.

Seth's smile was contagious and she found herself returning it as he backed out of the dirt driveway.

"Where are we going again?" she asked.

"It's a secret," he said, casting a quick look her way.

"A secret, huh?" She turned in her seat enough that she could see into the bed of the truck. There was a large to-go sack, a couple of fishing poles, and a foam container that she suspected contained worms. "Fishing maybe?"

She loved when he smiled like that. When he gave her that grin, she knew everything was going to be just fine. "Maybe."

She sat back in her seat, determined to relax and give today a chance. Last night, she hadn't known what to expect. Evidently neither had he, but today was a new day.

They had to learn to go with the flow, not read so much into every situation.

She chanced a look at him as he drove. She wanted that forever he talked about. And strangely enough, she wanted it with him. But when she added Chase back into the mix, she wanted nothing more than to hide under the covers like a child afraid of a storm.

The trip to the lake at the ranch took no time at all. Jessie had just enough time to get used to where they were going when suddenly they were there.

Together, she and Seth unloaded their lawn chairs, food, fishing poles, and bait and set up their camp for the afternoon.

A warm breeze stirred the tall prairie grass while birds flitted about and sang from the branches of the big oak tree.

"Here." Seth handed her a rod and sat down with the container of worms.

"Aren't you going to bait my hook for me?" she asked.

He looked up at her from under the brim of his hat, squinting those remarkable green eyes as he stared into the sun. "I happen to know for a fact that you are perfectly capable of baiting your own hook."

She plopped down into the chair next to him. "Maybe I would like for my husband to do it for me."

Seth thumbed back his hat and eyed her with mock wariness. "Are you flirting with me, Mrs. Langston?"

She tucked her hair behind one ear and pretended to think about it. "Yeah," she finally said. "I believe I am."

"Well . . ." Seth finished baiting his hook and handed the pole to her. "I think you should know that I am a married man. Flirting with me could be dangerous."

"Happily married?" she asked, wondering where the question came from.

The air around them turned suddenly serious. "I could be."

"Seth, I—"

He took the fishing rod from her and leaned in. His lips brushed hers like the wings of a butterfly, soft and teasing. Then as quickly as they came, they were gone again. "I suppose I could bait it for you. But just this one time."

Jessie opened her eyes, only then aware that she had closed them in anticipation of his kiss. Every kiss they had shared had been explosive, burning out of control within seconds of the first touch. She had expected this one to be the same. Though her lips tingled where his had touched, he had kept their kiss to a mere brush of the lips. The fact made her frustrated and hopeful all at the same time.

He stood and stretched out his long legs, then tossed his line into the water.

"Seth, I—"

He turned. "Are you going to fish or just sit there?"

She shook her head. "Is that a trick question?"

"No." He smiled and started to reel in his line.

A hundred questions crowded into her mind. "I—I . . ." She had nothing.

He pulled his line from the water and took her hand into his own, tugging her to her feet. "We've got our entire lives to make this marriage work. We don't have to rush into anything. Just relax and enjoy the ride."

She ran her gaze over his handsome features. No deceit hid there. No dishonesty or pretense. Was it as simple as he said? Could it be? She wanted to find out. More than anything she wanted that truth for herself.

Finally she gave a small nod. It was as if the dam broke and the tension between them fell away.

Seth tossed his line back into the water and Jessie did the same. They settled back into their chairs and whiled the afternoon away doing absolutely nothing but being together.

* * *

D amn it."

Jessie sat up in the truck seat a little straighter, trying to see what was upsetting him. "What's going on?"

Seth pointed toward the gauges, though she couldn't see what he was referring to. "Truck's overheating."

She looked out the front, but unlike last time, no billowing smoke poured from under the hood. "Are you sure? It looks okay to me."

Seth nodded and pulled the truck to the side of the ranch road. "I'm sure. We need to give her time to cool off or we won't make it to the house."

Jessie wasn't sure exactly where they were, but she knew for a fact that they couldn't be more than half a mile from their new home.

He put the truck in park and cut the engine. "Sorry about that." He turned toward her, running one hand along the back of the seat while the other was braced on the top of the steering wheel. "Maybe it won't take too long."

Was that a sparkle of mischief she saw in his eyes?

"So we're stranded?" she asked, studying his expression as he responded.

"Afraid so." His dimple flashed, but for the most part his expression remained the same.

"I see," she said.

"Too bad." He gazed out the front window, drumming his fingers along the top of the steering wheel. "Not really sure how long we'll be out here."

His look was so innocent she almost laughed. "I would have never gotten into this truck with you if I hadn't thought you'd had the radiator looked at."

He shot her an "oh, please" look, but she could see the humor twinkling in his eyes. "I told you this is a fine truck."

"Yeah, when Lee Majors was on prime time."

He chuckled.

"Tell me, Sheriff." She slid across the seat closer to him. She wished she was brazen enough to tip his hat from his head and toss it onto the dash, then lean in and kiss him until his toes curled. But the art of seduction was completely new to her. "Did you do *this* on purpose?"

His grin widened. "Maybe. Maybe not."

"Well, which is it?" She scooted closer still.

"I'll never tell."

"So you did."

"Are you basing my guilt on the fact that I won't tell you that I'm innocent?"

"Something like that."

He gave a nod. "I see."

"Would you like to prove me wrong?"

"No." He shook his head and swallowed hard. "Maybe I just wanted to be alone with my girl."

Her heart gave a crazy jump. Was she his girl? "Weren't we just alone for hours at the ranch lake?"

He shrugged. "I guess."

She could almost touch him now. All she had to do was reach out and run her fingers down the side of his face.

"But?" she prompted.

"There's something about being stranded."

She sat back, doing her best not to laugh. "You mean you didn't have the radiator fixed on purpose so that it would overheat and we'd be stranded?"

"Or maybe I pretended that it overheated so I could do this."

Before she could suck in a surprised breath, he pulled her to him.

His kiss was like firecrackers and candy—explosive and sweet. And she wanted it to go on forever.

Had it only been a month since she was in this truck with him, unable to get enough of his lips, his touch? It seemed like years and yet she knew his hands as if his caress had been a part of her since the dawn of time.

He cupped her face in his palms, holding her in place as he deepened the kiss. His tongue swept into her mouth, searching and exploring. She whimpered as he took his time learning every recess and crevice.

Where was that explosive need? She could feel it simmering just below the surface. He held himself so carefully in check that his hands were shaking. She was shaking, wanting—*needing*—more from him than he was giving.

"Seth," she protested, scooting even closer to him. If nothing else, they had this. They had volatile passion, the one thing that connected them above all else. It wasn't a lot, but it was a start.

He broke their kiss and leaned his forehead against hers. She touched her lips with the tip of tongue, relishing the taste of him.

He groaned. "You're not going to make this easy on me, are you?"

"Make what easy?" she asked.

A small part of laughter escaped him. "Courting you."

Even though she wanted to be as close as possible, she couldn't help drawing back. She needed to see his eyes. "Courting me? Is that what you're trying to do?"

He shook his head, that dimple flashing in the corner of his mouth, and he shot her a look of dread. "If you have to ask, I guess I'm not doing it right."

She shook her head. "We're married." She held up her left hand to show him the ring he'd placed there just yesterday, which was winking in the Texas sun. "Remember?"

"I remember," he all but growled. "But we did it all backward."

Truer words had never been spoken. She sat back farther into her seat to allow them to sink in.

She and Seth had done everything backward. They had known each other their entire lives, it seemed, and yet they had never been on a date. They had never made love in a bed. They had never just made out in the movie theater. So many things that normal couples experienced that had never been theirs. How could they make it to forever?

"I think you're doing all right." She shot him a mischievous smile.

"Just all right?" He had the cheek to look disappointed.

She gave him another smile, one she hoped would come across as a little seductive. "Well, try kissing me again, see if that helps."

Only in his dreams had she ever uttered that remark. "Oh, yeah? You think that will help?"

She scooted a little closer and clasped his face in the palms of her hands. "I don't know," she said. "But it never hurts to try."

Jessie felt his kiss from her lips all the way to the tips of her toes. Sweet and sassy and not too far from a certain kiss in a certain truck that had dumped them into the situation they were in now.

Yet now it was different. They were married. Having a baby. There was nothing standing in their way. Not even Chase.

In a heartbeat she was straddling him, enjoying a closeness with him that she hadn't felt since the afternoon after Wesley's birthday party.

She ran her hands down his chest, tugging at his buttons as she went. She wanted to touch him. So badly.

He pulled away, groaning as her fingers found skin. "Jessie," he rasped. "You have to stop this."

She smiled. "I do?"

He winced and shifted in his seat, increasing her need for him. "You do." Before she could utter even one protest, he set her back into her seat and adjusted his crotch. "I'm not going to do this here."

She sighed. "Then take me home."

He shook his head. "We're courting, remember?"

Surprise flooded her. "And people don't make love when they are courting?"

He started the truck and put it in gear. "Nope."

She wanted to ask if she could get a second opinion, but she had been forward enough for one afternoon. And there was something special about him putting the brakes on their make-out session. As if he was in it for more than just sex. . . .

Maybe forever was in their grasp after all.

Chapter Fourteen

꧁ ✸ ꧂

A re you nervous?" Jessie asked two days later as she and Seth sat side by side in the doctor's office.

"No, why?" he asked, though he was bouncing his knees to some unknown rhythm and thumping his thumbs against his thigh.

She placed one hand on his leg to stop his incessant movements. "You seem a bit agitated." And that was the understatement of the year.

"I'm fine." He glanced nervously around the office. "I didn't realize Doc Stephens was still delivering babies."

Jessie used her forefinger to mark her place in the three-month-old magazine she was reading and shook her head. "His son took over his practice."

"What?"

Several heads turned in their direction.

Seth nodded, then lowered his voice. "Your appointment is with Gary Stephens."

"He's the only obstetrician in Cattle Creek."

Seth was on his feet in an instant. "Come on. Let's go."

Jessie frowned at him but remained seated. "Go where?"

"Somewhere else."

"But it's almost time for my appointment." She checked the clock hanging on the wall behind the reception desk. "Past time," she corrected.

"You are not going in there." At least this time his voice was at a level that only drew a couple of looks of consternation.

"Will you sit down?"

"No," he said. "We have to find you another doctor."

"Sit," she said sternly.

Surprisingly enough he did, though he perched on the edge of his seat as if he wanted to spring up at any minute.

"He can't be your doctor," Seth protested. "I went to school with him, and I know he cheated on his biology tests. And I can't tell you how many times he copied my homework. We need to get you out of here and to San Angelo or Midland."

"We aren't going anywhere, Seth."

"Jessie—"

She leaned in closer. "I don't have a car. I can't go to another city to a different doctor. Gary Stephens is a perfectly fine doctor. He's been delivering babies here for years."

"But this is my baby."

"Our baby." The words sent her heart pounding.

"But—" he started again.

"No buts, Seth. Everything's gonna be fine."

"Jessie?" the nurse called from the door.

She stood and tossed the magazine into her vacated chair.

Seth was back on his feet in a heartbeat.

"You're coming in with me?" she asked.

"I think I should." The look in his eyes said he wasn't backing down.

Jessie sighed. "Come on."

* * *

Hey, Sheriff," Millie greeted as Seth stepped into the office later that afternoon. He had taken Jessie home after the doctor's appointment, arguing the entire way about going to Midland for her prenatal care. Her main point was that she didn't have a car to get to and from the appointments without someone taking her and that there'd be a chance he would be too busy or unable to get away. Not to mention, she might not be able to make the hour trip once the labor pains started.

Finally he had relented, though he still wasn't sure he trusted Gary Stephens with the lives of his wife and child. But what choice did he have?

"Hey, Millie. Anything happening today?"

She shook her head. "How'd the appointment go?"

Seth shrugged. "Fine, I guess. It's too early to hear the baby's heartbeat. So it was just a lot of talking about due dates and that sort of thing."

"And?" Millie rolled one hand as if to keep him talking.

"April second."

"A spring baby. That's nice." She smiled. "Oh, did you order something? This package came for you today."

Seth took the padded envelope, noting it was from an online bookseller. "Yeah." His very own copy of *Your Body, Your Baby*, a pregnancy book that was all the rage. Or so he had been told. "What do you think of Gary Stephens? As a doctor, I mean."

Millie pulled her reading glasses a little farther down her nose. "I've only been back in town for a few weeks, so I can only go on past experience. He wasn't much of one when we were ten."

Seth propped his hands on his hips. "Be serious. Jessie wants to use him, but I think she should go into San Angelo or Midland."

"Why?" She leaned back in her seat and waited for his answer.

"I think she would get better care." He was crazy worried about her and the baby. "What if something happens and Stephens can't take care of it?"

"Seth," Millie gently started, "you might get better care in a bigger town or with a different doctor, but it's not going to guarantee Jessie's or the baby's health."

She was right. Damn, he hated that she was right. Jake's wife, Cecelia, had gone into Midland and died. There were no sure bets when it came to babies and doctors. "You think Jess will be okay here, then?"

Millie nodded. "Just keep an eye on her. If she needs better care, then you can switch doctors later."

"Okay," he grudgingly agreed.

"You haven't given Jessie a lot of control over how things are going to be during this pregnancy. Let her have this."

Damn if she wasn't right again. "Fine," he all but snarled. He grabbed his package and headed for the door. "Call me if you need anything. I'm headed over to the Ford dealership."

"They having a problem today?" Millie asked, slipping her glasses back in place in order to get back to the filing.

Seth shook his head. "I'm going to buy my wife a car."

He ignored the shocked look on Millie's face and headed out once again.

Are you looking for anything special?" Bill Coleman asked as Seth eyed the brand-new cars all lined up neatly in the parking lot. Overhead, the vinyl banners flapped and snapped in the wind.

"Something for Jessie to drive," Seth said, trying to give the man his full attention, but unable to stop his gaze from looking down the line of shiny new Fords.

"Jessie McAllen?" Bill asked.

Nothing like small-town gossip. "Jessie Langston." He liked the sound of that. Especially since the name change was associated with him and not his brother.

Bill thoughtfully stroked his chin. "Yeah, I heard something about that."

"We need something reliable and big enough for a family."

"I've got just the thing."

He and Bill walked down the rows of new cars, but Seth couldn't picture Jessie driving any of them. She needed something smart and dependable, big enough for the baby, but small enough that she could maneuver it easily. Bill showed him all the new models with televisions and Wi-Fi connections, and as much as he would love to give her the world, he knew he had to tread lightly with this gift. She was going to have a hard enough time accepting the car itself, but she surely wouldn't want to be driving around in one that cost more than the house she grew up in.

Seth took one look at the brand-new shiny red Edge and shook his head. "You have anything less . . . fancy? I want Jess to have something she's comfortable in."

Bill thought about it a moment. "I might have something." He led Seth around the side of the car lot to the service department. Sitting next to the garage doors was an older-model Jeep Liberty. Dust and grime covered most of the outside, but Seth was pretty sure the vehicle was a beautiful, conservative, navy blue.

"This just came in this morning. I got it in a vehicle trade. It's got less than a hundred thousand miles, and for an '04 that's outstanding. Of course it doesn't have all the bells and whistles that they put in cars today, but she's solid. Runs like a top."

"How much?"

Bill named a price that was fair, but Seth pretended to think it over.

"Throw in a tune-up and you've got a deal."

Bill smiled and stuck out his hand. "I'll throw in a tune-up and a car wash."

Seth shook his hand and returned his smile. "That sounds fine."

"Give me just a minute, and I'll get the papers together."

"Take your time."

With a quick nod, Bill was gone.

Seth walked around the little SUV, noting any cosmetic problems. There weren't many, and the tires looked relatively new.

"I thought that was you." Darly Jo Summers-Eden Burnett eased out of the garage, a surprised smile stretching her pink painted lips.

"Hi, Darly Jo." Inwardly Seth cringed, but somehow he managed to keep his true feelings from showing on his face.

"I hear congratulations are in order."

He nodded. Ever since word of his and Jessie's wedding ran through the town, most of the casseroles and pies had stopped coming, but Darly Jo still managed to stop by the station at least once a week with some sort of foodstuff in tow.

"Now, ain't that something else?" She took a step closer to him, smiling as she did. He couldn't help noticing that her smile seemed a little put-on as she grabbed his hand and studied his wedding ring.

"You're a good man, Seth Langston." She raised those heavily mascaraed eyes to his but didn't release his fingers.

"Oh, yeah?"

"Everybody in town is talking about it. You and Jessie, that is."

"Why's that?" Did he really want to know? The people in Cattle Creek talked about a lot of things, and only a small percentage of them were true.

Darly Jo spread his fingers apart with hers and laced them together as if testing the fit. "How you married Jessie to give the baby a name."

What was it with people? It was over a decade into the new millennium and people still had hang-ups about babies and parents and when they got married. Wasn't the important thing that there was a marriage and a tiny person to carry on?

He gently untangled their hands and moved out of her reach. He cleared his throat while he searched for a suitable response. "I did what any man would do."

She took a step closer to him. "I seriously doubt that. And it's so sexy." She straightened his collar and allowed her hands to linger on his chest.

He picked them up and returned them to her sides. "Would you like to explain that?"

"What?" She batted her eyes. "It's very sexy for a man to marry a woman to give her baby a name."

"It's our baby."

"Oh, go on with yourself, Seth. Everyone in town knows that it's Chase's baby."

He closed his eyes and counted to ten.

"Seth?" Her fingers brushed against his cheek.

Capturing her hand in one lightning move, he somehow managed to keep her from pawing at him further. "Listen, Darly Jo. You are a lovely woman, always have been. But I am a married man."

"Well, I know that, but you don't have to pretend with me."

"I'm not pretending. I love Jessie, and she's having my baby. *My* baby. Not Chase's. If you want to start a rumor in this town, start that one. At least the girls at To Dye For will be telling the truth for once."

Jessie clipped on her headphones and started to work. Who knew two people could have so much stuff? She had gotten almost everything essential put away before the wedding, but there was still a ton of boxes to deal with.

Her mementos, Seth's keepers, and she hadn't even sorted through her grandmother's house yet.

The idea filled her with acute dread. Moving in with Seth had been a big enough decision, but it was at least one she could make herself. But closing down her grandmother's house, choosing what to sell and what to keep . . . the thought was daunting at best. But more than anything, it filled her with heartbreak and brought back the pain of her loss.

But now you have Seth and the baby.

She straightened from taping up the box and pressed her hand to her abdomen. She had Seth and the baby.

With each passing day she became more and more accustomed to living with Seth. And living was all they were doing. She slept in the master room on the iron bed she had brought over from her meemaw's house while Seth had taken to sleeping in the next room. Sometimes at night she could hear him roll over in his sleep or pad quietly to the kitchen for a drink of water. There were even times when she lay awake and listened for signs that he was there. Never before had she wished for a husband who snored, but how funnily enough, she wished she had one now.

Her music player changed songs, and Kenny Chesney sang to the world about his girlfriend thinking his tractor was sexy. Filled with joy, Jessie sang along. She danced a little sideways step to get to the next box. This one came from Seth's, and she had no idea what was in it.

As she bent to open it, a hand touched her shoulder. She screamed and whirled around to find Seth there, grinning like an idiot while her heart dang-near pounded out of her chest.

"Seth," she breathed, pulling the buds from her ears. "What are you doing home?"

"I brought you something, but if I had known that I was going to get a show, I would have come home an hour ago."

"Ha-ha," she said; then what he'd said sank in. "You brought me something?"

He nodded as she noted that he looked quite pleased with himself. "Come on. It's outside."

He led her through the house, Sadie trotting along behind them.

"Are you ready?" Seth paused at the door, blocking her view to the outside.

"Yes," she said, trying to peek around him yet not wanting to appear as if she were actually doing it.

"Ta-da!" Seth moved to the side and opened the screen door for her to step out onto the porch.

Jessie couldn't begin to imagine what he had brought for her, but never in her wildest dreams had she imagined . . .

"A car?" She looked from the shiny blue SUV to her husband.

"Yep."

She shook her head. Was this really happening? Or had her mind simply overloaded on all the changes that had come into her life these last few weeks? "For me?" she asked.

"I wanted you to have a good way to get around. All the talk about Midland got me to thinking. You don't have a way to get anywhere you need to go."

His words sounded as if she were walking down a tunnel. He had bought her a car. A car!

"Well?" he asked as she continued to stand on the porch and look at the vehicle.

"A car," she whispered.

"Do you like it?" he asked.

"I love it!" She threw her arms around him and nearly knocked them both over backward. "It's the most beautiful car I've ever seen."

"I wouldn't go that far. . . ."

"I would." She tipped off his hat and rained little kisses all over his face. Sadie danced around their legs, and Seth chuckled. His arms came up and slid around her waist, holding her close.

"There is one little problem."

She stopped kissing him long enough to meet his gaze. "What's that?"

"Can you drive a standard?"

"Of course not. Who drives a standard these days?"

Seth removed one arm from around her and held up the keys. "You do."

This was going to be the death of him.

"Release the clutch slowly. Slowly," he repeated as the Jeep lurched and died.

"I am releasing it slowly," Jessie moaned.

After their sweet session of kisses and thank-yous, Seth had driven the Liberty into one of the pastures and turned Jessie loose with the keys. The only problem was they hadn't managed to go more than two feet before she popped the clutch and the SUV stalled.

"Then go slower than slowly. Try again."

She pressed the brake and the clutch, then cranked the Jeep once again.

"Now ease up on the brake and press the gas. Slow . . . slow . . . don't let her die. . . ."

Finally the car actually moved yards.

"Push the clutch in again and shift her into second. Let up easy."

Jessie did as she was told and somehow managed to find the rhythm in driving a stick shift.

"I'm doing it," Jessie cried. "I'm doing it!"

Seth smiled at her. She had never looked more beautiful to him than she did in that moment. "Okay, bring her to a stop and do it again."

He had Jessie accelerate the car a couple more times and run through all the gears before he called a stop to the lesson.

"Wait a minute," he said, giving her a sidelong look. "You do have a valid driver's license, right?"

She shot him a look. "Of course."

"Just asking. The sheriff's wife can't be going around town driving without a license."

She laughed. "No, we couldn't have that."

"Then this calls for a celebration. Why don't you drive us into town for supper? We could pick up something at the Chuck Wagon. Or maybe Manny's."

"The Chuck Wagon's fine. It's rib night."

"Then let's go."

He managed not to leave too many finger indentations in the dash as she drove them into Cattle Creek. And the best part was she only let the Jeep die once. Unfortunately it was at the light at Third and Main, but she got it started quickly enough and they were on their way with hardly anyone noticing.

"Thanks for teaching me how to drive a standard," she said as they sipped their iced tea and waited for their order. "And for dinner."

"You're welcome." He punched down his ice and pushed the extra lemon wedge a little deeper into his glass. "How about this weekend we head over to San Angelo and pick up a few things for the baby's room?"

"Like stuff stuff?"

He nodded. "He's going to need furniture and such. I've been looking a little online, and babies need a helluva lot of stuff."

She laughed. "*She* may not need near as much as you think."

Seth smiled. "He's going to have everything he needs and more. Twice that."

Jessie laughed. "We haven't even heard her heartbeat and already you're planning on spoiling her."

Seth decided to let her last gender reference slide. "Of course. That's what daddies do."

"That's sweet, Seth, but you don't have to take me shopping. I mean, I can go by myself, or maybe get your mother or grandmother to go with me."

"I want to."

She studied him for a moment as if trying to decide if he was being sincere. "I'd like that," she finally said.

"Good. It's a date, then."

"So we're up to two dates now. Wow, we're rolling right along."

He grinned. "That's the plan."

She returned his smile, then frowned at something over his shoulder.

Only years of training kept him from turning around to see what it was. "Everything okay?"

"Sissy Callahan." She made a face. "She's staring at us."

Seth shrugged. "Why would that bother you?"

"She just . . ." She stopped, then blew the hair out of her face. "I don't know. It shouldn't, right? I shouldn't care that everyone in this town is talking about me—us—wondering about the baby and why you married me."

He covered her hand with his. "You can't let this town get to you, Jessie. Small towns are known for gossip and busybodies, but it sure beats the indifference of the big city."

She sighed and propped her chin in her hand. "Do you miss it a lot?"

"San Diego?" He shook his head. "I miss a few of the friends I made there and the beach now and then, but no, I don't miss the city itself."

"I think it would be heavenly not to have everyone going around town talking about all the mistakes I've made and taking bets on what I'm liable to do next."

He leaned back as Debbie Ann slid the plate covered with a half rack of steaming barbeque ribs in front of him. "Thanks," he said, shooting her a quick smile before grabbing the pepper shaker and adding a liberal dose to his french fries and coleslaw.

Then he looked up at Jessie. "Trust me. Small-town life is so much better than anything else out there."

"It sure is quiet without you around here, Jessie,"

Debbie Ann said as she set Jessie's plate in front of her. She had ordered the chef salad.

"Y'all need anything else?"

"We're good," Seth said, and Debbie Ann left to see to her other customers.

"That looks . . . satisfying," he said, shooting a pointed look at the salad in front of her.

She shook her head. "Calories, you know."

"You're not afraid of gaining weight, are you? I mean, you should enjoy yourself and being pregnant."

"Yeah, but now that I'm not working I'm not getting as much exercise." She trailed off with a shrug and didn't meet his gaze. She loved ribs, always had.

"Well, you have a way around now. You can drive into town and walk on the track at the high school or the park. You could even use the pool at the ranch."

Her eyes lit up. She loved to swim, and he knew it. "That would be heavenly."

"Remind me to call Mama when we get home. I'll give her the heads-up that you might be stopping in."

Jessie smiled big enough to light up Main Street, then picked up her fork. The look she gave her dinner was enough to make a grown man cry.

"Tell you what," Seth said, holding one saucy rib toward her. "You eat all your veggies, and I'll share."

She snatched the meat away with a satisfied grin. "Deal."

Chapter Fifteen

꧁ ✶ ꧂

One day slipped into the next and before long another month had passed. A minor problem between Amos and Chester had wrecked Seth and Jessie's plans to go to San Angelo and buy baby furniture. But they had time; she wasn't even showing yet. Instead she had stayed at home that weekend and worked on the closets, cleaning and organizing.

Jessie knew she needed to get over and start cleaning out her grandmother's house, but it was so much more fun to play house with Seth than it was to say good-bye to her last relative.

Seth was her future, the rest was her past, and she didn't want to dwell there any longer than necessary. Yet there was something so isolated about being at the old ranch house all day every day. Sure, she had a way into town now that Seth had bought her a car, but it wasn't like she could go bebopping into town every time she had the thought to. She wasn't working and bringing any money into the household. That was how Seth wanted it, but still it bothered her that she wasn't doing anything to contribute to their budding family. Or maybe it was not having a job after working nearly all her life. She had gotten her first job at twelve. She babysat, mowed lawns, and cleaned the church every Saturday morning. If she needed something she had gone out and worked for it. Her class ring, graduation pictures, cap and gown, new boots or jeans. She had worked her fanny off to get the basics. She appreciated what she had and only bought the necessities. It just wasn't in her to waste gas just because she was unaccustomed to being alone so much of the time.

Of course if she went into town, she would feel obligated to stop by the house on Larkspur Lane, and she just wasn't prepared for that. She still had a couple of months before she had to get everything out and the bank took possession. It would keep for a few more days.

"Are you ready?"

She looked up as Seth came into the kitchen. His hair was darkened to nearly black, and he smelled like a dream. After all the trials and tribulations in her life, she wasn't sure what she had done to deserve a man like Seth Langston to take care of her and her baby. Whatever it was, she was grateful all the same. Good, strong, handsome, caring. That was Seth in a nutshell. Just call her blessed.

"Yeah." She stood and took her coffee cup to the sink. At her last appointment the doctor had suggested she cut way down on her caffeine intake. These days she had allowed herself only one cup of coffee each morning and she nursed it as if it were the last one on earth. "Are you sure it's a good idea to buy furniture this early?"

"You still think it's bad luck?"

She shrugged and dried her hands. "No. I guess not, but it seems like we're moving fast. What if we buy the furniture and I decide I don't like it two weeks before the baby comes?"

He flashed her that killer smile. "Then we'll buy new furniture."

"Seth." She shifted from one foot to the other. "Be serious."

"I am serious."

"We can't do that. It's such a waste."

He crossed the room and took her into his arms. She could almost get used to him holding her close, kissing the tips of her fingers, trailing his own across her flat belly whenever she was in reach. Was this how it was supposed to be?

She had never had any male role models in her life. Her mother had never dated, or if she had, Jessie had never known about it. Her grandpa Larry was long gone by the time she was born. She just didn't know.

"We can do whatever we want. Whatever you want." He planted a quick kiss on her lips. "I read in *Your Body, Your Baby* that sometimes it's hard for a woman to make decisions when she's pregnant. I can help or we can do this later. I'm just afraid that it's not going to get any easier as time goes on."

Had she heard him right? "You're reading *Your Body, Your Baby*?"

His cheeks flushed a sweet shade of pink that almost had her giggling. Almost. "Well, yeah. I thought that it might give me insight into what you're going through, and—"

His words were trapped as she reached up and pressed her lips to his. It was without a doubt the sweetest and sexiest thing he had ever said to her. That anyone had ever said to her.

His arms tightened around her and for a moment she was lost in the magic of being held in his arms.

"So," he said, after he had taken over the kiss and shown her exactly how it was done, "do you want to buy furniture or not?"

When he looked at her like that, she would do almost anything to make him happy. She tapped down all her doubts and fears. "Let's go furnish the baby's room."

* * *

It was almost dark when Seth pulled the ranch truck to a stop in front of the house. He had been worried about driving his own truck all the way into San Angelo, especially with its tendency to overheat, and if they bought a lot they wouldn't be able to fit it all in the back of Jessie's Jeep. In the end he'd borrowed a truck from the Diamond, in case they found what they were looking for.

And they had, he thought as he put the truck in park. A beautiful mahogany changing table and a matching crib that turned from baby bed to a toddler bed and then into full size with a few adjustments. It would be the only bed the baby would ever need, the salesperson had proudly proclaimed, looking expectantly from Seth to Jessie.

In the end it was the look on Jess's face that made the decision. She had walked around the bed, trailing her fingers over the slick, dark wood as if she could already imagine their baby nestled there. What could he say after that?

He had wanted to get everything they would need or at least as much as possible while they were there, but Jessie told him that there would be baby showers and gifts galore. They shouldn't buy everything at once. Other people would want to give the baby Langston presents too.

They had picked out bedding. He had read in *Your Body, Your Baby* that most women like to have a theme in the nursery. He found the perfect sheets complete with gold stars, cowboy boots, and revolvers, but Jesse simply rolled her eyes and showed him soft white sheets with pale gray elephants and tiny gold stars. In the end he had agreed to bow to her expertise, or maybe he fell under the spell of her smile.

Seth cut the lights, only then realizing how dark it had gotten since they hit Langston property. Jesse had laid her head against the window a while back and now seemed to be in some sort of trance. She might have even fallen asleep. They had shopped all day. She had to be exhausted.

"Jessie?"

She stirred, and Seth could tell that she was neither asleep nor in a trance. Her lips were pressed tightly together, and she looked pale even in the dim light of the cab.

"Are you okay?"

She looked as if she was going to open her mouth and speak, but then she shook her head, opened the door, and fell out of the truck.

"Jessie!" He was out of the truck and around on her side in an instant.

He stopped short when he saw her there. She was on the ground on her hands and knees. Her head was down, and her body heaved.

"Jessie?" he whispered. "Let me help you up." He reached out to pull her to her feet, but she smacked his hand away.

"Don't touch me," she snapped.

She was sick. Dry heaves continued to rack her body. She had one hand pressed to her stomach while the other held her up. Maybe food poisoning. They had eaten together at his favorite place there in San Angelo, a little hole-in-the-wall that served to-die-for Tex-Mex. But they had eaten the same thing: chips, salsa, guacamole, and enchiladas. If she had food poisoning, then why wasn't he sick as well?

The answer hit him like a wet bag of manure.

"The baby," he whispered.

She gave a small nod, then coughed as another spell overtook her.

"You've got to get into the house," he said. She couldn't stay out here all night.

"I can't move," she admitted. "If I move, I'll be sick."

"You're already sick."

"Don't touch me, Seth."

This was one thing he couldn't give her. "It'll only take a minute. Right into the house and straight to your room. I'll go as quick as I can. You need to lay down and rest. You can't do that out here."

"No," she gasped.

"Jessie, let me help you."

"Seth," she breathed.

"Quit being prideful. This is our baby, and our pregnancy. I may not be able to carry the baby or suffer through morning sickness." He looked around at the indigo sky. "Er, night sickness, but I can damn sure carry you into the house and get you settled someplace more comfortable than the overgrown grass in our front yard."

He could almost feel her defeat. But it wasn't about winning. It was about teamwork. Yet now wasn't the time to lecture her about that. He needed to get her into the house and settled.

"Ready?" he asked.

"Ready," she finally said.

He lifted her as gently as he could, feeling as if she were the weight of the world in his arms. In a way she was. She was the weight of *his* world. He had done this to her. His desire for her had created a baby that currently seemed to be at odds with the rest of her body.

Somehow he managed to open the door with one hand and keep his wife steady against him.

Sadie barked in greeting as he entered the house with Jessie cradled to his chest. He took the time to acknowledge the confused pup who followed behind him through the living room.

"Just a couple more steps," he murmured as he continued down the hallway to her room.

It was dark inside, and for that he was grateful. He wasn't sure if light would hurt her eyes, but it wasn't worth finding out the hard way.

Ever so gently he laid her on the bed.

She rolled to her side, retching as she moved. At least she wasn't getting physically ill, but he'd had enough benders in his life to know that dry heaves could be worse than the other kind for sure.

He gave her a sympathetic look, then moved to the bathroom and wet a washrag.

Returning to her side, he pressed it to her cheeks, then laid it against her forehead. That task complete, he moved to the foot of the bed to remove her boots.

He set them next to the trunk at the foot of the bed.

Once she was still with the rag cooling her skin, her crazy stomach seemed to settle down. She lay quiet in the darkness of her room.

He wanted so badly to crawl into that bed beside her and pull her close. He wanted to hold her and never let her go. Let her know that they were in this together. He would be there for her come what may. But he knew she needed rest and quiet. He blew a kiss toward her freckled cheek, then let himself out of her room.

Bright sunlight filled the room. Jessie rolled onto her back. Why did she feel so twisted up and confined?

Ever since she had found out that she was pregnant, it seemed that her dreams had grown increasingly more vivid. Consequently she usually woke up bound in her own covers from a nighttime of tossing and turning.

She reached around her waist to release whatever cover she had twisted herself up into, only to discover that it was her own clothing that was causing her discomfort. Had she slept in her clothes last night? It was certain that she had slept in her jeans. She remembered San Angelo, then feeling a little sick as the sun started to go down, then turning into the ranch house driveway bouncing along, then Seth cradling her to his chest as he carried her into her room. Last night he had been her knight. More than her knight. Her hero, who had come to her rescue and had done everything right.

She sat up in the bed and pushed her hair back. The curls surrounding her face felt like a tangled rat's nest, but that was to be expected. Her curls plus wet rag equaled hot mess every time. Still, she was grateful for Seth and his tender, loving care.

She pushed off the bed and went to the bathroom. Her stomach felt empty and yet crampy at the same time. She supposed half an hour of dry heaves could do that to a person, but she hated it all the same.

At least with the new day came a renewed sense of health and well-being. She hadn't gotten sick at all until last night. Maybe it had more to do with the car ride instead of the baby. Whatever it was, she was glad it had passed. In fact, she felt energized, full of life, and . . . happy. Yes, she was happy. Was it okay to admit that now?

She had lost her grandmother and alienated Chase, and his family would never look at her the same, but she had Seth and their child that she carried. Today was a beautiful day. They had a lovely—in a vintage sort of way—home and so much more. Yes, she was happy.

"Good morning."

Seth was seated at the table when she breezed into the kitchen. Somehow her coveted cup of coffee didn't seem appealing this morning and instead she opted for hot tea.

"Good morning," he returned as she popped a cup full of water into the microwave and added a lemon zinger tea bag. Now, that sounded good. She went to the fridge and searched the shelves. Maybe some milk, a little sugar . . .

"Did you sleep okay?" Seth asked.

She grabbed the milk jug and set it on the table as she addressed her husband. Dang, he looked good in the morning, all stubby and sweet, sleepy and sexy. "I did. You?"

He shrugged and folded over the morning paper and set it to the side of his place mat. "I was a little worried about you."

She smiled and eased into the chair opposite him. "Thanks for taking care of me last night." She reached a hand across the table and squeezed his fingers.

"Of course."

"No, really, Seth. I don't know what I would have done

without you and . . ." She stopped as she remembered how stubborn she had been the night before. She hadn't wanted his help. Not just because she was a little uncomfortable with the situation, but also because she hadn't had to rely on anyone other than herself for so long that it was near impossible to do so. "Thank you." She leaned in and gave him a lingering kiss on the mouth.

Unlike the ones of late that seemed controlled and almost orchestrated—though nice, very, very nice—this one was wildfire and gasoline. In an instant, she felt as if her entire body had been engulfed with flames. She wanted him now more than she ever had. She wanted him inside her, all around her. She wanted him to be a part of her, together until they became one. One mind, one body, one soul.

He wrapped his fingers around her arms and put her away from him. His green eyes blazed with desire. She might not know a great deal about men and desire, but that much was obvious. How long were they going to court before he made her his once again?

"Seth?" If only she could get the courage she needed to ask him outright. But she was afraid she might not like the answer. No, it was better by far to wonder than have her heart shredded.

"Not yet, Jess." He placed a kiss on her forehead and set her from him. "What do you want to do today?" he asked.

She thought about it a minute and allowed him the subject change. "We could work on the nursery."

"I was thinking more along the line of going into church."

Jessie shook her head. "Maybe we should wait until people start to accept us as a couple before we do that."

"How are they going to accept us as a couple if we don't?"

"I don't know, but please." She couldn't handle another episode like the one with Sissy Callahan. Of course, they didn't have to go to the same church where Sissy's father preached, but one thing that Jessie had learned in life, there was a Sissy Callahan for every occasion. Or in this case, denomination.

"Whatever you want," he said in that wonderful Seth way of his, but somehow his bending to her every whim and desire was beginning to wear a bit thin. Or perhaps she was merely a little on the hormonal side. Or it could be the pent-up desire that flared to life whenever he was around. Once again, it could be chalked up to hormones. Her husband might have wanted her once. But he was holding back from her now. And she had no idea why.

"I want to get the nursery ready."

"Are you sure you're up for that?"

"You just said whatever I want."

He nodded. "So I did." He pushed to his feet and took one last drink of his coffee. "The nursery it is. Just promise me you won't overdo it."

Jessie sighed, though secretly she loved that protective streak of his. "Fine," she said. "I promise."

They spent all day working in the nursery putting together the furniture and washing the baby sheets. Seth figured she'd have to turn around and wash them again before they brought the baby home, but he wasn't about to interrupt her nesting.

She stood by the nursery door and looked at where he had placed the crib and the changing table. "Do you think the bed should go along that wall instead?" She pointed to the far window.

"Only if you want him awake with the sunrise. That window faces east."

She thought about it a second, then nodded. "I guess. It just seems . . . not right. Maybe it's not balanced."

"You want me to get one of those books on feng shui?"

She shook her head. "I don't even know what that is."

"It's a Chinese way of placing your furniture so that it brings wealth or happiness into your home."

"And they have these for baby furniture?"

He shrugged. "I would imagine. They have them for everything else."

"Like how to make her vice president?"

"I was thinking more along the lines of making him a cowboy."

She gave him that look he loved, somewhere between the little girl he once knew and the seductress he had met once or twice. "That won't be a problem," she said. "Not with you for a daddy."

Chapter Sixteen

❧❖❧

S he wanted everything to be perfect. Jessie slid the garlic bread into the oven and gave the spaghetti sauce one last stir and a quick taste. Perfect. She set the spoon to one side and turned down the heat.

Seth would be home any minute, and she wanted to present him with a wonderful, tasty, perfect spaghetti supper.

Yesterday they had spent the entire day together working in the nursery, putting the final touches on their home. Then last night Seth had been so kind and caring when the nausea set in. He made it easy to pretend that they would last forever. Or maybe he made it seem as though they could. He made it easy to believe that this marriage was what they both wanted. But the more he acted that way, the more confused she became. He wanted to court her, to give them time, and she . . . well, she wasn't sure what she wanted anymore. She loved this time of getting to know each other better, but yesterday morning she had wanted . . . more.

The timer for the pasta beeped, and she grabbed a couple of pot holders to pull the pot off the stove. She had no more gotten the water and noodles poured into the colander than a pungent smell filled the air.

What was . . . "The bread!" She raced to the stove and opened it just in time for the buttered slices to burst into flames.

As quickly as she could, she pulled them from the oven and tossed them into the sink.

Right on top of the pasta.

The pan sizzled, and plastic melted, adding yet another smell to the growing stench in the kitchen. Burned bread, hot plastic, and . . .

Scorched spaghetti sauce.

Jessie spun around toward the stove. The perfect sauce was bubbling out of control. She must have turned the temperature up instead of down. She switched off the eye, for real this time, and scooted the pan off to the side. That was one thing that she hadn't gotten used to since moving out to the old ranch house. She'd had a gas range at her meemaw's house. Not that the type of stove she was cooking on had anything to do with the disaster that had been the perfect dinner for her husband only a few minutes ago.

From outside she heard a truck door slam. Seth was home. She waved a pot holder in front of her face to clear some of the smoke away. The front door opened; then the smoke detector let out a shrill ring.

Seth took one step into the house, only to be greeted by the smoke alarm. "Jessie?" He took off running toward the kitchen. "Jessie!"

But the sight that met his eyes when he entered the room was not what he'd expected.

Jessie in cutoff jean shorts and a pink-and-white baseball shirt was something to behold, but after that, the kitchen left a lot to be desired. She looked okay, intact and whole, but the stove was covered with splatters of tomato sauce, something that looked like chunks of coal smoldered in the sink, and the smell of burned plastic invaded his senses. "What the hell happened in here?"

She whirled on him, jaw clenched, and then she collapsed onto the floor like a rag doll. At least she was sitting up. Her head was down, and her legs were crossed Indian-style.

"Jessie?"

She lifted her chin, and his heart skipped a beat as tears trickled down her freckled cheeks. "I just wanted tonight to be perfect."

Her expression was so pained he almost laughed. But he managed to pull himself together. He hooked his hands under her arms and hoisted her to her feet. "It's okay," he said as he wrapped his arms around her. "I'm sure dinner can be saved."

"It can't," she sobbed. "And I ruined it. It's all my fault."

"It's just dinner," he said as he rocked her from side to side. This must be what the book was talking about when it said pregnant women had mood swings and emotional outbursts. The authors' advice to husbands was to be kind and considerate and let the mom-to-be know how much she meant to him.

"It's more than dinner," she blubbered. "I wanted to do this for you."

"Shhh . . ." He pulled away from her and cupped his fingers on either side of her sweet face. "It's food, Jessie. Just food."

"But . . . but . . ." She pulled away and surveyed the mess. "What are we going to eat tonight?"

Seth smiled. "We'll find something."

Maybe this was why people fell in love before getting married. It made it easier to overlook all the little mistakes and blunders, Seth thought as he patted his stomach. "Thanks for dinner, Jessie."

She shot him a look, but it was more playful than angry. After her meltdown, they had scrounged though the cabinets and found the makings for a Frito chili pie. Not exactly a gourmet meal, but it was quick and easy and having an alternative helped to dry Jessie's tears.

"Let's go out on the porch and sit in the swing."

She set their dirty plates on the counter and gave him a look, half-confused, half-suspicious. "Let me clean up this mess, and I'll be right there."

"That'll take too long." The quicker he got her outside and sitting by his side, the quicker he could put Operation Seduce My Wife into motion. It was time. They had been married for six weeks, and he was pretty sure Jessie was ready to move to the next step. Lord knew, he was. Yesterday morning just proved it, but he wanted everything to be perfect, and laying her down on the kitchen table was far from a fantasy. Well, his maybe, but she deserved better. The best.

"It'll take half that time if you help me."

She had a point there. "Hand me an apron."

Side by side they scrubbed pans and pitched out burned hunks of bread and rubbery noodles. The plastic colander would have to be replaced, and he wasn't sure if his saucepan would ever be the same, but it didn't matter. That was just stuff. She was so much more important to him than kitchen accessories. And she needed to know that. Her meltdown this evening was a prime reason to take their relationship to the next level. It was time to let her know how much she meant to him. That she didn't have to worry about convincing him to like her. Even if he only told her with touches and kisses.

Half an hour later, they finished cleaning the mess. He pushed open the screen door and held it for Jessie.

She sat in the swing and steadied it as he joined her.

The night was perfect. This was all part of his plan, watching the sunset with Jess while the cicadas sang and the bullfrogs called to their mates.

"The baby's room looks nice," he said as he rocked them back and forth with his heels.

"I think so."

When had things gotten awkward?

Or maybe it was just him.

He felt fourteen again, trying to figure out a way to kiss a girl and hoping the whole while that she wouldn't slap him across the face.

But this was Jessie. All he had to do was scoot a little closer, wrap his arm around her, and—

"Are you okay?" he asked.

She gave one vigorous shake of her head, then doubled over.

"Jessie?"

"Sick," she gasped.

"Do you need help getting inside?"

"Is this going to happen every night?"

"I can't say for certain, but I'm thinking yes. This is three nights in a row." He couldn't be too upset about his plans being shot, not with Jessie wheezing and gasping and doing everything in her power to keep her dinner inside.

He rubbed her neck, wondering what he could do to make her feel better. He had wanted them to have a special time. He wanted to show her with his body that he loved her. He had been a patient man, but now that patience was wearing thin. But she was sick, and all because of his baby.

"Can you make it to your room?" His plans would have to be put on hold for a while. Maybe months if she was going to get sick as soon as the sun went down.

"I think so." She stood and swayed like tall grass in a strong wind. "Can you help me?"

He rose and wrapped one arm around her. As slowly as he dared yet as quickly as he could, he walked her to her room.

He helped her into bed, pulled up her covers, then got her a wet washrag just as he had the night before.

"Just rest," he murmured, bending low to plant a chaste kiss on her cheek. Not exactly how he had imagined their evening would end.

He started toward the door.

"Seth," Jessie whispered.

"Yeah?" He stopped, waiting for her to continue.

"I'm sorry."

"Aw, Jess. You don't have to apologize. Just feel better, okay?"

"Okay."

"I love you," he said with one last look at his wife before letting himself out of her room.

J essie woke the next morning feeling as right as rain, as Grandma Esther said. She had slept nine straight hours and felt refreshed after her bout of "morning sickness" the night before. Of course Seth's words didn't hurt either. He loved her. For a man who had trouble expressing himself, he sure knew the right thing to say.

The thought was satisfying and scary all at the same time.

It's going to be a good day. She pushed herself from the bed, a little stiff from her long sleep. As she stretched, her muscles cramped. What did she expect after three nights of dry heaves?

She could hear Seth moving around getting ready for work. Taking care of her bathroom business as quickly as possible, she washed her hands and face and met him in the kitchen.

His eyebrows rose in surprise at the sight of her. He had one hip propped against the counter as he sipped his coffee.

"Good morning," he said.

Normally she would have headed straight for the

coffeepot for her shot of morning caffeine. But this morning she had something else on her mind.

"Good morning." She stood in front of him, contemplating her next move. "Last night," she started, inching a bit closer. She wanted to reach out and touch him, but she told herself to wait. "Last night you said that you love me."

"Yeah." His jaw tightened and his eyes grew a bit guarded.

"Did you mean that?" she asked.

A moment hung suspended between them; then his mask cracked and fell away. "Yeah."

She rose on her toes and pressed her mouth to his. He loved her!

His lips were stiff beneath hers. Then they softened as she continued to kiss him.

He loved her and yet he pulled away.

"Jessie," he said, his voice choked and strained. "I need to go to work."

"You mean now?" she asked, deciding that if he wasn't going to let her kiss his lips, she would move her efforts to his jaw and that crazy pulse beating in his neck.

"Soon," he croaked.

"How soon?" she asked, sliding her hands down his chest. He had been so diligent in his courting efforts, but enough was enough. There was something between them. She couldn't say exactly what it was. But he loved her and she was beginning to think that she loved him in return.

Scratch that. She did love him. She had loved him her entire life like a brother, but ever since that afternoon in his truck . . .

He had been thoughtful and angry. Her rock, her nemesis, her savior, and now her husband. What was not to love?

"Fifteen minutes."

She continued to kiss her way down his neck. How could one man smell so good?

"Half an hour," he corrected, swooping in to capture her lips with his own. The kiss was searing and curled her toes. She loved every bone-melting minute of it. "Forty-five minutes. I got forty-five minutes before someone comes looking for me."

She laughed as he captured her lips once again. They could do a lot in forty-five minutes. Her arms snaked up and circled his neck, holding him closer and closer. His kiss was delicious, electric, and she couldn't get enough. She never wanted it to end.

He walked her backward until her behind bumped the kitchen counter, then lifted her up and nestled between her legs.

"Much better," he murmured as he continued his possession.

She was on fire, consumed by this need she had for him. "Is it always like this?" she asked as she tipped his hat from his head and tossed it onto the kitchen table.

"Yes," he said, his teeth capturing her bottom lip and tugging. "I mean, no."

She pulled away so she could look into those incredible green eyes and see the truth. "Which is it?"

"It's not always like this," he admitted. "But it is when I'm with you."

That was good enough for her. She tangled her fingers in the hair at the nape of his neck and pulled him in for her kiss.

The explosion was back. That out-of-control desire that had been there from the start. She might be inexperienced, but she could tell that Seth was holding himself in check, touching her as if she would break at any moment. He was gentle and caring, but she wanted more of that wild ride they'd shared on the seat of his truck.

"Touch me," she whispered.

"I am touching you." His fingers brushed across her breast, pebbling the nipple and sending tingles throughout.

"Touch me like you mean it." She pressed herself into his hand. She wanted him real. She wanted it real. Everything between them needed to be real. So much had happened and yet nothing. She needed him to stop holding back. He needed to be himself. Love her naturally.

He moved that hand up to cup the side of her face.

"Are you doing this because you're afraid?"

"I don't want to hurt you. Or the baby."

"People have been making love since the dawn of time. I'm sure a few of them have been pregnant."

"I suppose." He dipped in for another kiss.

"Would it help if I told you that the doctor said it was okay?"

"Gary said that?"

She nodded. "He said making love in the first trimester is perfectly safe as long as there are no other issues."

"He's a good doctor."

Jessie laughed and pulled his lips back to hers.

She smiled against his kiss, running her hands into his waistband and untucking his shirt from his jeans. "Kissing a man with a gun is tricky," she said, bypassing his weapon to ease her eager fingers under his shirt and up his warm torso.

"You have no idea." He shivered as she made contact, then moved in a little closer. "But if you keep this up, I won't have any self-control left at all."

"Isn't that the point?" She hooked her heels behind his legs to hold him in place.

"No, I want to love you like you need to be loved."

His words shot a thrill through her greater than the desire that filled every pore.

"I want to lay you down in a soft bed." He planted a quick kiss at the corner of her mouth. As he talked, he moved his hands over her, tugging at her cotton sleep shorts and the other pieces of their clothing.

"I want to kiss every single inch of you," he continued.

"Your chin, collarbone. Each breast." His mouth covered her through the fabric of her shirt, the cotton clinging to her as he wet the cloth.

"I want to touch every part of you and make you mine." His hand slipped between them as Jessie fell into his words.

"I want to be yours," she said. She had always been his. She just hadn't known it until recently. She scooted closer to him, realizing that her shorts were half off, dangling from one leg. He was a clever man, her sheriff husband.

"And you will be."

His fingers found her, slipped inside. She was ready for him, so ready. She had been ready her whole life.

"Seth," she gasped as he pushed farther inside. Touched her like no man before. "Seth, please."

"Seth, please what?" he asked. He pulled away just enough for her to want him back.

"Please love me." This friction was killing her.

"You know I do."

Unable to take any more, Jessie fumbled with his zipper. She left his belt in place, needing him so desperately. She needed him now, five minutes ago, since the dawn of time.

It seemed like forever before her trembling fingers freed him. She brushed her fingers down his length, soft, hard. So much like the man.

"Jessie." Her name was between a prayer and a curse, gritted from between clenched teeth. His control was slipping. She could see it in his eyes.

His hands came around and cupped her bare bottom. He lifted her and pressed for entrance. She used her hands to guide him home.

He filled her wholly and completely, the solid length of him taking her breath.

"Got to slow down," he panted. She needed to move. She wiggled, urging him deeper.

He groaned. She gasped.

"No." She buried her face in the warm crook of his neck. She wanted to stay that way forever, locked as one with him. But she needed that sweet friction even more. She pushed against him, urging him to complete their union.

His fingers dug into the soft flesh of her rear as he used his hands to pull her closer, closer, and then he moved away, only to come crashing in again.

Jessie kept her ankles hooked behind him, refusing to let him leave her for even a moment.

She met his thrusts with one of her own, finding an ancient rhythm with him that she hadn't known existed. He was more than she'd expected, and yet she needed him more and more.

"Don't," she panted. "Don't . . ." But she couldn't get the words out as he loved her so fully.

"Am I hurting you?" He stopped, and Jessie bucked against him one last time.

"Don't ever stop loving me," she finally managed.

"Never," he said. Then took them over the edge of sanity.

And just as the last pulsing wave of their shared desire quaked through her, Seth's phone rang.

Jessie floated through the morning on the euphoric high of their lovemaking. They hadn't even gotten their clothes back to rights before Dusty called wondering where Seth was. Jessie supposed that was what five years of being punctual and never missing a day got him. Caught with his pants down. Almost literally.

The first pain hit just after lunch. At first Jessie thought she had to go to the bathroom, but soon it became apparent that something else was wrong.

Please don't let it be the baby. Please don't let it be the baby.

She needed to call Seth. She needed Seth. He was her rock. He would know what to do.

She grabbed her purse and fished out her cell phone. It was dead. Unaccustomed to having the phone, she had forgotten to charge it. There wasn't a landline at the house. She would have to go to the big house. Someone there would help her.

One hand pressed to her lower stomach, she grabbed her keys. She had to stop at the front door and wait for the pain to subside. There hadn't been anything about searing abdominal pain in any of the books that she had. She had flipped through them all twice just to be sure.

Sadie whined as Jessie let herself out of the house and stumbled over to her Jeep. The ranch truck was still there in the yard. Seth was going to take it back this afternoon. Maybe she should drive it over, but she had grabbed the keys to her car and she wasn't going back now.

She slid behind the wheel of her Jeep and headed for the big house.

Wave after wave of pain washed over her as she drove.

She still had her appendix. Maybe it was her appendix. She wasn't sure how surgery would affect the baby, but the doctors would take care of her. She just had to get to the hospital. And pray that the baby was okay.

Jake waved as she pulled her Jeep into the drive. She tried to wave back but wasn't able. She had one hand pressed to her cramping stomach and the other in a white-knuckled grip on the steering wheel.

She stopped the car, somehow managing to get out though she clung to the door like a lifeline.

Another pain doubled her in half.

"Jessie!" Jake yelled from his place in the corral. She could hear the pounding of his boots as he ran toward her. Then the warm, sticky gush between her legs. She barely registered the stain of blood on her jeans before she slipped unconscious.

Chapter Seventeen

꧁ ✹ ꧂

W here is she?" Seth skidded to a stop on the hospital's overwaxed tile floor. "Where's Jessie?"

The waiting area was strangely empty, but he didn't have room in his thoughts for the whys. He needed to find out about Jessie. "Where's my wife?"

Jake stood. He was pale, his expression grim.

Seth looked to his mother for some reassurance, but there was none. Grandma Esther sat next to his mama looking as grim as his brother.

This couldn't be happening.

He turned. He had to find her. He had to find her now. "Where is she?"

"She's sedated and resting," Jake said.

"The baby?" His voice was barely above a whisper. He didn't need to ask to know.

Jake shook his head. "I'm sorry, Seth."

He collapsed into the seat nearest him, his feet unable to hold him any longer. He braced his elbows on his knees and stared at the floor. "This is all my fault." He shouldn't have made love her to this morning. Sure, all the books said it was okay, but what else could have caused her miscarriage?

"It's not your fault," Jake said from beside him.

"It is," Seth snarled. "This morning—" He stopped, unable to share. But Jake didn't need to hear the intimate details of their relationship. And Seth didn't need to hear that it wasn't his fault. He was responsible. He knew it.

"Seth?"

He looked up as Gary Stephens approached. He wore the same grim expression as everyone in his family. Seth was beginning to hate that look.

Gary—Dr. Stephens—stopped in front of him, reaching out to shake. "I'm so sorry for your loss."

Seth looked at his hand for a full three seconds before giving it a shake. It wasn't the doctor's fault. It was his. "Thank you," he murmured, realizing as he said the words they were the dumbest response he could have made.

"Do you have any questions?" Dr. Stephens asked.

He thought his head might come off. "Yeah," he all but snarled. Then he tempered his voice to a normal tone and continued. "Why?"

Gary shook his head. "No one knows for sure. Twenty-five percent of pregnancies end in miscarriage. And with first babies . . ." He shook his head. "Sometimes the body isn't exactly sure what to do with it. Sometimes it's a matter of early developmental deformities. The body recognizes that the fetus is not developing correctly and stops supporting it."

Jesus. Did he say fetus? Was that what they were down to these days? It was a baby, for God's sake. Did he think calling it by another name would lessen the pain?

You know why this happened.

Seth stood. As much as he wanted to believe all the reasons the doctor had outlined, he knew the truth.

"Seth, this isn't your fault," Jake consoled.

Gary looked from one of them to the other. "Why would it be your fault?"

Jake had the decency to take a few steps back and allow Seth the privacy he needed.

"This morning we, uh, made love. We shouldn't have. I know that now."

Was that what it was? Making love? He had taken her on the kitchen counter. The first time had been in the cab of his truck. Was he destined to continually fail where she was concerned?

"Stop blaming yourself, Seth," Gary said. "In most cases, sexual intercourse during the first trimester is perfectly safe. These things happen. It's unfortunate and sad, but they happen. It's not your fault."

"Can I see her?"

"She's pretty out of it right now. She was in a great deal of pain. So we gave her something to help her sleep. She lost a lot of blood. I want to keep her overnight just to be on the safe side."

"I want to see her."

Gary nodded. "Follow me."

Seth walked behind the doctor all the way to Jessie's room. Everything seemed magnified, the lights were too bright, the sounds of their shoes against the tiles too loud, the walls too beige.

"Stay as long as you like," Gary said. "But don't be surprised if she doesn't wake up, okay?"

Seth nodded and pushed into the dim room.

Her red curls contrasted starkly with the white of the pillows, and her freckles stood out against her pale skin. Dark circles underlined both eyes.

Tears stung the back of his throat and made conversation impossible. Like there was anything to be said.

She looked as though she was asleep. He crept into the room, careful not to disturb her. He checked the rise and fall of her covers as if the doctors would lie about her being okay. He just needed to see for himself. She was breathing. Aside from being wan and going through a horrible ordeal, she was fine. Or at least she would be.

He sat in the seat next to her bed. He wanted to hold her hand, kiss her fingers, but he was afraid of waking her. Gary had said that she'd had a lot of medication and would probably sleep the entire time he was with her, but Seth needed to be at her side.

Ignoring his own vow not to disturb her, Seth took her hand into his. She didn't move as he pressed little kisses on each fingertip. "I'm so sorry, Jessie." The tears that had threatened earlier made good on their promises and slid down his cheeks. "So very sorry."

By three o'clock the next afternoon, Jessie was released from the hospital. She felt numb and hollow.

She still couldn't believe that the baby was gone. How could everything be fine and dandy one minute and then completely fall apart the next?

Seth helped her into his truck and shut the door. She leaned her head against the window. Now what happened?

She closed her eyes as Seth started the truck and backed out of the parking lot.

He didn't say a word to her all the way back to the ranch house. She was just beginning to think of it as home. But now . . .

Seth had married her because she was pregnant. Now she wasn't. Where did that leave them?

And what must he think of her? She was a failure. She couldn't even grow a baby. Wasn't that what being a woman was all about? Bringing in the next generation?

Suddenly she wished she could call back every conversation they'd had about gender. She only wanted a healthy baby. Boy or girl, it didn't matter to her. And now she had none.

She could feel Seth's eyes land on her from time to time, but she kept her head against the window as she watched the world pass by. Out of Cattle Creek and onto the Diamond. She didn't move until he pulled to a stop in front of the old ranch house.

She got out before he could help her. She winced as her feet hit the ground. They told her the pain would be like an extremely bad period. Having not suffered from cramps like some other women, she wasn't prepared for the back-breaking pains that seared through her.

Seth led the way to the house and held open the door.

"Where's Sadie?" Jessie asked. The pooch was strangely absent.

"I took her over to the big house. I thought you might want a little more peace and quiet for a couple of days."

She nodded. That was Seth, ever thoughtful, but Jessie would have preferred to have the pooch there. She could use a bit of that canine unconditional love.

"You want to talk about it?" Seth's question was softly spoken, nearly hesitant.

She shook her head. "I think I'll go lay down."

He looked as if he might protest, but in the end he gave a quick nod and let her go. She walked down the narrow hallway, faltering when she got to the baby's room.

They should have never bought the furniture so early in her pregnancy. It was bad luck. Everyone said so. But she had wanted to spend time with her husband; she had wanted to please him. So they had picked out the crib and brought it home. Now it would remain empty forever.

She closed the door and continued to her room.

A tired sigh escaped her as she turned down the covers. She removed her boots and crawled into the bed, still wearing the clothes she had come home in. They weren't the clothes she'd had on yesterday. She didn't ask what had become of her blood-soaked jeans. She didn't want to know.

She needed to cry, but she couldn't. She had been a fool. A crazy, self-centered fool.

She was married to one of the greatest guys in Page County. But for how long was anyone's guess.

He had only married her for the baby, but now that it was gone, it was only a matter of time before Seth would want his freedom. He'd had a pretty sweet deal before he married her. Eligible women bringing him cakes and casseroles. He could have had his pick, and he got stuck with her.

Last night he'd told her that he loved her. And fool that she was, she didn't stop to ask him to explain. She heard only what she wanted to hear. He admitted that he wasn't good with words. How else could this have fallen so easily from his lips? They had known each other practically their whole lives. He had been trying to make her feel better and said those sweet words, but he couldn't mean them. Especially not now, now that she couldn't do the most basic of womanly functions. Now that the baby that had forced them together was gone.

A shudder shook her, but no tears came. She raised her knees to her chest and wished she could cry herself to sleep.

Jessie?" Seth hated to wake her, but he was worried. She had barely gotten out of bed the day before. Now it was nearly lunchtime and she hadn't been up at all.

The doctor had said there would be mental and physical adjustments, and now Seth understood what he meant. Jessie was depressed, not at all the vivacious girl he had fallen in love with.

Maybe if he could get her up and interested in doing other things, that depression would pass and the healing could begin.

Gary had also told him that there was no reason for her not to be able to get pregnant again. "Give it a few months and then you can start trying again."

Seth hadn't bothered to point out to him that he and Jessie hadn't been trying to have a baby in the first place. But now that the opportunity was gone, he realized just how much he had been looking forward to being a father and raising a child with Jessie at his side.

He lightly shook her shoulder. "Jessie," he said again. "I made you some coffee."

She stirred and finally sat up in the bed. The covers fell around her hips and he noticed she still had on the same clothes as the day before. Seeing her like this broke his heart. He would do anything to bring that light back into her eyes.

Give it time.

He handed her the cup and watched as she took a sip.

"What time is it?"

"Eleven thirty."

"In the morning?"

He gave her a gentle smile. "Yes."

She nodded, then took another sip of her coffee. "I guess I don't have to nurse this cup now, huh? I can have all the caffeine I want."

He didn't know what to say to that. "How about I make you some breakfast?"

She shook her head. "Thanks anyway."

"Will you come sit on the porch swing with me?"

For a split second he thought she would tell him no, but then she gave a quick nod. "Don't you have to go to work?"

"I took a couple of days off. Dusty can handle it."

"What about Chester and Amos?"

"There are some things that are more important than a half-a-century-old family feud."

His heart soared when she smiled. It was a sad smile, but

the first one he had seen from her in over two days and he was thankful.

"Come on," he said. "Let's go enjoy the day."

She couldn't say that she enjoyed the day. She felt listless and sad. She was numb. There was no baby. The baby that had brought her and Seth together was no more. Where did that leave them?

But she had to snap out of it.

"Are you sure you'll be okay today?"

"Yeah." She tucked her hair behind her. "I thought I might go over to Meemaw's and start packing up."

Joy chased concern across his face. "Are you up for that?"

She wasn't, but she knew that she needed to put some effort into moving forward. Or at least pretending that she was. Maybe if she pretended hard enough, it would come true. "It's time," was all she said.

Thankfully Seth didn't question her about it.

If he was pretending alongside her, then surely they both couldn't be wrong.

She managed to drag herself into the shower and put on clean clothes. But before she went into the kitchen she had to sit down and rest. She could do this. She *had* to do this.

One foot in front of the other and soon it wouldn't seem so hard.

Her first stop was at the liquor store to pick up some boxes.

Shonda Preston was behind the counter. "Jessie McAllen," she greeted her as she walked through the door. "Oh, wait, I guess you're a Langston now," Shonda corrected herself. Her father owned the store and she had always felt that she had an edge over everyone in their class. Of course, now that they were all over twenty-one, that edge was gone and Shonda was in search of another one.

"Yeah," Jessie said. "I'm looking for some boxes."

"Trouble between you and Seth already?"

"I'm cleaning out my grandmother's house." Why was everyone in this town so mean?

"Oh." Shonda nodded. "Come around back, and I'll see what I have."

Half an hour later, Jessie pulled up to her grandmother's house and cut the engine. She wasn't ready for this. Too many changes, too much loss. Seth had told her to wait a couple more days and he would come with her. Dusty had gone to training in San Angelo and would be back by then, but she wanted to do this alone. It was her responsibility, and she was tired of postponing the inevitable.

She sighed. It had to be done.

The porch steps creaked as she made her way up to the porch and let herself into the house. It smelled the same, like cigarettes and menthol.

"Meemaw, I'm home," she said to no one in particular.

Everything was just as she had left it. Somewhere in the back of her mind, she'd hoped that it wouldn't be as bad as it was. She didn't know where to start. She walked into the kitchen. Some things could be donated to charity. She wasn't up to a garage sale. Or maybe that was the answer: pull everything out into the yard and take the best offer.

She didn't need the dishes. Or the pots and pans. She poured a glass of water from the tap and gave a drink to the four little pots of herbs that grew in the windowsill. She should take them back home with her.

Home. This used to be home, but now she lived with Seth. For how long?

She had been mulling it over for days. Seth was a noble man. He had said forever and that was what he would deliver. But was forever in their cards?

It wasn't. She knew that. This morning with Shonda was

a prime example. Jessie didn't belong here, the one place she had lived all her life. It was time for her to go. She knew that.

She needed to get her money together and get out as she had always dreamed. Only then Seth could go on in the life that was truly destined to be his.

She hadn't decided where she wanted to go. That would have to be her first decision. Then get her job back at Chuck Wagon. Seth wouldn't like it, but he couldn't cry pregnancy as a reason for her to be a housewife. With any luck, she'd have enough to leave by the beginning of the year.

She opened the cabinets and started pulling out the cans of food. Take them back to the old ranch house or donate them to the food bank? The thought of lugging them out to the Diamond sounded like way too much effort. Not when she could load them up in paper grocery sacks and leave them on the porch for someone else to deal with.

She stacked all the can goods on the countertop, then started for the cabinets holding the dishes. She stacked them next to the canned goods, then reached for the coffee cups.

Jessie went into town every day for two weeks. She got up each morning and took a shower, shared a cup of coffee with Seth on the porch, then drove behind him all the way to Cattle Creek. Seth had never felt more separated from her.

"Chester," Seth started, doing his best to defuse the situation. "Why would Amos come over in the middle of the night and paint your mailbox pink?"

Better yet, why would he want to?

"I know he did it." The elderly man spat to one side, and Seth winced as the old birddog dodged to avoid it.

"I'll talk to him," Seth promised. "Just do me a favor."

The old man thought about it a minute, then gave a quick nod. "What?"

"Don't retaliate." He had too much to do to have to run back over here because Chester was missing his mailbox.

"Bah." Amos waved him away with one hand, then hobbled back to his front porch. A shotgun sat propped up next to his rocking chair.

"And put that gun away."

"Rabbits," Amos said without turning around.

Please, Lord, let that be all he's shooting at.

His cell phone jangled as he slid back into his service vehicle. He grabbed it up as he pointed his truck back toward town.

"How's Jessie?" his mother asked without preamble.

Seth bit back a sigh. "Healing," he said. Such a lie. He didn't know what was going on in Jessie's head. He hadn't been by her grandmother's house to see if she had made any progress. He just knew that she was going there every day, and every day it seemed that the chasm between them was bigger than the day before.

"Why don't the two of you come out to the house tonight for supper? Grandma Esther is making chicken enchiladas."

"That sounds good." He wasn't sure if he could get Jess out of the house, but he would do everything in his power to. Maybe a night out was exactly what they needed.

Maybe this weekend he would take her into Midland. Maybe catch dinner someplace nice and a movie, her choice. He had let her wallow in her grief long enough. Now it was time to move forward.

"We'll be there," he said, then turned his truck down Larkspur Lane.

Her Jeep was out front when he pulled into the gravel driveway. The house looked so different to him now. Yet the only thing that had changed was that Naomi McAllen was no longer there.

He took the steps two at a time and let himself inside. "Jessie," he called, his gaze bouncing around the room. For a moment he wondered if the house had been burglarized. Most the pictures were off the walls; knickknacks were stacked in boxes and strewn about the floor. Papers littered the rug between the rooms. "Jessie?"

She came out of the kitchen. "Seth? What are you doing here?"

"I came by to see how you were doing." His gaze bounced off the mess spread out in front of him. "Do you need some help? I told you I would give you a hand."

She shook her head. "I've got it under control."

"Yeah, sure looks like it."

Wrong thing to say. Immediately her hackles were up, but facing her anger was much more satisfying than dealing with her indifference. Perhaps she was healing after all.

"This isn't easy, you know."

"I know."

"Coming here every day and trying to decide what to keep and what to give away. These are her *things*."

"I know."

"I can't go into her room. I can't go into the nursery."

And now they were at the crux of the problem.

"Do you want me to take a couple of days off and come and help you?"

"Don't you understand?" Tears rose into her eyes. It was the first time he'd seen her cry since she lost the baby. He wasn't sure if it was a good thing or a bad one. "She's gone."

"I know." He moved toward her, needing to comfort her, let her cry, then dry her tears.

She flung herself into his arms, clutching him to her as if he were a lifeline and she was going down for the last time.

"It's okay, Jessie." He smoothed a hand over her hair. "We'll hire someone to pack everything up. We can store it all in the barn until you're ready to sort through it, okay?"

As quickly as she grabbed him, she let him go. "I'm okay." She dabbed at her eyes, but as she wiped the tears away, they reappeared.

"You're not." He wanted to hold her in his arms once

again, but even as he reached for her, she took a step back.
"Maybe you should go talk to someone."

She shook her head. "I said I'm fine." Her chin tilted to
that stubborn angle he knew so well. Her shoulders
straightened, and her eyes blazed with determination.

"I just need a little more time."

"I know." He tried his best to sound supportive, but he
had his doubts.

Yeah, she would be fine. But what would happen to
them in the meantime?

"Mama invited us to the ranch tonight for supper," he said
when he got home later that evening. It had been a
helluva day. After the incident with Chester and Amos and
his time with Jessie at her grandmother's house, there had
been a problem at Manny's. At least this time neither Jessie
nor Chase was involved. Thank heaven for small miracles.

She took so long to answer that he was afraid she was
going to tell him that she wouldn't go. "Do I have time for
a shower before we leave?"

It was on the tip of his tongue to say that he would join
her, but it was too soon. "Sure. I'll go after you."

She nodded and headed for the bathroom. On her way
down the hall, he heard her close the nursery door. How
had it gotten open? He needed to check the latch to make
sure it was working right. Otherwise Jessie would be closing that door . . . forever.

The pipes thumped as she turned on the water.

She was slipping away, he could feel it. And the worst
part of all, he didn't know what he could do about it.

Chapter Eighteen

❧ ✶ ❧

Dinner at the ranch was always a special occasion. Jessie had enjoyed many suppers at the Langston table. The food was always tasty, but it was the sense of family that she loved most.

"I'm glad you're here, Aunt Jessie," Wesley said. "Can you come out to the barn and see the kitties that Uncle Seth brought over? I asked Daddy if we could keep them. He said he'd think about it, and he's been thinking about it so long I think he'll say yes." She stuffed a tortilla chip into her mouth and grinned.

"Of course," Jessie replied. She wasn't really up for a trip out to the horse barn, but she couldn't tell that sweet little face no.

It was all part of her plan to continue. Or at least pretend she was. Fake it until she could make it. Fake it until she had the money to leave everything behind.

She took another bite of her enchiladas as Evelyn frowned. "That dog." Evelyn shook her head. "He never stops barking."

"He's just lonely," Wesley said.

"How can he be lonely?" Jake asked. "There's five kittens and half a dozen horses out there."

"Is that the puppy Chase brought home at the wedding?" Seth asked.

Evelyn shook her head. "He came by this week with this little guy."

"I'd like to keep him," Jake said. "He's at least half cattle dog. I thought he'd be good around here, but it's almost too much for him. Seth, why don't you take him for a while? Then once he gets used to the ranch, I'll bring him back over. All he's doing now is upsetting the horses."

"Sure. Is that okay, Jess?"

But Jessie couldn't find her voice to answer. Chase had brought home another dog, another stray. Just like Sadie. Just like her.

How many times had Chase dragged home a stray only to make Seth be the one responsible for its care?

In a heartbeat she was back on that faithful day when she met the two of them. Heather Clemens's dog had come out of nowhere. Jessie had turned to run and tripped over her own shoelaces. Down she went, skinning the palms of her hands and both knees. Chase had come over to help her up. She had been so thankful to him for his assistance. She remembered staring at him and thinking how cute he was. For a boy anyway. Chase had held her arm as he escorted her back to his brother. She had always attributed Chase for her rescue, but in truth, it was Seth who had cleaned her wounds and given her a cherry ice pop, still her favorite to this day.

She was just another one of Chase's strays.

"Jess? Are you okay?" Seth asked.

"I'm sorry. I don't feel very good. Can you . . . can you please take me home?"

She ignored the concerned looks that rippled around the table. Only Wesley's expression remained the same.

"Does that mean you won't be able to come see the kittens?"

"Can I do that another day?" Jessie asked.

"I s'pose," she replied.

"Wesley," Jake said, his voice low with reprimand.

"I mean, that'd be fine, Aunt Jessie. I'm sorry you feel bad."

She trailed her fingers down the girl's cheek. "Thank you, sweetie."

"Let me get you a plate to go." Grandma Esther started to stand, but Jessie waved her back down.

"That's okay. Thank you anyway. I think I just need to lay down."

She refused to look at Seth as he said his good-byes and walked with her to his truck.

She got in without a word and nothing was said on the short trip back to their house. But she could feel him winding up to talk. And that was the last thing she wanted to do.

He pulled the truck to a stop, then turned to face her. "Jessie."

She leaned her head back against the seat and closed her eyes. "Do we have to do this now?"

"What's wrong?" His voice was so soft and filled with concern that tears clogged her throat.

"I just need a little time," she managed. But was she talking to him or herself?

"I just want to—" He stopped. "You can have all the time you need."

She couldn't open her eyes. She couldn't look at him. She was so afraid of breaking down right there in front of him.

She had been so excited when he told her that he loved her. She had just never considered the many definitions of love. Yes, he had known her his entire life. Yes, whenever he kissed her it sizzled, but that didn't mean he harbored romantic feelings for her. He could have any woman he wanted in Page County. Why would he pick wild child Jessie McAllen?

"Thank you," was all she said as she slipped from the truck cab.

* * *

S eth sat in his truck and watched Jessie make a break
   for the house.

Damn it all to hell! He smacked his hand against the steering wheel and debated on whether or not to go after her. He wanted to chase her down, kiss her like crazy, and make love to her until that lost look faded from her eyes.

But it was too soon for that, both emotionally and physically. She needed time to heal, time to get her mind straight, but he was afraid that by the time that happened she would be lost to him forever.

He gave her enough time to hide out in her room before he got out of the truck and followed her inside. As he expected, she was nowhere around. He grabbed a beer from the fridge and settled down to watch the last of the Rangers game.

But he couldn't keep his mind on anything but Jessie. He had come right out and told her that he loved her, but he didn't think she believed him. He had done everything in his power to let her know that he would be by her side forever and always, baby or no baby.

He slipped off his boots and propped his feet up on the coffee table.

Sadie climbed up next to him and laid her chin on his thigh, staring up at him with those questioning brown eyes.

"What am I supposed to do, girlie?"

She didn't answer.

"Did she shut you out of her room?" Normally Sadie slept curled up next to Jessie, a place that Seth wished he could claim for his own.

He scratched her behind one ear. She closed her eyes and sighed, but he knew she would rather be in there with Jessie.

"That makes two of us."

He drained the last of his beer and switched off the television. The Rangers were getting beat anyway. No sense in adding insult to injury.

"Come on, girl." He made his way down the hallway to Jessie's room. He gave a small rap on the door and quietly peeked inside. It was still pretty early, but Jessie had already crawled into bed. From her lack of response he figured she was also asleep.

Sadie looked up at him, then over to the bed, quickly deciding on joining her mistress rather than hanging out with him.

What he wouldn't give to be able to slip into bed beside her and hold her close all night long.

As if they had a brain of their own, his feet carried him to the bed. What harm would there be to just lay with her for a while? Hold her close and pretend that everything was right with the world.

It might not be wrong, but it was pathetic. Still he climbed into bed with her.

He just wanted to hold her. She was facing away from him, so he curled one arm around her waist and spooned to her back.

She felt so good, warm and sweet. And he never wanted to let her go.

She sighed in her sleep and snuggled a bit closer to him. He grew hard as her behind pressed against him, but tonight wasn't about that.

"Down, boy," he muttered, and buried his face in her hair. She smelled like strawberries and sunshine. He breathed in her scent and knew that he could never let her go. Finally—finally—he had her in his arms and he would do whatever it took to keep her there.

If only he knew what that was.

Jessie woke the next morning realizing that she'd had the strangest dream. She had been standing in line to get on a plane. She had no idea where she was going, but Seth came up behind her and pulled her close to him.

Somehow with his arms around her the trip didn't seem quite so important. She had missed her flight, but she didn't care. Not as long as she had Seth.

But in the light of day she could see the dream for what it was: her mind's pitiful attempt to keep Seth close. But he could only be hers in dreams, and she would do well to remember that.

"You have any plans for today?" he asked over their morning cup of coffee on the porch. She would miss this when she left. She would have to make a new tradition to follow to keep her mind off him. Like that was going to work.

At least she had a while before she would have enough money to head out. "I thought I would go up to the Chuck Wagon and see if I can get my job back."

He looked up, clearly surprised. "You don't have to go to work."

"I want to."

"Are you sure you're up to it?"

She nodded.

For a minute she thought he might protest, but then he seemed to relax. "Just promise me that you'll take it easy and rest if you get too tired."

Just another reason why she hated her lie from the night before. Physically she was fine. Emotionally she was a wreck and it wasn't only from losing the baby. With the baby she had lost Seth. And that was the worst part of all. "I promise." She took a sip of her coffee. "I probably won't start until next week. I still have so much to do at the house."

"Why don't you postpone getting a job until after you get the house cleaned out?"

Because that meant it would take that much longer before she could set them both free. "It'll be better this way. Give me motivation to get the house finished this week."

"It was in pretty bad shape when I was there yesterday. Are you sure you'll have enough time?"

"Yeah," she said. "I have a plan."

* * *

Her plan was simple. She'd make three piles: keep, donate, and throw away. Touch an item once and don't second-guess.

With the new plan in place, it took the rest of the week to get most everything in order. She called the Baptist church to come pick up the donations. Then she loaded all the trash into the can and pulled it to the curb for the next pickup day. Now all she had to do was take the keepers to her car and she was done.

She had saved three large boxes of things. Most were pictures mixed with a few keepsakes. She had kept it minimal. She would be leaving soon. The less she kept, the less she would have to move when the time came.

She moved two of the boxes to the Jeep, then went back into the house to get the third one. She placed the old black-and-white picture of her mother and her grandmother on top. Meemaw had told her so many times to make sure she kept that picture. How could she leave it behind? She ran her fingers across the glass, over the frozen images of the two women who had raised her. Now was not the time to get overly sentimental. She picked up the box and started for the door. She stopped just inside the house, unable to leave without one last look around. This was the last time she would be there. The bank would take possession and sell the house. And this part of her life would be over. She looked at the nearly empty room. Only a few pieces of large furniture remained. She left them for whoever bought the house. She had no need.

"Oh, Meemaw," she whispered to the empty house. "I hope we're both going on to better things."

She raised one shoulder to wipe the tears from her eyes. The picture frame on the top of her box unbalanced and fell.

Jessie tried to catch it but only succeeded in almost dropping the box she held.

The picture frame hit on the corner. The wood split and the glass shattered.

"Oh, no!" She set the box down next to the mess and started separating the stack of pictures that the frame held. She had never known there was more behind the picture of her mother and grandmother.

She shook the glass from the photos, realizing that there were only two photographs. The rest were merely paper, some sort of documents. She looked them over, nearly forgetting about the mess of glass that still needed to be swept up.

The papers were old, though how old she had no idea. Carefully she peeled them apart and gently unfolded them. Jackson Tractors, Midland, Texas, the first one said. She had never heard of them. Another was Southwestern Bell, and the third was for Rigley Produce. They were bonds, she finally realized. Was that why her meemaw wanted her to keep the picture, for these documents? The Southwestern Bell one had to be worth a little, but the other two were probably worthless. Only one way to find out. She'd take them over to Carson Accounting. Dale Carson was the only CPA that Cattle Creek had and most likely the one person in town who could track down the bonds' value, if there was any.

She shook them one last time just to make sure there were no other lingering shards of glass, then stacked them and the other photos on the top of her box. Careful to step over the glass, she took the last box to her car, then went in search of a broom.

Carson Accounting sat near the end of Main, directly across from the Tenth Street empty lot.

Jessie parked her Jeep in front of the gray-painted building and pulled the bonds from the box.

She had decided not to tell Seth until she knew something. There was no sense getting him excited if there was nothing to be excited about. Chances were the bonds were worthless. Or worth very little. Whatever she made from them she would add to her escape fund.

The thought made her stomach hurt. Seth had ruined her. She wanted to stay so bad. Wanted to give the two of them a chance, but too much was stacked against them.

Susie Baker waved as Jessie headed toward Carson's office. Jessie waved back and then wondered what Susie whispered to Sissy Callahan beside her. Let them wonder what she was doing in the accountant's office. She didn't care. But she did. She was so tired of being talked about at every social gathering Cattle Creek had from the weekly PTA meetings to Cattle Days. She had thought when she married Seth that maybe some of that talk would settle down, but it had only increased the speculations on whether or not the baby she carried was really Seth's or if he was merely covering for his brother.

In the end, what did it matter? She had lost the baby. Chase hated her more than ever and Seth . . . Seth said he wanted to be married to her forever, but that was before she miscarried. Now he was only trying to be polite. How long could forever last if there was nothing holding them together? Not even love.

If he was going to divorce her, she would have to leave. She couldn't stay in this town knowing that he was so close yet out of reach. And the gossip! No, thank you.

"Hey, Jessie," Pam Carson, Dale's wife, greeted her. "What can I do you for today?"

Pam was about the same age as Jessie's grandmother had been, but neither she nor her husband seemed ready to retire. That was good, since there were no more accountants in Cattle Creek. And Main Street just wouldn't be the same without them.

"I was cleaning through Meemaw's house and I found these." She handed the bonds to Pam. "Can you tell me if they're worth anything?"

Pam looked them over. "I'll need to show these to Dale, but I would say Southwestern Bell is probably your best bet."

"Yeah, that's what I was thinking. I wanted you to look at them. You know more about these things than I do. And I surely don't want to throw them out if they're worth something."

"Amen to that," Pam said. She looked down to the blinking light on the phone. "Let me show these to Dale. He's on a call right now. Not sure how long he'll be. Can you wait around?"

Jessie shook her head. "I need to be getting home."

"That's all right." Pam waved a dismissive hand. "He'll probably have to research them anyways. You just leave them with me, and I'll make sure he gets right on it."

"Thanks, Miss Pam."

"Anytime, dear."

Chapter Nineteen

⚜

"Did Seth ask you to do this?" Jessie smiled to take any suspicion from her words. She asked the question, but she knew the answer. Who else would have called his mother and asked her to invite Jessie out to shop and eat lunch?

After three stores, Jessie was ready to have a margarita and rest. She had never been much for shopping and carrying on, so she steered Evelyn into the Cantina for a healthy dose of chips and salsa and a little bit of tequila.

Evelyn stirred her margarita and took a tentative sip. "Of course not, dear. I thought you might could use a little girl time."

Jessie wasn't sure what she needed, but she didn't think it was girl time. She felt as if she lived on a different planet than Evelyn Langston. The woman had never been anything but nice to her, always looking out for her and her kin. Yet despite Evelyn's cordial mannerisms and bend toward charities, the last thing Jessie wanted to be was one of those people who depended on others for every little thing. She refused to be Evelyn's next charity case.

"Girl time is always nice," Jessie lied. She wanted nothing more than to be tucked safely at home and not worry about anyone or anything else. Funny, living outside town had made her see that she had the perfect hideout in the old ranch house. But she couldn't afford to hide any longer. Next weekend was the garage sale at her grandmother's house. She had decided that was just that much more money she could use to help her when she left. Not that she had any concrete plans on when that might be. But one day soon . . .

The thought of leaving Seth behind made her stomach hurt, and that pain had nothing to do with the lingering cramps. She would miss him terribly, but it was getting harder and harder each day to face him knowing that she was just another one of the messes Chase left for Seth to clean up. How she wanted to be so much more to him than that. But how would she ever know that she was?

"I think so too." Evelyn smiled. "We should make time to do this more often."

Jessie made a noise that she hoped sounded like an agreement.

"That's another reason why I wanted to come out with you today," Evelyn started.

"Oh, yeah?" Jessie asked. "And what is that?"

Evelyn sat up a little straighter in her seat and made a perfect pleat in her napkin, a sure sign that she was uneasy. The great Evelyn Duvall Langston was uncomfortable. "I don't know what happened between you and Chase, but I want you to know that you are a welcomed member in this family. Of course, the holidays may be a little strained, but somehow we'll make it through. We're Langstons after all."

Jessie cleared her throat and pushed to her feet. She didn't know if she was even going to be here come Christmas. "I need to use the restroom," she said. "I'll be right back."

Evelyn drew back, looking a bit shocked. "Of course, dear."

Jessie walked toward the back of the restaurant where the bathrooms were located. She didn't have to go, but she needed a minute. Anxiety had taken her breath. She knew what it was, but identifying it didn't make it any easier. She didn't want to talk about Chase, but even more she didn't want to talk about spending the holidays with the Langstons.

She pushed inside and decided she'd go while she was in there. At least then her words wouldn't be such a lie. As she shut the door behind herself, she heard someone else come into the restroom.

"Did you see her over there?"

Jessie knew that voice. Lindy Shoemake. They hadn't been in the same class at school. Lindy had been a senior when Jessie started high school, but everyone knew Lindy. Her father had been mayor as long as Jessie could remember.

"Ugh. I know, right? Sitting there with his mother like nothing in the world is wrong. Makes me sick."

Darly Jo.

And they were talking about her!

Jessie held her breath.

"I just wish I'd thought of it before Jessie. Pretending to be pregnant and then losing the baby. Brilliant."

"Everybody in town knows that baby was Chase's."

"If there even was a baby. Then she trapped Seth and made him marry her. It's a cryin' shame, really. I mean, Seth is such a great guy."

"Yeah. He's too decent to ask for a divorce. And why should she file? She has everything she wanted and more."

Tears stung her eyes. Jessie would never live down this place. Cattle Creek was her home and her hell.

The door to the restroom opened and Jessie was alone once again. She dashed away her tears with the back of her hand and let herself out of the stall.

This town.

She splashed cold water on her cheeks and tried not to look at her reflection. She couldn't even face herself. Was that what this town was saying about her?

It had become so hard to hold her head up. Now it was dang near impossible. Her neck was about to break under the strain. She needed to get out and as soon as she could manage.

She headed back to the table and slid into the booth.

"Are you okay, Jessie? You look pale."

Jessie shook her head. "I'm fine." A total lie, but Evelyn seemed satisfied.

"Now, where were we?" She shifted in her seat as she started folding her napkin again.

"You know I went to Seth about it, and he actually told me that he loves her." Darly Jo's voice floated to them from a nearby booth.

"Do you believe that?" Lindy. Of all the luck. They were practically sitting right next to them.

"Not for a minute."

Evelyn looked up from her folding and caught Jessie's gaze.

She would not cry. She would not cry. She would not—
Screw that.

Jessie stood. "Excuse me." She started for the door, noticing that of course she had to walk by the table where Lindy and Darly Jo sat in order to get there. Just her luck.

She could hear Evelyn behind her, but she wasn't about to stop. She needed to get out of there. If she had ever thought that she and Seth had a chance, this just proved how wrong she could be.

"Your folks would be ashamed if they could hear you now."

Jessie looked back over her shoulder to see Evelyn had stopped next to Darly Jo and Lindy's table and was giving them a dressing-down as only she could.

And as much as she appreciated whatever support she could get, Jessie knew deep down the problem wasn't the lack of people on her side, but that she had a side to begin with.

Evelyn caught her just as she swung herself into her Jeep. "Jessie, wait."

She cranked the engine and rolled down her window. "I know what you're going to say."

Evelyn propped her hands on her slim hips. "And what is that?"

"Something along the lines of 'Keep your chin up and don't let the people of this town get to you.' Well, you know what? They do get to me and I've had all I can take. There'll never be a day when I can hold my head up in this town and not have whispers trailing behind me. The quicker I accept that and move on, the better off we'll all be."

"That's not true, honey. Give it some time. You'll see."

Jessie nodded, but not because she agreed. She nodded because she knew the truth and accepted it. She had to get out of Cattle Creek as soon as she could. Go somewhere she could start over. Someplace where no one knew her name.

Evelyn squeezed her hand in that reassuring manner that Jessie so desperately wanted to believe. "You and Seth come out to the ranch tomorrow. Maybe I can talk Jake into grilling some hamburgers."

"Sure." She flashed her mother-in-law a cheeky smile, hoping the gesture bought her escape.

Evidently it worked. Evelyn kissed her cheek and gave her a quick wave.

Jessie breathed a sigh of relief. But the break was cut short by the jangle of her cell phone.

"Hello?"

"Jessie? It's Dale Carson. Is this a bad time?"

"No," she lied. She rolled up the window. "Did you check over those papers?"

"Yes, I did."

"And?"

"Are you sitting down?"

Jessie stared at her lap. "Yes."

"We had figured the Southwestern Bell would be worth a little money. It's the small tractor company. They sold to a national chain, and from the terms of the original stock, that transferred and you retained ownership. It's worth a small fortune."

Jessie started trembling. "Define small fortune."

"I'm thinking close to half a million dollars."

She nearly choked. "Half—half a million?"

"Give or take. Of course I won't know for sure until I contact a broker. But somewhere in that neighborhood."

"That's some neighborhood." Was this really happening? Should she pinch herself to make sure? Would it work if she was truly dreaming and she pinched herself?

Dale chuckled. "I can't imagine this happening to a better person."

"Thanks," she murmured.

"So, does that mean you want me to find a seller for these?"

"Yes, please." So much money just hanging on the wall all these years. Money that she could have used to make her escape long ago. But deep down she knew the real reason she'd never left. She had never really wanted to go. But now . . . she had nothing to keep her there and money wasn't an obstacle. She couldn't even pretend that it was.

"It may take a little bit to unload. I'll call you when I get something worked out."

"That sounds great." Great? It was stupendous. Wasn't it? "And, Dale, just one more thing."

"What's that?"

"Please don't tell anyone about this. I don't want this to get around."

"Sure thing." If he thought the request was strange, he didn't say.

Jessie hung up the phone, the weight of what had just happened dropping on her like a half-ton boulder. She had all the money she would need. Maybe enough to last her entire life.

She had no reason to remain in Cattle Creek. She was free to go.

Chapter Twenty

❧ ✴ ❧

Y ou want to watch a movie?" Seth asked. It was too
quiet in the house. Like a movie would make more
noise than the baseball game. But Jessie was curled up on
the end of the couch reading a magazine. At least if they
watched a movie they would be doing something together.

"I thought you were watching the game."

He shrugged. "The Rangers aren't playing tonight."

"Whatever you want to do," Jessie said.

What had happened to the sassy-mouthed redhead who
everyone in town believed was behind half the mischief
that took place inside the city limits?

"I asked you what you wanted to do."

She looked up from her magazine once again. "I don't
care, Seth."

"Are you trying to fight with me?" He didn't know
where the bee in her bonnet came from, but he wasn't about
to argue with Jessie over something as trivial as what to
watch on television.

"No, but you're making me crazy with all these questions. I'm trying to read."

"I'm trying to spend time with you."

She placed the magazine on the couch between them and crossed her arms. Something was wrong. He didn't know what. Something that transcended magazines and baseball games.

"Jessie?"

She stood. "My head hurts. I'm going to bed."

He watched, confused, as she made her way to her bedroom. He had talked to Gary that very afternoon about Jessie's roller-coaster moods. The doctor had attributed them to the drop in hormones coupled with all the loss and change that Jessie had suffered in such a short time. He told Seth to be patient and if she was still having trouble in another week to let him know. Seth had hung up the phone not feeling any better about the situation. He wanted his Jessie back.

They had the perfect—okay, not so perfect—chance to start over. But it was still a chance, and she was slipping away. He wanted nothing more than to put that spark back in her eyes. He just didn't know how to do it.

He eased down the hallway and creaked open her door. "Jess?"

She mumbled something from the bed, though he couldn't make out any words.

"Did you take something for your head? Do you want me to get you a Tylenol?"

"Don't, Seth."

"Don't what?"

"Don't be nice to me."

What was she talking about? "Why shouldn't I be nice to you and take care of you?"

"I don't deserve it."

His heart broke in two. "Of course you do." He wasn't

about to let her browbeat herself over nothing. "I'll be right back."

She mumbled something else.

Seth let himself out of the room and made his way to the kitchen for some pain relievers and a glass of water for her.

As quickly as he could, he took them back to her. She seemed to be sleeping, and he didn't want to disturb her. He set the pills and the water on the nightstand next to the bed and bent close to press a kiss to the side of her face, just above her ear.

He wanted to whisper that he loved her, tell her how much she meant to him. Let her know that whatever this was that plagued her, they would get through it together. But those were just words. He had said them before and she hadn't believed him. Saying them now wouldn't bring her back to her happy self.

Instead he smoothed down her hair and left the room.

Forget the yard sale. She had to get out of here while she still could.

Last night, Seth standing over her, touching the side of her face as if he couldn't get enough of her. He was only trying to convince himself to stay in this thing. He didn't have to treat her like that any longer. Like he truly cared. Especially when they were alone. It wasn't necessary. It was over. When she got settled she would send him the divorce papers and set him free. It was the only thing she could do.

She looked around the bedroom that she had never shared with Seth. She supposed that was a good thing. She didn't know what would have happened to her feelings for him had they been so intimate as to share the bed. They'd made love twice, and leaving was about to kill her now as it was.

The hardest part was knowing that it was for the best. She had to get out to save both her and Seth—him for staying married to her and her for loving him to forever and beyond.

Sadie whined, jumped on the bed, and flopped down next to her suitcase. The poor pooch wore a worried frown as she watched Jessie throw her clothes in.

"I'm sorry," Jessie said to the dog. "But this is the only way. As much as I hate to admit it, Darly Jo was right. Seth is too noble. He won't ever divorce me. But he doesn't love me. Not really."

She sat down next to the pup and scratched her behind one ear. "See, there's only one thing worse than being in love. And that's being in love alone." She had heard that once before, but she couldn't remember where. At the time she hadn't understood what it meant. Today she knew all too well. "We both deserve better than that."

She stood and grabbed the rest of her clothes and stuffed them into the suitcase before zipping it closed. Then she carted everything to her Jeep.

It took three trips to load her car. It was a shame for sure that her entire life would fit into the backseat of her small SUV.

But it was just the start of her new life, she told herself, not the end of the previous one.

So why did her heart feel shattered into a million bruised and bleeding pieces?

She kissed Sadie on the top of the head, then let herself out of the house.

She had debated leaving Seth a note, but in the end she had decided against it. What could she say? *I don't want to be in love alone*? Or how about *I don't want to be in love with someone who needs to pretend to love me back*?

He was a smart man. He would figure it out soon enough. Like five minutes after he got home from work.

It was time to go. No doubt about it.

Jessie took one last look at the house, then started the Jeep.

Sadie jumped up onto the table in front of the window and braced her paw against the glass. She barked and barked as Jessie stared at the house.

She wasn't sure how long she sat there before she got out of the car and made her way back to the front door. She opened it, and Sadie flew toward her, wagging her tail the entire time.

Seth had never wanted Sadie; she had become his by default. So had Jessie.

"I guess we're just two of a kind," she said, holding the dog close.

Without releasing Sadie, Jessie shut the door and headed back to her Jeep. "Come on, girl. Let's go start our new life."

She tried not to think about how Seth would feel when he came home and she wasn't there. Maybe she should have left a note. But she wasn't sure she could complete the chore without breaking down and begging him to love her.

He would figure it out for himself. And maybe even one day when he was married to someone he truly loved, he would thank her for the sacrifice she made for him. She, on the other hand, would live life alone, but it would be a fresh start in a place where no one knew her name. No one knew her mother or her grandmother, and no one talked behind her back about her relationships with the Langstons.

It would all be worth it. And maybe if she kept telling herself that, she would eventually come to believe it.

She was almost to the highway when she saw one of the Diamond's trucks on the side of the road. Should she call and let someone know? The driver should have a cell phone. She had no reason to get involved.

Then she slammed on her brakes when she saw Jake come around the front of the truck.

He shielded his eyes and gave her a wave.

Unable to drive on past, Jessie rolled down her window. "Having problems?" she asked.

Sadie barked in echo.

He shook his head. "Just releasing a tortoise. Wesley made me bring him out here so he could find his way to the creek."

"Hi, Aunt Jessie." Wesley waved from the backseat.

"Hi, punkin'." Lord, she would miss that little girl.

"Where are you headed?" Jake asked.

He was just being friendly, nothing more. The rest was her guilt talking.

"Just running into town to pick up a couple of things."

"With the dog?" He nodded pointedly toward the Yorkie.

Jessie shrugged as if to say of course. "Like any girl, she needs to get out of the house from time to time."

Jake planted his hands on his hips and looked up at the sky. "Pardon me for saying so, but isn't town that way?" He pointed in the direction she had come from.

"Well, yeah." She shifted in her seat. "I'm low on gas. I, uh, thought I would go around to the Shell station and fill up. It's closer, you know."

"Uh-huh." He wasn't buying it. Not at all. He eyed her as if she were about to run. "What's really going on, Jessie?"

That man was too smart for his own good. "I'm leaving."

"Seth? Cattle Creek?"

She nodded, tears clogging the back of her throat.

"Why?" The one word was simple and complex all at the same time.

"He doesn't love me."

"You're wrong about that. He told me himself."

Oh, how she wanted to believe that to be true. But it was just typical Seth. The peacemaker. Always making the best of everything. He'd go around telling everybody he loved Jessie. He might even start to believe it himself. But she knew the truth. "He doesn't."

"So you're going to leave. Just like that."

"Just like that."

"Without saying good-bye."

She turned to face him but couldn't look him in the eye. "Good-bye." Her heart lurched in her chest.

"What about Seth?"

"He'll figure it out." It was a coward's way out, but she just couldn't handle any more. She'd call him in a day or two, once she had time to settle in, collect herself, understand it. Like that was ever going to happen.

"Are you sure about this? Maybe you should give it a couple more days."

"I'm sure." She smiled reassuringly, then added a nod for extra emphasis.

Sadie barked as if to say *make that two*.

Jake slapped his hand against the side of her car as if to send her on her way. "Be careful, then," he said.

"I will." She waved and pasted on a fake smile as she pulled away.

What do you mean she's leaving?" Seth covered his free ear with his hand, doing his best to hear his brother over the running noise of the small waterfall created by a thick wooden dam. It wasn't the biggest dam he had ever seen. But it was sure serving its purpose.

"I mean she's leaving," Jake said. "She has a bunch of stuff packed into her car, and she's headed out of town."

"Are you kidding me?"

"She had the dog with her."

That can't be. They were a couple, weren't they? Were they? He loved her so much it hurt. Every day his love grew, and he knew eventually that it would consume him whole. His only hope was to have her by his side come what may. She couldn't leave. He had to stop her.

"Seth?"

"I'll get over there as soon as I can."

"You better hurry," Jake said. "She was almost to the highway."

Seth muttered a curse under his breath and swiped his phone off. He had to get out of there and find out what was wrong with his wife. The good Lord willing, Jake had misread the situation and Jessie would be waiting for him at the ranch house tonight.

You know that's not going to happen.

Jessie had been pulling away from him ever since she lost the baby, and he had been helpless to stop it. They had been so close, so close to the love they both deserved. After the baby, he'd wanted to give her time. Time to heal, time to see the truth for what it was.

Damn it! He'd told her he loved her! What else was a man supposed to do?

He made his way over to where Chester waited, his black slacks looking strangely crisp against the muddy banks of the creek.

"Well?" he asked, raising one brow in an echo of his question.

"Listen, Chester. I'm pretty positive that Amos is not responsible for this dam."

"He most assuredly is." For all of Chester's Texas upbringing, the man sounded a lot like an extra for a British sitcom. Dressed that way too, with a brocade waistcoat and pocket watch. "Who else would do something so diabolical?"

"Beavers?" Though he knew good and well that there weren't any beavers in Cattle Creek. At least not counting the ones that lived on Basin Road, and Seth was fairly certain that Royce and Imogene weren't responsible for the load of firewood that had been dumped in the creek.

"Poppycock! Beavers aren't diabolical. It's man . . ."

Seth had heard the talk so many times he started to tune it out. It was the same every time. Man was the downfall of man. And teenagers had made the dam, but knowing Chester the way he did, even that answer wouldn't satisfy the man. He wanted Amos strung up. Plain and simple.

But right now he had something more important to do. "Chester. I've got something I need to take care of."

"You need to take care of this."

How close had she been to the highway when Jake called? He wished he knew. He was running out of time.

"Let me get Dusty out here. Or even Summers." Bradley Summers was his latest deputy, fresh-faced and eager. Brad was the grandson of the previous sheriff and nephew to Darly Jo, but even with all that stacked against him, he still wanted to be in law enforcement.

"What's he, twelve?"

"Twenty," Seth corrected. "And he loves the law. I'm sure he could straighten this out for you." That was a lie, but Seth needed to go; time was wasting.

"Sheriff, you gotta do something about this." Amos came barreling through Chester's pasture.

"You need to get off my land," Chester countered.

"It ain't enough that he violated my mailbox and other private property. Now he wants to go and . . ."

Seth blocked out the two and thumbed his cell phone to the address book. He was going to need backup. "Millie, get Dusty out here to the Gibson place. Jessie's leaving, and I need help."

"Jessie's leaving?"

"Just get Dusty out here. Now." Somehow he managed to keep his cool when he wanted to do nothing more than yell, scream, and jump up and down.

The line was silent for two whole seconds as Seth waited. "He'll be there ASAP."

"Thanks, Millie."

"Sure thing, Sheriff."

He dialed his second number and did his best to ignore

the dueling seniors behind him. This was far more important to him than pink mailboxes and faux-beaver dams.

"Yello," the young voice on the other end greeted.

"Brad, it's Seth."

"Oh! Sheriff." He could almost hear the boy's heels
click together in military fashion. "What can I do you for?"

"I need you to find my wife."

"Jessie?"

"She would be the one, yes." He used one finger to plug
his ear as Chester and Amos continued their arguing.
"She's heading toward the Shell station out on the
highway."

"Yes, sir."

"I need you to find her and stop her."

"Stop her from what?"

Seth closed his eyes. "Stop her from leaving town."

"Jessie's leaving town?"

"Can you do it?" Seth asked.

"I think so." His tone did not inspire Seth's confidence.

"Don't think," Seth instructed. "Do. Do whatever it
takes but don't let her leave town."

"Roger that."

"And, Brad?"

"Yes, Sheriff?"

"Don't answer the phone 'Yello.'"

"Yes, sir." There went that military click again.

Seth hung up and eased back over to the two men. They
hadn't even known that he was gone.

"And furthermore," Chester was saying with a flourish
and a brandishing of his long pointer finger.

"Furthermore, nothing," Seth interrupted. "This has
got to stop, and I need it to stop now." He turned to Amos.
"The Nolan twins painted your mailbox. They thought it
would be a good joke and no one would care because they
put a pink ribbon on it. You know, the whole breast cancer
awareness thing. They also painted Miss Gleeson's, the

fire chief's, and the one in front of the hospital. They're doing two weekends of community service and will be putting up new mailboxes in all four places."

He turned back to Chester. "The basketball team built that dam. Well, more than likely. They've gotten into more mischief this summer than I care to recall. It's time you got that through your head. Amos has a bad back and couldn't get down long enough for that sort of construction without spending weeks in traction afterward. I'll call the coach and have a talk with him. He'll have the boys come out and dismantle it for you. Until then, leave your neighbor alone. *Capiche?*" Seth asked.

"What exactly does that mean?" Amos asked.

"It means understand, you imbecile," Chester said.

"I'm the imbecile? At least I speak American."

Chester rolled his eyes.

Seth would have laughed, but daylight was burning. "I'm leaving, gentlemen. I trust this incident is over."

He waited for them both to give a nod of agreement before tipping his hat, turning on his heel, and heading back for his truck.

He could only hope that Brad could hold the scene until he could get there.

The blue-and-red strobe lights flashed in her rearview mirror.

Jessie glanced back, hoping against hope that it wasn't Seth. Surely he would know his own vehicle. It was probably the highway patrol. Had she been speeding?

Her heart was breaking, so she hadn't been paying the best attention to how fast she was going.

She rolled down the window as Bradley Summers came up to the side of her car.

"Can I see your driver's license and registration please?"

Sadie let out a bark from her perch in the passenger's seat. Then bared her teeth and emitted a low growl.

"Hi, Brad. Is there a problem?"

"Just driver's license and registration."

"I understand that." Jessie fished her wallet out of her purse and handed her license to him. "But why did you stop me?"

"We can talk about that after I see your registration."

What had Seth done with the registration papers? She leaned over and dug around in the glove box, but there was nothing. She checked over the visors—passenger's side and driver's side. Nada. "Let me check under the seat."

"Ma'am, do you have a registration for this vehicle?"

This was growing more bizarre by the minute. "I don't know what Seth did with it, Brad, and why are you calling me ma'am?" She fished around under the seat and came back with a folder of papers. Thank heaven, the registration for the Jeep was right on top.

She handed it to Brad.

"Thank you, ma'am."

"I babysat you, and you tried to kiss me at church camp. Why are you calling me ma'am like you don't even know me?"

"Wait here, ma'am." He walked back to his car, and Jessie wondered what the odds were that he would follow her if she floored it.

Only two things stopped her. One was the fact that she had Sadie in the car and she wouldn't risk the pup's life in a potentially high-speed car chase. And two, she might have known Brad Summers her entire life, but that didn't mean other agencies wouldn't get involved in whatever was playing out right now.

Oh, and it was against the law. There was that too. She certainly didn't want to spend the afternoon in jail. One night there had been enough.

She checked her rearview to see if Brad had taken her

documents into his car or if he had done something else.
With the way this day was turning out, she wouldn't have
been surprised if he had set fire to them both and was now
performing the Mexican Hat Dance around their smoldering remains.

Thankfully he had slid behind the wheel of his car and
was talking on the radio. To Millie? To Seth?

Maybe she should take her chances.

"Great," she muttered as Seth pulled up.

She watched in the mirror as he came up to the car. She
didn't get out.

"What are you doing?" he asked. He looked as if the
devil himself had taken up residence. His eyes blazed, his
cheeks were red, and his breathing was labored.

"I'm leaving, Seth." She had said it three times now and
it hadn't gotten any easier.

"Why, Jessie?"

"Don't make me say it." She closed her eyes, but they
snapped back open again as he responded.

"Say it."

"You don't love me, and I can't make you stay married
to me. Not now."

"You're wrong. I do love you. More than you will ever
know."

"And this is why I didn't want to say it." She shook her
head. "You're a great guy, Seth. One of the best I know.
Maybe *the best*. But I can't trap you into staying married
to me. Let me go. There's somebody out there for you to
love. I can't keep you from that."

"Jessica Langston, what the hell are you talking about?"

"I'm talking about words, Seth. Don't tell me you love
me when we both know that's not true. They're just words,
Seth. Only words."

"Get out of the car, Jessie."

Something in his voice made her comply. She slid from
the cab of the Jeep and immediately wished she hadn't.

He towered over her in both height and anger. Maybe this wasn't such a good idea.

Next thing she knew, he had confined her hands in cuffs, and she was on her way to his service vehicle.

"What are you doing?"

"I'm taking you to jail."

Chapter Twenty-one

❦

"Y ou're what?"
Seth escorted her past the shocked deputy, then opened the back door of the car. "Watch your head."

Had the entire world gone insane?

"You can't do this," she said as he urged her inside.

"Oh, but I can. You see, you stole my car."

"I thought it was a gift," she mumbled.

"Tell that to the sheriff."

"You are the sheriff."

"Hmmm."

She looked to Brad. "It was a gift. Help me."

"Was it a gift?" Brad asked Seth. She had to hand it to the kid. He had a pair for sure.

"Maybe. Maybe not," Seth answered, slipping his sunglasses back into place.

"I'm not sure if you can arrest someone for taking a gift, sir."

"Fine." Seth pressed his lips together and gave him a

curt nod. Then he turned back to Jessie. "You're under arrest for stealing my dog."

Seth was surprised that he had any molars left by the time he got Jessie to the jail. This had to be one for the history books. How many sheriffs had had the great honor of arresting their wives? Not once, but twice!

He opened the door and helped her from the backseat.

All eyes were on them as he escorted her inside and to one of the holding cells.

"You have anything you want to tell me?" he asked.

"Now, why would you go and ask a fool thing like that?"

"Nothing in your own defense?"

She tossed back her head like an angry filly. "Nope."

"Then you have the right to remain silent—"

Jessie shut the door before he could even finish. "Lock me up, Sheriff."

"Are you bad to the bone?" he asked, repeating her words from that fateful night just a couple of months ago.

"Damn straight."

"A smart man once said, 'Pride goeth before a fall.'" He watched her reaction as he locked the cell door. Damn, but she was full of piss and vinegar.

"Bible," she mumbled.

"I beg your pardon."

"It was in the Bible."

He nodded thoughtfully. "I believe you're right."

"You think I'm being prideful?"

"Honey, I know you are. But it's okay. I've got all day." He sat down in his chair and propped his booted feet on the desk. "Hell, I've got at least another year before election time comes around again."

"What do you want from me, Seth?"

"I want you to admit that you love me."

"Why, so you can rub my nose in it? One more notch on the bedpost for Cattle Creek's most eligible bachelor."

"No, because it's a terrible thing, to be in love alone."

"Who said that? Grandma Esther?"

"Nah, it was on that box of herbal tea you left in the pantry."

"Sage advice from Lipton."

He snorted.

"You don't love me, Seth. Just let me go."

"You don't know what I feel. You've never given me a chance to explain."

She crossed her arms and huffed. "Fine. Explain."

The straight line of her shoulders and the set of her jaw looked dangerous.

"What do I have to do, Jessie? What do you need from me?"

"I need the truth."

"Never mind." He had tried, and he was all out of ideas. He couldn't make her believe. Not when she didn't want to so badly.

He started toward the door.

"Does this mean you're going to let me out of jail?"

"No." He said the one word, then turned to Millie. "Whatever you do, don't let her out of that cell." That said, he walked out of the building.

Jessie flopped back onto the cot and mulled over her options. There really weren't any. Not until Seth decided to let her out of jail.

Unless Seth hadn't considered Millie as a weakness. . . .

She was on her feet in a heartbeat. She wrapped her fingers around the bars and said a little prayer this would work.

"Why is he doing this, Millie?" He was only making it harder on them all.

Millie didn't look up from the papers she was reading.

"Millie," Jessie tried again. "Just let me out of here. I won't tell."

She turned the page but didn't acknowledge Jessie's words.

"I know you know where the keys are."

Millie didn't answer.

"It's better this way," Jessie said. "It's time for me to go. All I want to do is start over. Millie?"

She turned another page, not taking her eyes off her reading.

Time to pull out the big guns. "I love him, you know. But it won't work between us. We've tried."

"I'm not taking sides, Jessie."

"But if you're not taking sides while I'm in jail, doesn't that mean you are—in a sense—taking Seth's side?"

Millie shook her head, but then she met Jessie's gaze. "What?"

Jessie didn't have time to answer as Dusty came into the station.

"You get everything taken care of with Chester and Amos?" Millie asked.

Dusty gave a quick nod, then looked from Millie to Jessie. "Are you kidding me?" he asked.

Millie shrugged. "I just work here."

"Why did he arrest her this time?"

"Stealing his dog." Jessie and Millie said the words at the same time.

Sadie barked.

Dusty muttered something under his breath that didn't bear repeating.

Jessie cringed as he stalked to his desk, rummaged through the top drawer, and removed a key. Still muttering under his breath, he stalked over to the key cabinet, opened it, and retrieved the key to the jail cell door.

He unlocked it with more force than necessary, the ring of keys jingling like a string of bells.

"You're free to go." He stepped back from the door.

She had plenty of room but was hesitant. "Is this some kind of trick?"

"No."

"Dusty," Millie started. "I don't think—"

"It's okay, Millie," Dusty said. "Come on, Jess. You want to leave, leave."

When he put it like that, it made her seem cold and heartless. Didn't he understand? She was doing this for her and Seth. But mostly for Seth. He deserved to find his one true love. Not the girl he got pregnant and had to marry.

"But Seth said—" Millie tried again.

"I'm not worried about Seth. Go on, Jessie."

Left with nothing else, she slipped from the cell. "Do I need to sign anything?" she asked.

Dusty shook his head. "Just go."

She nodded, her throat suddenly constricted with tears. She picked up Sadie and started for the door. The pooch didn't need to stay with Seth any more than she did. They were the same; just a couple of strays that had once been Langstons.

With a sniff, she picked up her purse and started for the door.

"Why'd you do that?" Millie asked Dusty as Jessie reached for the handle. "Seth will kill you for letting her leave."

Jessie paused.

"She won't make it out of town."

She pushed out of the sheriff's office, looking first one way and then the other, Dusty's words ringing in her ears.

It was leaving time. Yet how?

Seth had taken her keys. She didn't have time to get another car. She needed to get out of town. Once that was accomplished she could take her time in building her life back one piece at a time.

Did Dusty think she had no means? Okay, so maybe

she didn't have any way of leaving now. But she still had a few friends in this town.

"Come on, girl." She walked across the street to the Chuck Wagon, praying the whole while that Sheridan would still be at work.

She pushed into the restaurant, her gaze darting around until it landed on her friend.

"Honey, are you okay?"

Jessie swiped at her cheeks, only then realizing that she had been crying. "Yeah. I will be." But how long it would take was still undetermined. Six months? A year? Forever?

"Come sit down. I'll get you something to drink. You want a Coke?"

Jessie shook her head. "I need a ride. Can you help me?"

"A ride? Where?"

"To the bus stop."

Sheridan pressed her lips together and shook her head. "Jessie."

"Please," Jessie begged, her tears starting anew.

Sheridan thought about it a minute; then Chuck came out of the back.

He took one look at Sadie and shook his head. "Jessie, get that mutt out of here."

"Sheridan?" She turned her attention back to the waitress. "Please. I need your help."

She shook her head. Her blond ponytail swinging from side to side. "Let me get my keys."

"You want to tell me about it?" Sheridan asked as they headed out to the bus station at the edge of town.

"No." Jessie looked out the window and watched Cattle Creek roll by. How long had she dreamed of this moment? Forever. And now that it was here she didn't want it anymore.

"He's a good man, Jessie. Maybe you should talk to him."

"It's not about him."

Sheridan stopped her car at the light at First and Main. Jessie could feel her gaze on her, but she kept her eyes trained on the sights outside the window.

Then the light turned green and they were headed out again.

"You know, I didn't really know your mother that well. I mean, we were in the same class and all, but we didn't hang out with each other."

"You knew my mom?"

Sheridan looked at her for a second, then turned back to the road. "Yeah. But like I said, we weren't really friends, but there was something about your mother that you couldn't help noticing when you were around her."

"What was that?" No one had ever really talked to her about her mother.

"Her bravery." Sheridan smiled. "You make me think a lot of her. Your smile and spunk."

"Thank you," Jessie murmured, petting Sadie's head and thinking about what Sheridan had just told her.

"You're also the hardest-working person I know. So was she."

Jessie could hear a "but" coming, though she didn't say as much.

"But she never left this town," Sheridan continued. "Not until she had to."

Jessie tried to let those words sink in, but they kept bouncing around just out of reach.

Her mother had come back to this town from college, pregnant with no father in sight. She'd raised her the best she could in an unforgiving town. Jessie never remembered her mother's chin being down. Donna McAllen lived as if each day was a gift. And somewhere along the way, Jessie had forgotten that about her. Her smile, her laugh, the way she smelled when she just got out of the shower.

"She would've never given up on something she wanted."

But there was more to it. She had turned to tell Sheridan

that when she caught sight of the water tower and an image that had her shaking her head and rubbing her eyes.

"Oh, honey." Sheridan peered through her windshield, then pulled her older-model Chevy to the side of the road.

Jessie got out of the car and, standing in the V of the door, continued to stare.

"Is that really . . . ?" Sheridan asked.

"Seth," Jessie whispered.

The sheriff of Page County was standing on the water tower's catwalk. Next to the longhorn mascot in large red letters, he had painted SETH LOVES J. He had even spelled out the word *loves*. His paintbrush was working on the next *e* in her name.

"Oh, honey," Sheridan said again.

She had doubted his love for her all this time. What a fool she had been.

"You still want to go to the bus stop?" Sheridan asked.

Jessie shook her head, unable to take her gaze from Seth.

"Good. Because I wasn't going to take you. Not after that."

Jessie smiled and shaded her eyes to get a better look at her husband. He loved her. He had been telling her all along. But she couldn't believe. Those were just words, and he was a man of action. This was his way of showing her.

"Thanks, Sheridan." Jessie scooped Sadie into her arms, then went around the front of the car to give her friend a quick hug.

"I would say anytime, but I hope you never need another ride to the bus station."

Jessie smiled. "I don't think I will." She was staying right there in Cattle Creek. Right where she belonged.

"Go get your man," Sheridan said, then ducked back into her car.

Jessie carried Sadie over to Seth's patrol vehicle and climbed onto the hood. He hadn't looked down even once.

He was wholly concentrating on the task at hand while her heart was near to bursting with her love for him.

A car drove by and honked.

Jessie turned and waved, registering in that split second that it was a carload of high schoolers showing their support.

A classic Lincoln pulled to a stop next to Seth's truck and Miss Alma Brown got out. Miss Alma had taught almost every resident of Page County piano or violin at one time or another. She propped her hands on her pudgy hips and gazed up at the water tower. "Has he gone crazy?"

"No, ma'am," Jessie said. "He's just in love."

"With who?" she asked.

Jessie smiled. "Me."

Alma left, only to be replaced by the mayor, the principal, and Edward Ralston, who farmed tomatoes and sold them at the edge of town.

Everyone who passed by honked and waved, but for the most part, they were left alone. Jessie had needed a public confirmation of his love for her, but the town seemed to know that they needed as much privacy as a couple could get while painting the water tower in the middle of town.

Finally he finished his work with a big heart at the end and climbed down.

Jessie was waiting for him.

"Hey, cowboy, don't you know you can get arrested for defacing public property?"

He set the paint can down and gave her that ornery grin she loved so much. "It's okay. I know the sheriff." He swooped in and captured her lips with his. "I love you, Jessie Langston. I've loved you since the day of your mother's funeral. You were standing there looking all brave and tough."

She shook her head. "But you argued with me that day. You said—"

"Not your grandmother's. Your mother's."

"But that was—"

"Eight years ago."

"Why didn't you tell me?"

"Because you were Chase's girl."

She shook her head again. "I was never Chase's girl."

"Never?" he asked with an indulgent smile.

"Not even from that first day. You helped me up, cleaned my scraped knees, gave me an ice pop. From that moment on, I was your girl. It just took me a long time to realize it."

"Mine," he whispered. "Always."

His kiss sealed the deal. Regardless of the town and the rumors, the gossip and all the troubles that might be in front of them, they had each other. They always had, though it took her a while to understand that. They had each other and they always would.

"So you get it now?" he asked several minutes later when he raised his head. The love shone in his eyes. Love for her, Jessie McAllen Langston, wild child of Cattle Creek, Texas.

She shook her head, happy tears clouding her vision. "I get it. I'm sorry I didn't get it before."

"I know. You are a damned stubborn woman."

"Are you going to be able to handle that?"

He kissed the tip of her nose. "I'm looking forward to it."

He threaded his fingers through her hair and pulled her in for another kiss, this one hotter than the one before. All she wanted to do was get him home, figure out which bed they would share, then stay in it for two days straight. But . . .

She pulled away. "Seth, it's too soon for . . ."

He winced and adjusted his jeans. "I know. I'm just happy you're staying with me. We can wait. I can wait. Just imagine how much sweeter it's going to be."

Jessie couldn't imagine loving Seth being any better, any sweeter, but she could hardly wait to find out. "I don't know what I did to deserve a man like you, but I'm glad, whatever it was."

He laughed and hoisted her down from the hood. Sadie barked, demanding equal attention. Seth scooped up the pooch and placed her in the backseat. "Come on. It's time to go home."

"Home," she said, swinging into the truck beside him. "I like the sound of that." Her home. Their home. Where she would spend forever loving her lawman.

Epilogue

❧✳❧

Four months later

Bprotested. we've been married for almost six months," Seth

"I don't care," Jessie said. "You are not staying in here with me while I pee."

He let out an annoyed sigh, then ducked out of the bathroom. It was his baby, and he had the right to know. Especially after all that they had been through.

He heard the toilet flush and rapped lightly on the door. "Jess?"

She wrenched it open. "You're making me nervous."

"How do you think I feel?" He pushed past her and into the tiny bathroom. "Where is it?"

Jessie pointed to the cabinet where the little white wand rested on a folded piece of tissue.

"Is it pink?"

She shook her head. "This one is supposed to turn blue."

Seth raked his hands though his hair. "I wish they

would make all these things the same. How am I supposed to keep up with what color it needs to be?"

He looked down into the tiny side-by-side windows. One was marked with a blue *X* and the other . . .

"Is that it?" he asked.

Jessie closed her eyes. "I can't look yet. It's too early. We need to wait another thirty seconds."

"No, we don't." The blue checkmark they were waiting for had made itself clear. Bright and wonderfully clear!

"We don't?" Jessie's eyes flew open, her gaze darting from the test wand to him.

"We don't." He scooped her into his embrace, holding her as close as he dared. He wanted to squeeze her so tight she couldn't breathe, but he knew that wasn't a good idea. So he rocked her back and forth, basking in the joy they had found.

"Seth." Her voice sounded a bit strained as she pulled away. "Can we wait a little before we tell everybody? I mean, you know . . ."

He knew, and he was so glad she didn't actually say the words. Nothing was going to happen to this baby. He would take her to Austin if need be. Somehow he knew everything was going to be just fine. "If that's what you want to do."

"I think so, yeah."

"Or," Seth said, still rocking her from side to side, "we could tell everybody at Christmas."

Her eyes lit up at the thought. Christmas was still a couple of weeks away.

"What a present for our first holiday together," he said. Planting a quick kiss on her lips. "It would be sort of fun to tell the family when everyone's here for Christmas." At least Jake, Wesley, Grandma Esther, and his mother. Who knew if anyone else would make it in for the holiday?

"The best present ever," Jessie said, tightening her arms around him and pulling him from his thoughts.

But Seth knew, he already held the best present ever right there in his arms.

Read on for a preview of
the next Cattle Creek Novel,

Healing a Heart

Coming soon from Berkley Sensation.

❧ ✦ ❧

It was official. Jake ripped off his leather work gloves and shoved them into the back pocket of his jeans. He was going to kill Jessie.

This was all her fault. And she was going to pay for it one way or another.

He raised his binoculars to get a better look at the little white car that had so recently pulled into his drive. A convertible Volkswagen Beetle. Not a ranch car by any stretch.

How many did this one make? Seven? Eight? He didn't know. He'd lost count early on of how many "cowbride" wannabes had shown up on his doorstep—literally—to get a shot at Texas's fifteenth most-eligible bachelor. Heaven help them all if he had scored any higher on the scale. They'd have been wading through women. He had a ranch to run. He didn't have time to fend off ladies with wedding gleams in their eyes while his sister-in-law sat back and laughed.

Though this one seemed a little different. Field glasses still magnifying the scene, Jake peered at her. She wasn't wrapped in some slinky, stretchy second-skin dress that showed off every curve. Instead she wore faded jeans and a hippie-looking shirt with elaborate stitching on the front. Her leather sandals weren't appropriate ranch footwear, but it was a sight better than a pair of those god-awful heels women seemed to prefer these days. The word *hippie* sprang to mind once again.

He lowered his binoculars and cranked the four-wheeler, then whistled for Kota. His blue heeler perked up at the summons and ran ahead toward the ranch house.

Best he take care of this one on his own. The last time he'd left it up to whoever answered the door, Grandma Esther had invited the woman in and had all but interviewed her to be the next Mrs. Jake Langston. And down the aisle was one place Jake never intended to walk again.

She started for the door but stopped, apparently deciding to wait for him to greet her. She turned and shielded her eyes and his heart gave a painful thump. Something about the motion was so familiar . . .

He was only a few yards away when he recognized her. Austin. And that one fantastic night . . . But her name . . .

He killed the engine and slung his leg over the side of the four-wheeler, his hands suddenly sweaty, his mouth dry.

But she wasn't here to find him because she missed him. Or wanted a repeat of that one incredible night.

Damn that article. She was only here because she had realized that he wasn't a poor work-a-day cowboy, but one of the wealthiest men in West Texas—oil excluded.

She smiled.

He scowled.

Damn he wished he could remember her name. Had they even exchanged names? It would be so much easier to kick her gold digging rear off the property if he could call her by name.

"Jake." She said his name as if she were trying it on for size.

He stopped and propped his hands on his hips. He really didn't have time for this.

Kota had no such reservations and continued on toward the interloper. He sniffed his way toward her.

She held her ground but gave the dog a cautious glance. "Will he bite?"

"Only if you break from the herd."

She nodded, then a nervous laugh escaped her. "I—"

He broke in. "Let me save us both the trouble and the embarrassment. I know why you're here."

"You do?" Her brown eyes widened. He might not remember her name but those melted-chocolate eyes were burned into his soul. Along with the feel of her underneath him, on top of him . . .

"The article in *Out West* magazine."

A frown wrinkled her brow, and she tilted her head to one side as if needing a better angle on the situation.

You're going to need more than that, sweetheart.

The hot Texas sun glinted off the chunk of purple on one side of her seal brown hair. That he didn't remember. Purple?

"And you should know, you better just clear on out right now," he continued. "I'm not interested in it."

The frown deepened. "It?"

"It." He waved a hand in her general direction. The word had sounded so much more forceful in his head.

"I don't think you understand."

"I don't think *you* understand."

"Can we go inside and talk?"

"Nope."

"It's hot out here and I just—"

"If you don't like the heat, stay out of Texas."

She thought about it a second, then gave him a small smile. "That was a joke."

"I'm trying to be as nice as I possibly can, but I've had more women crawling around here in the last few weeks than I ever imagined. It's best you just go on home." He turned to walk away, hoping she took the hint. Maybe if he went back into the house without inviting her she would lose interest and leave.

Yet that feeling that something about her was different panged at his midsection.

"Jake?" Grandma Esther stood on the large stone porch. "Aren't you going to invite her in? It's mighty hot out."

"That's true, Grandma, so get on back in the air conditioning."

"Jacob Dwight! How are you ever going to find yourself a bride if you don't invite these women in?"

He closed his eyes and sucked in a deep breath, his feet stuck in the dirt somewhere between the driveway and the big house.

"Are the women coming here to marry you?" she asked from behind him.

"He is the seventeenth most-eligible bachelor in Texas."

"Fifteenth," he corrected, then winced at his own words. He wasn't making this easier on himself.

Her laughter rang, sweet and clear like a babbling brook. Wait . . . what?

The sun had to be getting to him. He whirled around, wondering why she hadn't left.

Then he realized what was so strange about the situation, why would a hippie chick want to marry a cowboy? True, he'd shown her a few tricks in the saddle, as they say, but one completely incredible, fantastic, amazing night did not a lifestyle change make. Or something like that.

"I don't want to marry you," she said. The light in her eyes told him she wasn't lying. "But I do need to talk to you about something."

Just as bad.

"Come on in this house, girl." Grandma Esther waved her in with the business end of her cane.

The brunette—why couldn't he remember her name?—edged past him.

Kota nipped at her heels.

She yelped. The cow dog had never actually bitten any-one, but Jake knew that his nips and nibbles could be a bit unnerving if you weren't used to them. He hid his smile as she skipped to the house.

Reluctantly, he followed behind.

Grandma Esther stepped to one side as she entered the house. He watched her rear disappear into the shadows of the cool foyer.

The porch offered a reprieve from the blistering sun, but another heat filled Jake. Memories of that one night when he had let his guard down. When he'd lost his resolve and tried once again to find the answers at the bottom of a bottle. He hadn't had a drink since then, but he didn't count days sober. It wasn't like that for him. But he knew with so many ghosts of could-have-beens and should-have-beens haunting him that the alcohol could take over in an instant and it was best to just stay away.

But that one night . . .

"Esther, what is going on out here?" His mother skidded to a halt when she caught sight of their visitor. But Evelyn Duvall Langston was nothing if not composed. She brushed down the sleeves of her rose-colored pearl-snap shirt. "Hello."

"Hi." The brunette flashed his mother a nervous smile. Bre? Was that her name? No, but it was close. Briana? Nope. That wasn't it either.

"I wasn't aware that Jake had a guest."

"She's not a guest." He frowned to silently instruct his mother to drop the matter.

Mom opened her mouth to speak—she never was much at following his wishes—but Grandma Esther stepped in, her cane rattling against the stone floor. "Come on, Evie. Let's give these two some privacy."

For once Jake was grateful for his grandmother's inter-ference. He certainly couldn't toss the brunette out on her pretty little behind with his grandmother and mother watching. Well, he *could*, but he would never hear the end of it.

He watched Grandma Esther lead his mother into her office, then turned back to his unwanted guest.

Once again she shot him that nervous smile. She hadn't been so nervous three and a half months ago when they had—

"I don't know how to say this except to just say it." She sucked in a deep breath. "I'm pregnant."

He went numb as his gaze flickered to her midsection hidden under her blousy, gauzy shirt. A bus could be parked under there. Or maybe that was the point.

"Pregnant?"

Was this true? Would she even be here if it wasn't? Maybe. He had become such a target lately. Slowly he raised his gaze to hers. She was telling the truth. Somehow, someway, he knew it.

His heart constricted and the air left his lungs even as he tried to speak.

His worst nightmare.

His stomach clenched and his fingers tingled from a combination of adrenaline and terror.

Nothing would ever be the same again.

"Get rid of it." His lips barely moved. Fear gripped him. Fear like he had only known once before. He was the dutiful brother. Reliable. Dependable. The caretaker. The responsible one. Always responsible. He'd never been careless. Never.

That night in June flashed through his mind and mixed with one fall afternoon down by the river with Cecelia. A picnic meant to bring the spark back into their marriage. And yet all it had brought about was her death.

The night with this stranger blurred and frayed until the two merged into one and all he could think about was the fear.

"I—I beg your pardon." Her voice was no more than a

whisper. But it held the weight of the ages. Betrayal, disbelief. He'd never meant to hurt her.

"Get rid of it."

She trembled, her own nervousness eclipsed by an emotion he couldn't discern. She opened her mouth, and when she spoke her voice was no more substantial than a wisp of smoke. "You mean like an . . . an abortion?"

"That's exactly what I mean." An invisible hand clutched and clawed at his throat until he could barely breathe. This couldn't be happening.

"Jacob Dwight Langston!"

His mother stormed into the room, but Jake couldn't think, couldn't move.

"I'm sorry, Miss . . . Miss . . ."

Evelyn looked to him.

"Bryn," he croaked. Oh, *now* he could remember her name.

"What my son means to say, Miss Bryn—"

"Talbot," she corrected, then shifted from one foot to the other and adjusted the strap of her enormous orange handbag.

"Miss Talbot," his mother started again, but Bryn shook her head.

"I . . ." She faltered. "I just thought you'd want to know."

She spun on one heel and headed for the door.

Out of all the possible scenarios she had expected, this was not one of them. Weren't cowboys supposed to be noble?

Bryn shook her head at herself and palmed her keys. What the heck did she know about cowboys anyway? Just that one sizzling night where she had done the unthinkable and hooked up with a man she didn't even know. A perfect stranger.

Not perfect at all.

She tripped down the steps and hurried toward her car. This stop had put her behind schedule. But she had thought he should know. Didn't every man deserve that much?

She just hadn't expected his reaction. Disbelief maybe. Denial, probably. Even anger.

Coldhearted bastard. Except he hadn't been so cold that night. He'd been more warm that night. Hot, burning up, dazzling.

As if.

"I should have never come here," she muttered. But she hadn't expected his reaction.

Still there was something in his eyes when he said the words, that unthinkable act. Sadness, remorse and . . . guilt?

She pushed the thought away and slid behind the wheel of her car. What did he have to feel guilty about? They had entered that hotel room together.

"Looks like it's just the three of us again." She pressed a hand to her rounded belly and glanced over at the urn sitting in the passenger's seat. "Just the three of us." She cranked the car and put it into reverse. The best-laid plans.

"Miss Talbot?" Jake's mother came rushing out of the door and over to where Bryn had parked. At least she thought she was Jake's mother and the older lady his grandmother, though neither one looked particularly like the man. Neither had those fabulous green eyes. Or that dark hair that just begged a woman's fingers to—

Bryn rolled down her window. "Yes?"

"Won't you come back into the house?" Mrs. Langston stooped down so she could look into Bryn's car. Her gaze flickered to the passenger's seat, then back to Bryn. She'd be damned before she would explain herself.

"I don't think so." She shot the woman her most polite Southern smile and turned to get a good look out the rear window as she backed up.

Jake's mother clutched her arm. "Please, Miss Talbot. Come in. Let me apologize for my son's behavior."

She whipped around, but shook her head even as she made no move to leave. "There's no need." He didn't want the baby they had created. So be it. She did. The child she carried was a new beginning. A fresh start. One she so desperately needed.

"I believe there is."

Something in the woman's voice had Bryn putting the car into park, had her cutting off the engine.

"Just for a bit." His mother smiled encouragingly, then moved back so Bryn could get out.

Her limbs were stiff and jerky as she opened the car door and stepped into the Texas heat once again. It was different from Georgia. Not as humid by far, but hot all the same.

Together the two of them walked back to the sprawling ranch house. It was a beautiful structure, though Bryn had been too nervous before to truly appreciate its majestic beauty.

"Let's go into my office where we can talk." She led the way, then turned back to face Bryn. "I'm Evelyn, by the way. Jake's mother."

"It's nice to meet you," Bryn murmured. Southern manners kicked in when all else failed. At least she had called it right. "This really isn't necessary," she said.

Evelyn ignored her and opened one of the large doors to a leather-and-bronze office complete with a gently worn sofa with a brown-and-white cowhide tossed over the back. Bryn was fairly certain it was the real deal and not a designer version from Pottery Barn.

"Go ahead and have a seat. Grandma Esther went to get us some refreshments."

"Really," Bryn gently protested one again. "This isn't necessary. I don't want anything from Jake. I—"

"Sit." The one word was spoken like a woman who was accustomed to getting her way. Always.

Bryn perched on the edge of the sofa, while Evelyn eased into the overlarge chair behind the desk.

"How did you and Jake meet?"

Bryn shook her head. This was not going at all as she had planned, but then again, what had she really expected? That she could come in, announce that she was having Jake's baby, and they would just let her waltz out the door without so much as a by-your-leave?

A girl could hope.

But when she got back to Georgia, she was having a long talk with Justin about personal boundaries and bad advice. A girl had to depend on her best friend to help her through tough situations. So far, he had encouraged her to latch onto a cowboy—the very same cowboy who'd gotten her pregnant—and then had pointed out his picture in *Out West* magazine, thereby negating her arguments that she didn't even know his last name. That night trivial matters like surnames had never come up.

"I was in Austin in June. I believe Jake was there for a weekend conference. He really didn't tell me." She shook her head. She was making a mess of this. She stood. "Listen, you don't owe me an apology. I'd rather just be on my way."

"Carrying my grandchild."

Bryn made a face. "She sort of has to go with me." She placed one hand protectively over her growing mound of a baby. No matter how much she watched what she ate, she seemed to be packing on the pounds.

"It's a girl?" Evelyn asked. Her voice was barely audible.

Bryn shrugged. "I just want it to be."

Jake's mother smiled. "So did I, but I ended up with five boys."

"Five?"

"I'm afraid so." But her smile took all the venom from her words. "Jake didn't mean what he said. He . . ." she started, then shook her head. "He had a tough time when his first wife died."

"He's a widower?" Of course he had been married. The women in Texas knew a good thing when they saw it.

"Cecelia—that was his wife—she died giving birth to their daughter, Wesley."

He has a daughter? Bryn sank back to the couch cushion. "I see."

"He just needs some time to adjust to the idea of being married again. And having another baby."

"I'm not marrying Jake." The idea was ludicrous. They didn't know each other. A baby did not a marriage make. "It was a mistake coming here." Bryn pushed to her feet and slung her purse over one shoulder.

Evelyn was on her feet in a heartbeat. "I told you, Jake didn't mean what he said."

Bryn pinched the bridge of her nose. "This has nothing to do with what he said. Well, maybe a little, but we don't know each other. We can't get married."

"You know each other well enough to have made a baby." Evelyn's words stung with the truth.

"That's not really the point, now is it?"

"Why are you in such a hurry?"

She spun around. Grandma Esther stood in the doorway with the promised refreshments.

"Oh, you know. I'm a busy girl with things to do."

"If you're going back to Austin, then I hope you'll leave your number and address so we can keep in touch," said Evelyn.

"I'm not going back to Austin."

"Your car has Georgia plates," Esther said.

"That's right. That's where I live."

"You're from Georgia?" asked Evelyn.

"That's right."

"You never did answer me," Esther pressed.

"I have a . . . meeting on the West Coast." That was a great way of putting it. Surely beat the heck out of "I'm dumping my baby sister's ashes in the Pacific." "I'm supposed to be there the day after tomorrow."

"Then you have plenty of time." Esther waved away Bryn's protests with a flick of one gnarled hand.

"That's right," Evelyn said. "You can have dinner and spend the night here."

"I—"

"We won't take no for an answer," Evelyn said.

"Besides," Grandma Esther interjected, "it'll save you the hotel charge."

Money wasn't an issue. But staying with these people . . . that was. She should get out now while the getting was good.

"Please." Evelyn's voice was filled with heartfelt emotions. "Please give us a chance. We need to get to know you. After all, you're having my next grandchild."

She didn't want anything from these people. In fact, if it hadn't been for that blessed magazine, she wouldn't be standing here now. But she had wanted to give them a chance, let them know that in six months' time another Langston was entering the world.

"How do you even know I'm telling the truth?"

Evelyn smiled. "If you weren't and you were just trying to trap Jake into marriage, why would you walk away?"

LOVE
ROMANCE NOVELS?

For news on all your favorite romance authors,
sneak peeks into the newest releases, book
giveaways, and much more—

"Like" Love Always on Facebook!
 LoveAlwaysBooks